Water's Edge

Genevieve Fortin

Bella Books, Inc.
P.O. Box 10543
Tallahassee, FL 32302

Printed in the United States of America on acid-free paper.

First Bella Books Edition 2017

Editor: Katherine V. Forrest
Cover Designer: Micheala Lynn

ISBN: 978-1-59493-553-4

Other Bella Books by Genevieve Fortin

First Fall
Two Kinds of Elizabeth

Acknowledgments

Water's Edge is a story that's been with me for several years, evolving. The research was intimidating and that's probably the only reason why it's my third novel rather than my first. Emilie, Angeline, and their families have been in my head for over fifteen years and they will stay there forever.

They were born after I became a research assistant on a large and important research project on Franco-Americans. Naturally, the first person I want to thank is Dr. Cynthia Fox, who trusted me to work with her team on that research project. I don't think I would ever have thought of this story without that experience. As I transcribed interviews with Franco-Americans who told their stories, how their families were compelled to leave everything behind in Quebec and move to New England to work in cotton mills and how they adapted to their new environment, I was touched. And I was curious. I'm from Quebec, after all, and I was living in the United States at the time, so I related to their stories. I even learned during that experience that my own grandfather had moved to Massachusetts to work in a cotton mill for a while, but that he'd returned home to Canada to marry my grandmother.

It was a part of my history I wanted to share and build on. I started to think and asked myself, what if two of these young French Canadian women, living in such restrictive conditions, fell in love? And then I wanted to tell their story in the most realistic and empathic way I could.

I also want to thank Denise, who encouraged me through the research as much as the writing process, who patiently listened to my doubts and fears, and who fell in love with Emilie and Angeline.

And I want to thank the wonderful Katherine V. Forrest. When I learned that she was my editor on this project, I was deeply honored. I was given the chance to work with the woman who gave us *Curious Wine*, a woman whose work made it possible for women like me to write about women like us. I couldn't believe it, and I was beyond happy. My happiness was all about me for a few hours, and then it changed. I realized that although working with Katherine V. Forrest was a great opportunity for me as an author, it was even more important for the story I wanted to share. I am most of all grateful that, with her help, my novel was given the chance to be the best it could be.

I'm proud of this novel, and I'm proud to share it with you. Thank you, dear reader, for choosing it.

Dedication

For Denise, my Rimouski

About the Author

Genevieve is French Canadian but claims her heart holds dual citizenship. Not surprising since she lived in the USA for thirteen years and still visits every chance she gets. Besides writing and reading, her passions include traveling, decadent desserts, fruity martinis, and watching HGTV. For now she lives in St-Georges, just a few miles north of the border between Maine and Quebec. She and her partner share a house with their two dogs, Spike and Betty.

FLOW

1888

CHAPTER ONE

Rimouski, Quebec
March 1888

Emilie Levesque sat on the top step of the narrow L-shaped staircase that led down to the small kitchen where her parents were having a discussion that seemed very serious to her eight-year-old ears.

So serious that she got up and went to awaken her older brother Joseph to listen to the conversation with her. He grumbled in protest but finally followed Emilie and sat with her on the top step, most likely wondering what kind of drama his sister was brewing this time.

All she'd heard before she went to get her brother was something about leaving their farm and she was scared. She would never admit it to ten-year-old Joseph but his presence as he held her tiny hand reassured her. She'd never been alone in her life. She had Joseph.

At the staircase Joseph protested, "This is a private, grownup talk, Emilie. Papa would be so mad if he saw us."

"Shh," Emilie said and covered Joseph's mouth with her free hand. "He won't see us if you shut up."

Most of the stairs could not be seen from the kitchen since they hid behind the wall that hosted a large cast iron woodstove. In fact, Emilie knew they could sit lower without being seen which would allow them to hear their parents much better, but she also knew that one more step down the pine wood stairs would make them squeak and they would get caught and punished. Emilie didn't get caught often because she knew how to avoid it. She glanced at her brother and grinned. Joseph, on the other hand, rarely disobeyed or attempted any mischief, but when he did he got caught every single time.

They were complete opposites, even physically. Her hair was as dark as a crow's plumage; his was blond, almost white in the summer. Her eyes were black as coal; his were blue as the clearest of skies. She often envied her brother's features. The only attribute they had in common was the pale skin they inherited from their mother. And the only advantage she thought she had over her brother was that her skin lightly tanned in the sun while his freckled. Other children often made fun of him because of his freckles and Emilie jumped to his defense any chance she got.

"We're losing the farm anyway, Mathilde." Her father's words brought Emilie's attention back to her parents' conversation. "I can't keep up with the payments. And it would be temporary. Just the time it'll take to make enough money to pay off this darn loan and we'll come back home."

Emilie noted shame in her father's voice and her heart broke. She looked down to a hole in her nightgown that her mother had just mended for the third time. The grayish white cotton nightgown was too long and she stepped on it all the time but it was the only one she had, a hand-me-down from an older cousin. She knew they didn't have money. She never had any of the pretty new clothes they sold at the general store. Her mother reminded her they had to make do every time she dared complain about eating potatoes for dinner again. Yes, she knew they were poor, but she had no idea they could lose their house. What were those payments her father was talking about and how could they force them out of their home? Her parents worked hard. She knew that too. Every day but Sunday. Wasn't that enough?

"How did we get to this point, Henri?" Her mother's voice cracked. She was crying. Emilie heard the scraping of a chair being moved across the floor and she imagined her father getting closer to his wife as they sat at the small square kitchen table where they ate every meal. When her father spoke again his voice was calm and soothing. Emilie closed her eyes and let it comfort her. She needed it as much as her mother.

"I'm not sure how we got here, darling. But we're not alone. A lot of folks got to this point in the past couple of years. They all did what I'm suggesting and they don't regret it. You read the boys' letters don't you? They love it in the States."

The boys were Emilie's five older half-brothers. She barely knew them. The youngest of the boys, Edouard, was ten years older than Emilie and had moved away when he was fifteen years old to join his older brothers who all worked in a cotton mill in Fall River, Massachusetts. Emilie remembered taking him to the train station with her father. That was the first and last time she'd seen a train. Emilie didn't know much about her half-brothers other than that. Emilie's mother was her father's second wife. His first wife had died while giving birth to a sixth child. The child had not survived either. They never talked about it.

The only reason Emilie knew was because she'd listened in to a conversation between her parents and the priest one night. Father Lavoie visited their home regularly. Emilie had missed most of what they'd said but she'd caught the end of it, when the priest had suggested it might be time for her mother and father to have a third child. Emilie had gotten excited at the possibility of having a little sister or brother. Her father had remained polite but when Father Lavoie had left she heard him say to her mother that the last time he'd let a priest convince him to conceive a child against the doctor's orders he had not only lost the child but his first wife and the mother of five living children. He added that the experience had taught him to take the word of a doctor over any priest when it came to childbearing and that it was more than likely God's will for children to grow up with a mother. Emilie had thought her father was brave for defying a man of cloth, but she'd also been scared he'd be punished for his bravery. The entire conversation had remained with Emilie and she'd often wanted to question her father about it but the pain she'd heard in his voice that night told her she should leave it alone.

The distinct shrill of the heavy door of the woodstove opening and closing forced Emilie out of her memories and back to the discussion that was still taking place in the kitchen. She knew her mother was the one adding wood to the fire. Her mother always kept busy, especially when something made her upset. "I don't like it, Henri. I don't like it at all. Rimouski's always been our home."

"I know, darling. And it always will be. We just need to get out of this predicament we're in."

"Promise me it's temporary. Promise me, Henri."

"I promise, Mathilde. We'll be back here in no time. But with a little money to do what we've always wanted to do. Can you imagine?"

Emilie heard her mother sigh heavily before she spoke again. "Fine, so be it then. Make the arrangements." There was a pause and then her mother added, as if she needed to keep some control over the situation. "We're not leaving until the end of the school year."

"Okay. That'll give me time to get everything organized."

Emilie felt her hand fall to her side as Joseph released it, stood up and whispered, "I've heard enough." She heard how defeated he sounded but couldn't move to comfort him. She heard more whispering coming from the kitchen but she didn't try to understand any of it. Her world was crumbling around her. She thought of the children at school she couldn't call friends but who were at least familiar. She thought of her aunts and uncles she wouldn't see anymore. Even the cousins she didn't like but were part of the world as she knew it. She thought of the animals on the farm, the few they had left, especially the big gray cat she called Misty and with whom she shared her dreams.

Then Emilie thought about all the books that grownups had let her put her little hands on. Some from her mother, some from her aunts and uncles, some books from school. All of her dreams came from those books and her own imagination. Dreams that included traveling on a train and finding people she might have more affinity with. In foreign countries where she could be whatever she wanted. Then she wondered if perhaps Fall River could be the beginning of her dreams coming true instead of the end of her world.

She grinned and went back to bed with a feeling she wasn't accustomed to: hope.

CHAPTER TWO

Fall River, Massachusetts
June 1888

When she woke up on the train and her mother told her they were almost there, Emilie was disappointed. She'd been so excited to be on board a train at last and wanted to take in every bit of the scenery the windows had to offer, but the sound and comforting movement of the train traveling over the tracks had soon put her to sleep. She glanced at Joseph and was relieved to see him asleep. Chances were he hadn't seen more than she had and couldn't tease her about it later.

Emilie looked at Joseph's brown wool pants and crisp white cotton shirt, then down at her own blue dress. They were not new but almost. Their aunt Rita had offered them the practically new outfits for their big trip to the States. Their cousins had thrown a fit over giving away their good clothes but were quickly reminded it was the charitable thing to do. Charity or not, Emilie was proud of her blue dress. It had short sleeves, a round collar, and a white sash around the waist. It was only slightly too big and more importantly it was not brown or beige. Emilie then looked at her mother and felt pride from knowing that her own long hair was gathered up into a loose chignon, just like her mother's. She often wished her own hair was the same light brown as her mother's, but knowing she at least wore it in the same style was comforting enough today.

When they arrived at the train station Emilie stood aside with her mother as Joseph helped their father carry one at a time the two large pine trunks in which fit all of their belongings. She was still amazed at how little they possessed. To pay for the trip and to get settled in Fall River, her father had sold the few animals they had left and some of the farm equipment he figured he could replace when they returned. As soon as they put the first trunk down Emilie sat on it and observed her surroundings.

She'd never seen so many people in one place. And not one single familiar face. She couldn't even understand what most of them said. The language they spoke was English, her father had explained, and he'd assured her that she and Joseph would learn it quickly. She caught herself smiling at a few other children who spoke French and they smiled back. She didn't know them but their shared language was enough to make them familiar. Emilie's father had explained that there were many families in Fall River who spoke French like them. Many even came from Rimouski or neighboring villages. She found that reassuring.

Her brother and father put down the second trunk and her father immediately started looking around in the crowd, searching for his older sons. "Where are they?"

"They'll be here, Henri. Don't worry. Oh, there comes Edouard," Mathilde said as she looked over her husband's shoulder. Edouard was the half-brother Emilie could remember best yet she barely recognized him. He wore a nicely trimmed beard and a three-piece suit with matching wool trousers, sack coat and waistcoat. He looked proud, yet tired. He shook his father's hand with a formality that didn't surprise Emilie. Yes, her romantic mind had imagined warmer greetings between a father and a son who hadn't seen each other for over three years, yet she realized her imagination and reality rarely matched. This handshake was, after all, much more in her father's character. "Where are the others?" her father asked Edouard.

"Still at work. I was able to come because I stayed late last night but the boss couldn't accommodate all five of us. I'm sure you understand." It was six p.m. on a Saturday. "They'll meet us at your apartment later." Edouard kissed Mathilde on the cheek and then turned to Emilie and Joseph, his face lighting up at the sight of them. "Hello there, little monsters. You both got so big."

"Hi, Edouard," said Joseph, and he shook his older brother's hand as a man would. Emilie didn't know what the most appropriate greeting was so she extended her hand as well. Edouard dropped to one knee and hugged her instead.

"Nice to see you again, Edouard," she murmured as she accepted his embrace. Right then the memory of Edouard carrying her on his back while he walked across the kitchen floor on his hands and knees flashed through her mind and she smiled. She'd been close to her half-brother once. Maybe she could be again.

Emilie was exhausted when Eugene, Louis, Alphonse and Jean-Baptiste arrived at their new apartment in the Flint section of Fall River. She greeted her half-brothers and then followed Joseph to the bedroom they would share, leaving the adults to catch up. She was tired yet she couldn't sleep. She focused on the stains she could see on the walls, even in the dark. Their apartment was one of six in what Edouard had called a tripledecker. It was on the third floor and it was stiflingly hot despite open windows. Their home in Rimouski wasn't much larger than this two-bedroom apartment but it was clean, and fresh air came through its open windows. She would help her mother clean these walls tomorrow, she was sure of it.

Emilie couldn't believe how many of these triple-deckers lined the streets of their new neighborhood, all of them the same. She didn't think she could find her way back to their apartment if she had to go anywhere alone. She couldn't believe how many people were piled up in so little space. Edouard had told her father that they were lucky to have this space just for the four of them and that most apartments hosted families of eight or more. Her father had replied that if any or all of the boys wanted to share the space they were welcome to since it would allow them to save more of their wages. Edouard had promised to think about it. Emilie wondered where the boys would sleep if they moved in, but trusted her father's judgment.

She heard Joseph's small bed squeak as he tossed and turned and sighed loudly.

"You can't sleep either?" she asked softly.

"No. I hate this place. I want to go back home."

Emilie turned to face her brother. Both beds were so close they might as well have been one bed. "I know it's not like home, Joseph, but did you see all the stores and the restaurants we passed on our way here? I'm sure we haven't seen the best of this place yet. Just wait and see."

"The ice cream did look good in that one store window, did you see it?"

Emilie could imagine a smile on her brother's face in the darkness of the room. "Yeah, it did look good. And did you see those cookies?"

They kept talking about the things they'd seen on their way from the train station to Flint and finally went to sleep in their new home.

CHAPTER THREE

August 1888

Two months after their move to Fall River, Emilie and Joseph were finally used to the fact that their mother left for the cotton mill with their father, Edouard and Jean-Baptiste six mornings a week. Eugene, Louis and Alphonse had decided to stay in their own apartment but Edouard and Jean-Baptiste had accepted their father's offer to stay with them. Emilie's parents had given the second bedroom to the older boys and the parlor at the front of the apartment had been turned into a third bedroom for Joseph and Emilie, with small mattresses directly on the floor. Emilie remembered her mother telling her as they'd first made the small improvised beds that they didn't need a parlor anyway since they never had time to use it. A kitchen to eat and rooms to sleep in were all they needed.

Emilie had turned nine in July and she was in charge of preparing dinner every night so they could eat in between six and six thirty p.m., as soon as the four adults came back from their thirteen-hour shift at the mill. She enjoyed cooking. In fact, of the long list of chores both Joseph and Emilie had to do every day, cooking was her favorite.

Their chores didn't leave Emilie and Joseph much time to play outside but they had an hour or two most afternoons to meet with neighboring children by the Quequechan River to swim or play or just chat. Emilie often chose to sit by herself and read an old book she'd already read. This time of day was her time. Besides, the children in Flint Village were almost exactly like the children in Rimouski. Emilie didn't dare tell her parents or even Joseph that she was quite disappointed with Fall River. It was too much like home, but without the aspects of the farm that she actually missed, like green spaces and animals, animals she could speak to without fear she'd be mocked or misunderstood. Joseph, on the other hand, had adapted to life in Fall River much better than he'd expected that first night. He'd made lots of friends in Flint and as soon as they left their apartment he didn't pay any attention to his sister, which saddened Emilie.

On this specific Thursday of August, however, Emilie and Joseph didn't go down by the river to play with the other children. Their mother had warned them that the apartment needed to be perfectly clean and the table needed to be set with their best linens, dishes and silverware. Father Robillard was coming for a visit, his first visit since their arrival. Emilie was surprised it had taken so long for the priest to accept her mother's invitation. Back home, Father Lavoie had visited often and without being invited.

When they'd left for the cotton mill that morning, her mother had seemed nervous and anxious to finally have Father Robillard over for dinner. Her father, however, had seemed less than pleased. He'd even grumbled something on his way out the door about the money this meal would cost them. Her mother had left Emilie in charge of the pea soup, which Emilie had made before, and had bought pork and beef for a stew. Emilie had made stew once with her mother but today would be the first time she made it alone. Stew was a meal they ate on rare festive occasions and Emilie prepared it with all the respect it deserved.

When her parents and half-brothers came home, she was busy selecting the dishes with the least number of chips.

Mathilde went straight to the stove and tasted the stew. "Mm, great job, sweetheart," she told Emilie, kissing her on top of the head. "You make me proud." Emilie smiled and watched her mother disappear into her bedroom. She knew her parents and half-brothers were hurrying to change out of their working clothes, covered in cotton dust, into their Sunday clothes. Emilie and Joseph had already changed into the same outfits they'd worn for the trip to Fall River. They hadn't waited for their mother to tell them. The visit of a priest called for it and Emilie took advantage of every occasion she had to wear her pretty blue dress.

Everyone changed quickly and Mathilde was fixing her chignon when Emilie heard a faint knock at the door. Her father opened the door and welcomed Father Robillard. He then introduced his children to the priest and the men all sat at the table. Emilie helped her mother serve dinner and when they finally joined the men at the table they all closed their eyes as their guest said a prayer.

"Thank you for inviting me. I rarely have the occasion to share a meal with my parishioners," Father Robillard said afterward. Emilie thought that was strange and from the expression of surprise on her mother's face, she wasn't the only one. It seemed some things, after all, were different in Fall River, and that made Emilie smile to herself.

They ate as the priest talked with Emilie's parents and her older brothers. Emilie focused on her mother as the conversation went on and she could swear she read more and more disappointment in her face.

The first letdown had come when the priest mentioned that he hadn't been to Canada in over a decade. The second came when he casually declared that he'd seen several families settle permanently in Fall River even though they'd originally come with the intention of going back to Canada. From her mother's grimace at the priest's casual declaration, it couldn't have been worse if he'd pierced her chest with a knife.

Fortunately for Father Robillard, her mother's smile came back when he mentioned how much he was looking forward to seeing Emilie and Joseph at Notre Dame's parochial school in September. Before her expression had a chance to fully change for the better, however, Emilie's father spoke. "Actually, Father, Emilie and Joseph are going to attend public school."

Emilie was as shocked as everyone else by her father's words. She immediately stopped observing her mother's reactions to bring her attention to her father, whose face was as stern and stoic as Emilie had ever seen it. His gray eyes had become black and his mouth was sealed into a tiny, lipless line, barely visible in the thick black beard studded with white hair.

It seemed to Emilie that the thin crown of gray hair on the priest's head tried to stand up, and in her mind she could easily see smoke coming out of the priest's ears. It made her smile, but her smile quickly disappeared as Father Robillard swallowed the bite of stew he'd been chewing and addressed her father directly at the other end of the table. "But Mr. Levesque, surely you want to ensure your children go to a school where their catholic religion and values are taught daily, and in their own language. It is, after all, the only way to maintain their culture and their religious beliefs, the only way to avoid the corruption that grows so easily at every street corner of this country. As the proverb goes, Mr. Levesque, tell me with whom you associate, and I will tell you who you are." The priest ended his speech with a nervous yet condescending laugh and a long silence followed.

Her father coughed and cleared his throat before he finally answered. "With all due respect, Father, I trust my children already know who they are, no matter who they associate with. Unlike those other families you've talked about, we're going back to Canada sooner rather than later, but I don't see how it can hurt my children to learn English while they're here and to be around other folks. I've seen plenty of corruption among us and I don't think paying the Catholic Church to send them to school is what will save them from it."

"Henri," Mathilde interrupted. "I think that's enough." She spoke in a voice that was soft but achieved her goal as he stopped talking and took another bite of stew. It was the second time Emilie heard her father defy a man of cloth and this time it scared her even more than the first because he'd done it right in his face. Emilie waited for God to strike their apartment with lightning or show his disapproval in some way. But there was only thick, uncomfortable silence.

Edouard and Jean-Baptiste asked the priest a couple of questions, creating diversion until the end of the meal, when everyone stood up and gathered at the door to bid farewell to their guest. Father Robillard thanked Mathilde for the meal and then brought his attention back to Emilie's father. She trembled at the disdain she saw in his eyes and figured the wrath of God had finally found a way to manifest itself. When he spoke, it was as if each word addressed to her father were like a weight over their entire family. "I hope you'll reconsider, Mr. Levesque. As your priest, I am convinced Notre Dame is the best option for your children. You do want their lives here in Flint to be as virtuous as possible, don't you? Not to mention how going to public school may affect their status, and yours, in this community."

Emilie saw her parents exchange a look before her father answered. "I'll think about it, Father. I bid you good night."

Emilie helped her mother with the dishes and went straight to bed with Joseph. Edouard and Jean-Baptise quickly retired to their bedroom as well. Her mother hadn't said a word while they washed dishes, which was not usual, but she was clearly, obviously upset.

Once everyone else was sleeping, Emilie listened to the argument between her parents. Her father would not back down. She argued that the priest was right, that they needed to go to a French-speaking, Catholic school to keep their virtue and culture intact. He argued that it wouldn't hurt them to be exposed to different children. But his biggest plea was that he wouldn't give any money to the Catholic Church when there were free schools available. His final words were, "I'm not going to change my mind about this, Mathilde." His tone was as rigid as steel. Emilie hadn't heard her father use those words often but she knew that when he did use them, they marked the end of the conversation. She heard a door slam and then nothing.

That night, Emilie took a long time to finally fall asleep. A small part of her still feared for her father because of his defiance, but a bigger part of her was pleased she'd be going to public school. She'd been told there were American children there, as well as Irish, Italian, Polish and even Russian children. She smiled at the possibility that she might finally stop feeling like the odd one out.

CHAPTER FOUR

September 1888

The first day of school wasn't at all what Emilie had expected. Her father had promised English would be easy to learn, but she didn't understand anything. She'd loved school in Canada, but here she felt like an idiot. How could she learn when she couldn't understand anything her teacher said? It was so frustrating.

The other children were different from the children in Rimouski and in Flint Village, that much was for sure, but she couldn't imagine finding kinship with any of them. Most didn't pay attention to her. They stayed with their own group and didn't seem to share her need to get close to anyone outside of their clan. Italians stayed with Italians, Polish with Polish, and so on.

The only group that paid any attention to her was the Irish and so far it was only to insult her. They'd called her "Peasoup" or "Frog" all day long and one had even yelled at her to go back home. He said other things Emilie couldn't understand, but she knew what "go back home" meant. Emilie ignored the comments but she didn't understand how children she'd never been in contact with could hate her so much just because she was from Canada. She'd known a couple of Irish children in Rimouski, but they were just like the others. Certainly not mean.

It had been a horrible day and Emilie was ready to go home, maybe not to Canada yet but at least to their apartment in Flint. She almost ran to the spot where she was supposed to meet Joseph so they could walk back together, but when she got there the scene she witnessed horrified her.

Joseph was on the ground and a group of four children his age were kicking him, spitting on him, and yelling at him words that Emilie couldn't understand beside the familiar names she'd been called herself all day long. Emilie's instinct was to defend her brother so she started yelling. "What's wrong with you, boys? Leave my brother alone right now or my five older brothers will kick your butts!" The boys briefly turned to Emilie but only to laugh at her before going back to Joseph.

Certain they couldn't understand her threat because she'd addressed them in French she was trying to think of English words when someone spoke French behind her. "That's not going to work. Between the four of them these boys probably have fifteen older brothers of their own." Emilie turned to see a girl slightly taller than she was. The girl walked past her and addressed the boys in English. They stopped beating on Joseph, grumbled, and went their way.

"What did you say?" Emilie asked the girl as she picked up Joseph's wool cap and they both walked toward him. She had long curly light brown hair and big blue eyes. Her cheeks were pink, her nose curved up just a little. She looked like the girls in that catalog her mother kept at home who wore all the pretty dresses she'd never have.

"I reminded them they're one warning away from getting kicked out of school and if they do get kicked out, jobs are already lined up for them at the mill where their parents work." The girl grabbed one of Joseph's arms while Emilie grabbed the other and they helped him up. "Are you all right?"

"Yes, I'm fine," Joseph mumbled as he shook the dirt off his clothes. "They're not that strong," he added with the little pride he had left even as he brought his hand to his side. He took his wool cap and put it back on his head with a forced grin. "Thank you," he said to the girl.

"Yes, thank you," Emilie added.

"You're welcome. My father always says we have to stick together, you know, us frogs." They all laughed, which made Joseph grunt in pain. "My name is Angeline Fournier."

"Pleased to meet you, Angeline. I'm Emilie Levesque, and this is my brother Joseph. Do you live in Flint? Do you want to walk with us?"

"Yes, I'd love to walk with you." Angeline bent forward to whisper into Emilie's ear, but made sure Joseph could still hear, "Someone has to be there to defend your brother." Emilie laughed.

"I'm perfectly capable of defending myself," Joseph quickly protested, his pride as obviously hurt as the side of his body. "It'd help if I could understand what they say."

"You will," Angeline reassured him. "You'll see. You'll speak English in no time."

The girls started walking together and Joseph walked behind them, kicking rocks as if they were the boys who attacked him. Emilie was grateful for the time it gave her to speak to Angeline alone. "How long did it take you to learn the language?" she asked.

"Oh, I didn't." The answer left Emilie confused and she showed her puzzlement because Angeline chuckled before she continued. She had beautiful laughter: unrestrained, yet not loud or obnoxious. She laughed like a lady. "I mean, I grew up speaking both languages. I was born here."

"But, aren't you from Canada?"

"Yes, my family is from Sainte-Flavie, but my parents moved down here before I was born. My seven older siblings were all born in Canada, though, and they always say it was easy to learn English. That's how I know."

Emilie knew that Sainte-Flavie was about twenty-five miles from Rimouski and she couldn't help but think it was ironic for them to meet over six hundred miles away from their homes. "Wow, you have a big family. Is that why we never saw you at the river with the other children all summer?"

Angeline looked down, hesitant. "Mostly I don't like to be around other children my age. I'm usually very shy. The two of you needed help; otherwise I may never have talked to you."

"Well, I'm happy you did."

"So am I."

Emilie couldn't even express how happy she was. Angeline was the only girl her age she'd ever felt like she could speak to. For the first time in her life she had a strong urge to make friends with another being, one that didn't walk on four legs. "My brother and I really can't thank you enough for what you did. Do you have any idea why they hate us so much?"

Angeline shrugged. "My father says it's sad that children fight at all. He says the fight should stay among grownups."

"What fight is that?" Emilie asked, genuinely curious.

"I don't understand everything; it's grownup stuff. Papa says that every time the Irish try to strike for better conditions or better wages, Canadians are there to do the work they don't want to do. Papa also says that's why the big bosses love us but that we might be better off joining in the strike because the working conditions really are awful."

"I see. My mother complains about the mill sometimes but my father always says it's still better than starving on the farm."

"I guess that makes sense. Did you like it? The farm?"

There was a sudden light in Angeline's blue eyes and Emilie knew her interest was sincere. "Yes, I liked it. I liked the fresh air and the animals, mostly."

"I loved everything about it." The declaration came from Joseph. He moved to the other side of Angeline. "There's so much space. And forests so thick it takes days to get to the other side, if you can get to the other side at all. And our river is not like this tiny Quequechan River you have here. The Saint-Laurent is so wide that you can't see the other side of it on most days. The sky has to be completely clear and even then you can barely see there's land on the other side."

Joseph went on about Canada and Angeline hung on to every word. Emilie missed her attention but couldn't help smiling. Her first day at school was ending much better than she'd thought possible. She had a friend, a friend that was both like her yet different. A perfect blend of a friend. Just for her. And apparently for her brother.

* * *

Later that night Angeline Fournier had dinner with her family just like every other night. There was just as much noise around her. Her four sisters and her mother talked about the eldest's upcoming wedding. Her three brothers and her father talked about work and politics. Everything was like every other night, except Angeline felt different. She didn't feel alone anymore. She had not one but two new friends, friends her own age.

Five years separated Angeline from the youngest of her older siblings. They all cared for her and took care of her in their own way, but she'd never been close to them like Emilie and Joseph were to each other. Angeline was used to feeling lonely. She never tried to tell anyone because she realized how bizarre it would sound for her to complain of loneliness while she grew up with seven siblings in an apartment where silence was impossible. But bizarre as it may sound, she still felt lonely.

She was the little one, the one no one ever seemed to speak to. Sometimes they spoke about her, but never to her. The only way she'd found to get their attention once in a while was her humor. A joke or a funny face would make them laugh before they went on with their own conversations. She'd craved attention her whole life. Until today. Joseph and Emilie both seemed eager to give her their attention. She smiled to herself as she ate her cabbage soup.

When she'd seen Joseph and Emilie after school she'd just wanted to help them. She figured she'd get the Irish boys off their backs and go her own way. But when Emilie asked her to walk with them, something happened inside her. Her heart opened up to this new girl, almost against her will. She would usually have said no thank you and walked away, but she couldn't help but say yes instead. Something stronger than her and her old habits wanted to walk with Emilie, talk with her and be with her for as long as she could. That skinny girl, with her straight black hair, her black eyes, and her pale skin, was definitely odd, but also interesting. The way she spoke was different, like a grownup. The way she asked questions, with that wrinkle between her thick eyebrows, told Angeline she was truly interested in her answers. When Emilie talked with her Angeline knew she had her undivided attention, and she loved every minute of it.

Joseph was something else. What she liked most in him was his love for Canada. The way he spoke about the home country they shared was fascinating. Angeline had always dreamed of seeing Canada some day and when Joseph described it she felt like she could see it through his eyes. To Angeline, Joseph was the personification of Canada. He even had the look. Square shoulders and a solid build. He was ten but could pass for thirteen. He looked like her brothers when they were younger, like most boys her father referred to as hard-working, strong Canadian boys.

Angeline helped with dishes and went to bed thinking about the Levesque children. They'd decided to walk to school together, all three, the next morning. Angeline's life had changed today. She was no longer the loner she'd always been. She was part of a trio she knew in her nine-year-old heart would stick together for a long time.

MAELSTROM

1891-1898

CHAPTER FIVE

June 1891

Emilie and Angeline waited for Joseph at their usual spot. It was the last day of the school year. The girls were eleven years old and they'd been inseparable since Emilie's first day of school almost three years ago.

"He keeps looking at you," Emilie announced as she looked over Angeline's shoulder toward Tony Berardi, the boy staring at her best friend like she was a juicy piece of roast beef. Tony was in Joseph's class. He was thirteen and evidently appreciated the way Angeline's body had taken the shape of a woman over the school year. Even with the modest skirts and bodices she wore, one would have to be blind not to notice the way her chest protruded now compared to the flat chest she had back in September.

Emilie looked down at her own chest, still flat as an ironing board. She had no hips yet either, while her friend had developed an hourglass shape the boys, especially Tony Berardi, shamelessly admired. No, Emilie was as skinny and odd-looking as ever. She hadn't even gained a whole inch in height since

September and Angeline was now towering over her by four inches, as tall as Joseph.

"He's not looking at me," Angeline murmured. She didn't seem aware of the effect she had on boys yet, which made Emilie smile. "He may be looking at you for all you know."

"Oh please, Angeline, there's nothing to look at." Emilie laughed, but she was disconsolate. Not because Tony Berardi looked at Angeline instead of her. She didn't care about Tony Berardi. She was convinced, however, that *no one* would ever look at her the way Tony looked at Angeline.

"Don't say that, Emilie. You're very pretty. You just don't have the looks that boys like Tony go for. And boys like Tony aren't worth worrying about. No, you'll probably end up with a doctor, Emilie Levesque. Or a librarian."

They both burst out laughing at Angeline's comment. Emilie thought being married to a librarian might be a lovely idea. She'd be surrounded with books then. Of course, the chances she'd meet a librarian in Flint were slim. And a doctor? The only doctor she'd met in her life was old Doctor Michaud in Rimouski and that was only in church on Sundays.

"Is Tony bothering you?" Joseph asked Angeline as he joined them, glaring at Tony. Joseph had started shaving a couple weeks ago. At the age of thirteen he almost looked like a man. His shoulders had broadened, his jaw had squared off, his muscles had started to show. He looked good in his white shirt and suspenders, his sleeves rolled up to his forearms. He was handsome, Emilie thought. She was proud of her brother, especially when he acted protective toward their friend, and she secretly wished he'd put Tony Berardi in his place the way she couldn't.

"No, he's not bothering me, Joseph. Let's go now."

They walked back down the dirt roads that took them to the triple-deckers of Flint like they did every day. Had Emilie known the news that was waiting for them at home, she thought later, she probably would have taken better notice of this specific walk home from school.

Emilie and Joseph did their chores and had dinner with their parents and half-brothers. After dinner, Edouard and Jean-Baptiste uncharacteristically retired to their bedroom. They would usually play cards with their father while Mathilde and Emilie did the dishes. Joseph moved to go to the front room where he and Emilie still slept every night, but Henri stopped him. "Stay here a minute, son. I have something to say to you and your sister."

Mathilde placed her hand on Emilie's shoulder and jerked her chin in the direction of the kitchen table. "I'll finish this by myself, sweetheart."

Emilie sat next to Joseph, both of them facing their father. It was hot in the kitchen. Emilie's hair stuck to her forehead with sweat, but she knew the difficulty she had to breathe was not related to the heat. The nightmare she'd feared for a year was about to become reality. She knew it.

Her father spoke in a lower voice than usual. "Children, as you know we came down here to get enough money to pay back our loan so we can all go back to the farm. That's what we all want, right?"

Joseph immediately nodded his agreement.

"Emilie?"

At her father's insistence, she finally nodded. Going back home to Rimouski was what everyone in her family wanted, most of all her mother. She had no power to oppose their wishes.

"Good. I don't see that happening any time soon with just your mother's and my wages. We need your help."

Emilie glanced at her mother. She was looking down at the dishes she was drying, her back to them. Emilie looked back to her father.

"We got you jobs at the mill. Emilie, you'll be a spinner. Joseph, you'll be a doffer. You both start tomorrow."

There it was. The nightmare. In the past year Emilie had seen dozens of Flint children her age leave school to work at the mill. She knew her turn would come, but she always thought that since he was older, Joseph would be put to work before her, leaving her more time to prepare. Her father stood up and started leaving the kitchen table. Emilie could see the announcement hadn't been easy on him, but she still had one very important question. "Papa?"

"Yes, Emilie?"

"We'll be working at the mill all summer, then, right? Until school starts again?"

Her father sighed deeply. "You'll be working at the mill until we go back home, Emilie. No more school." With that, he left the kitchen and went outside.

Mathilde came up behind Emilie and placed both of her maternal hands on the small shoulders. "I'm sorry, Emilie. We know how much you love school, but you're old enough now. I'm sure you understand."

Emilie nodded as tears fell freely to her pale cheeks.

"We do understand, Maman. It's time we contribute to the family's effort." Joseph's voice was firm, determined, without a hint of regret.

"Thank you, Joseph. We knew we could count on you. On both of you," she added, taking off her apron and folding it over one of the wooden dining chairs.

"Of course, Maman," Emilie finally said. It took everything she had not to let her voice break and show her heartbreak. When she turned to her mother, she met a comforting smile.

"Well, you should both go to bed now. Tomorrow will be a long day."

Joseph went to the front room but Emilie hesitated.

"Yes. I just need to run to the outhouse first."

"All right, but be careful out there."

"Yes, I will."

While Emilie and her family occupied an apartment on the third floor of the triple-decker where they lived, Angeline's family lived on the first floor of their building, making it much easier for Emilie to knock at the window of the room where she knew her friend was sleeping. Angeline shared her room with two of her older siblings, but judging by the animated conversation and laughter that came from their kitchen window, Emilie was almost certain Angeline would be the only one in the bedroom now and she was right. Angeline came to the window wearing an ample nightgown and her face immediately showed concern when she recognized her friend. She frowned and opened the window as quickly as she could. "Emilie, what are you doing here so late? What's wrong?"

Emilie had run the two streets that separated her apartment from Angeline's. She was still slightly out of breath when she spoke. "I just wanted to let you know that I won't be able to meet you at the river tomorrow as we planned."

"Oh? Why not?"

Emilie watched as Angeline looked down, disappointment mixed with worry on her beautiful face. Emilie couldn't help but caress her friend's soft cheek with her long and slim fingers, forcing her to look back at her. "I'm sorry, Angeline. It's not that I don't want to spend the time with you, you must believe me. It's just that…"

"That what?" Concern once again took over Angeline's expression.

"It's happening, Angeline. Joseph and I are starting at the mill tomorrow." Emilie could no longer hold on to her tears.

Angeline reached through the open window and grabbed both of her friend's hands. "Oh, no. Already? But you're my age!" Angeline paused, firmly holding Emilie's hands as she sobbed. "So we won't have much time together over the summer, I assume?"

Emilie cried even harder at Angeline's words. "It's worse than that," she finally said through her sobs. "I'm not coming back to school in the fall, Angeline." Emilie slowly calmed down, as if stating the words out loud had made them so true that there was no point fighting her fate.

"But…but you love school so much." Angeline's voice was small, incredulous.

"I know, Angeline. I do love it. But none of us gets to go to school very long around here. Why would it be different for me? I'm not special."

"Don't you say that, Emilie Levesque. You hear me? You are so very special. Oh, I can't believe this is happening. When am I going to see you?" Angeline leaned her forehead against Emilie's as they held hands.

Emilie's heart broke at the thought of not swimming in the river with her best friend or sitting by their favorite buttonwood tree every day, chatting about the books Emilie read, the drama *du jour* in Angeline's large family, the Flint children they didn't care for. And their walks to and from school. Oh, she would miss those most of all. She couldn't lose all of her beautiful friendship with Angeline because she was becoming a mill worker. It had taken her nine years to find a true friend, and no one could take that away from her now. She wouldn't let that happen.

"On Sundays? We could spend every Sunday afternoon together if you want, and we could find a few minutes after dinner like tonight. Could you do that?"

"Yes, of course I could," Angeline answered.

Emilie was pleased to see her smile for the first time during her unannounced visit. Angeline's whole face illuminated when she smiled, even in the dark.

"I would love that very much, Emilie."

"Great. I will see you tomorrow after dinner, then. Good night, Angeline."

"Good night, Emilie." Emilie kissed her friend on the cheek and ran back home, her heart a little less heavy now that she'd made plans to see Angeline, but her spirit still dragging behind with the knowledge that life as she knew it, her childhood, was officially and irrevocably over.

Angeline stayed in bed but couldn't go back to sleep after Emilie left. She tried to make sense of this new development and simply couldn't. Why would a girl who loved school as much as Emilie did be forced to stop and go to work while she, who really didn't care much for school at all, got to keep going? Angeline could still hear her siblings talk loudly in the kitchen. Two of her older sisters and one of her older brothers were now married and had their own apartments, but she could swear every time someone left the familial home the ones that stayed got louder to make up for it.

With all the commotion going on, she barely heard a knock on the bedroom door. "Angeline?" Her father's voice, even when he whispered, carried over any other noise in the apartment. "May I come in?"

"Yes, Papa."

Her father came in and closed the door behind him. He walked to Angeline's bed and sat by her feet. "Was that your friend I saw running in front of the house a little while ago? That little Levesque girl?"

"Yes. She came to tell me she couldn't meet me at the river tomorrow because she's starting at the mill."

"I see." Her father looked genuinely upset by the news. "Is it just for the summer?"

"No. She says she won't be coming back to school in the fall."

"I see," her father said again, this time with more weight in the two simple words, and Angeline knew he understood all the implications behind her statement. "I guess you'll miss her a lot, huh?"

"I will, Papa, but that's not the worst part."

"It's not?"

"No, not even close. The worst part is that of all the children I know, Emilie's the one who loves school the most. She loves it so much, Papa. And she's so good at it. It's so unfair that I get to keep going to school and she doesn't. So unfair. And I feel so guilty about it."

"Oh, Angeline. I understand," her father said as he rubbed Angeline's hand with his large, callused fingers. "It really is unfair. You see, we can afford to keep you in school longer because we have seven wages to pay for this household and still save some money. Your older siblings didn't go to school as long as you did either, Angeline. We needed help. Just like Emilie's parents need help. It's unfair, perhaps, but that's the way it is. You're the lucky one, Angeline."

"But I don't want to be the lucky one, Papa," Angeline said as she felt tears welling up in her eyes. "It makes me feel terrible. Please. Can I go to work with Emilie?"

Angeline felt her father wrap his strong arms around her and she cried against his chest. "Do you think that's what Emilie would want, my girl?"

"I don't know," she answered weakly.

"I do. Your friend wouldn't want you to leave school, Angeline."

"Are you sure?"

"Yes. Emilie would want you to go to school and learn everything she can't learn in school with you. She'd want you to work hard and remember everything so you can share it with her. That's what she'd want. I'm sure of it."

"Really?" Angeline asked as the tears subsided.

"Really. That's how you can make what's unfair a little bit better, my girl. That's what you want, isn't it?"

"Yes. You're right, Papa."

Her father hugged Angeline again and kissed her forehead before leaving the bedroom. Angeline turned in her bed to face the window, armed with a new sense of purpose. She would not disappoint Emilie.

CHAPTER SIX

June 1891

Emilie was used to the sound of the siren calling mill workers every morning at five a.m. and she was used to being up that early. Her mother helped her prepare for work while her father helped Joseph. The preparation was brief. Emilie's mother gave her an apron to wear over her everyday brown skirt and a short-sleeved white blouse. She explained that the short sleeves were to make the heat more bearable but also to avoid getting a sleeve caught in machinery. To protect her hair from the same machinery, she wore it in a tight chignon on top of her head, just like her mother.

Joseph wore denim overalls and a white shirt and rolled up his sleeves. Henri told both of them that all they needed to do was exactly what they were told and wished them luck on their first day. Then they walked to the mill together.

The large granite building had been there all along, but it was as if Emilie really noticed it for the first time. It seemed like all of Flint was moving in its direction, like the ants she'd observed at the farm, all lined up and following each other until they disappeared under a large rock. The cotton mill was their rock. Their enormous, granite rock.

When they entered the building, the heat and humidity stopped Emilie in her tracks. She'd thought the apartment was hot, but it was nothing compared to the thick, suffocating wall of breathless air she'd just walked into. She started sweating right away. She looked at her brother and saw droplets of perspiration on his forehead as well. Her mother had told her the humidity was necessary to keep the cotton thread from breaking, but Emilie wasn't expecting this much. She had to tell herself to take another breath before she could keep following her mother to the spinning room with Joseph. Their father, Jean-Baptiste and Edouard disappeared in the direction of the blowing room where Emilie knew they worked even though she wasn't sure what they did.

As she slowly adapted to the heat and humidity, Emilie realized that the cotton dust floating everywhere probably didn't help her breathe any easier. The cacophony of the machinery and the strong smell of sweat, cotton and machine oil aggressed her other senses, yes, but she kept thinking that if she could at least breathe a little easier, she could get used to the rest of it. Her mother assured her she would get used to breathing in the air of the mill as well, but Emilie thought she didn't look that convinced herself.

The spinning room was divided into fifteen long rows of machinery. Mathilde started working immediately while Emilie and Joseph had to follow a man who started explaining what their job would be. The man didn't say what his name was or ask what theirs were. Names were not important. He yelled his instructions, partly because he had to over the noise of the machines, but also partly because, Emilie imagined, he seemed to enjoy yelling through his thick mustache.

The man explained that the bobbins on top of the machines were filled with roving, a cotton fiber that was clean but not tight enough to be weaved into cloth yet. The spinning process took that roving and made it pass through rollers at high speed, literally spinning it. Spinning tightened the fiber into thread. As a spinner, Emilie's job was to move quickly up and down a row of machinery and repair breaks and snags in the roving. She would wear around her waist a case to carry a pair of scissors, her only tools.

As a doffer, Joseph's job would be to replace empty bobbins with new ones as quickly as possible. No matter what their job was, their first and most important duty was to keep the machines going at all times. When a machine had to be stopped temporarily, their job was to get it started again, and fast. "Stoppage means loss. Stoppage means loss." The man repeated the words a few times, looking straight into their eyes. His goal was to scare them and it worked. The man's speech lasted no more than ten minutes but Emilie already felt more pressure than she'd felt her entire life.

Before he left to do more important things, the man told them they would be observing for the rest of the day but were expected to be fully functional and productive by Monday morning. The job was not, after all, that hard to learn, he added. Joseph was paired with a boy barely older than he was, Martin, who had been a doffer for two years already. Emilie was lucky enough to be paired with her mother.

She realized very quickly that observing was indeed the way she would learn her job. Her mother had to keep her working speed and didn't have time to stop to answer a question. Besides, the machines were making too much noise for a question to be heard in the first place. No, the only information available was visual and the only tools she was given to assimilate that information were her eyes. She watched as her mother moved up and down the row she was assigned to, cut roving that was problematic, made knots at lightning speed. Everything happened so quickly that at first Emilie couldn't see the problems her mother spotted so easily or understand how they were repaired. Slowly, though, she started to notice the same problems her mother did and understand how to repair them. Toward the end of day, she attempted a few repairs of her own and although they were not perfect her mother seemed happy with her progress.

Joseph appeared to learn just as quickly. She saw him replace a few empty bobbins by himself as Martin watched. He was not as fast as Martin, of course, but he wasn't as slow as some of the other boys she'd seen either. Emilie didn't hate her first day of work as much as she'd feared. She was learning. It wasn't the kind of learning that required books or school. But it was learning nonetheless. The hours went by fast and when the sirens announced the end of the day, Emilie was surprised to find out she was almost used to the thick wet air she was breathing.

Until she stepped outside and fresh air penetrated her lungs. She took a few deep breaths and smiled. She was free. She would go home and have dinner and then go visit Angeline for a few minutes. That was the plan. But Emilie was so exhausted she fell asleep at the table in the middle of dinner and barely was conscious enough to notice her father lifting her up and taking her to bed. Tomorrow was Sunday, she thought as she yawned, her eyelids too heavy to open her eyes. She would see Angeline tomorrow.

The buttonwood tree Angeline and Emilie called their own was located by the river but far enough from the water's edge that they were rarely bothered by any of the other children. They usually sat on the ground by the large trunk, the generous foliage above acting as a roof over their heads. Protected by their tree, their sanctuary, they felt like they could say anything they wanted and no one could ever hear them.

Right after lunch on Sunday Angeline ran to their tree, anxious to see Emilie and hear all about her first day at the mill. She was disappointed that Emilie hadn't visited her the night before as promised, but realized she might have been too tired. She hoped she was indeed just too tired and not hurt by the machinery, as accidents were common. She'd stayed awake part of the night worrying about her best friend. Both disappointment and worry rushed back to her when she arrived at the buttonwood tree and didn't find Emilie sitting there, leaning against the trunk, reading a book as she waited for her. Emilie always beat her to the tree. Something had to be wrong.

Angeline was seriously considering walking to the Levesque's apartment to find out when Emilie finally arrived.

"I hope you haven't been waiting too long," Emilie said anxiously.

"I just got here. I'm so happy to see you."

"Me too," Emilie declared with a weak smile.

Angeline hugged her friend, instantly relieved to see her. Emilie had always been smaller than her but now in her arms she seemed even more delicate. Angeline held her at arm's length and examined her. Emilie also looked paler than usual. She wore a dark brown skirt and close-fitting brown blouse, her everyday, severe attire contrasting with Angeline's own white Sunday dress, embellished with thin light blue stripes, pleats over her bosom, and a slight puff in the sleeves. "Are you all right, Emilie? Was it awful? I was so worried about you."

"I know, I'm so sorry. I really wanted to see you, believe me, but I couldn't even stay awake through dinner. I don't think I'll be able to see you as often as we planned."

Angeline saw Emilie's eyes well up with tears and her heart sank. So unfair, she thought again for the thousandth time in three days. Emilie was too small, too fragile for such hard work. She looked up at the thick leaves of their buttonwood tree, realizing that, just like herself, they were powerless to protect Emilie from this situation. Angeline closed her eyes in resignation. She couldn't change what was happening. All she could do was support her friend the best she could. So she put on a smile before she looked at her friend again in an attempt to reassure her. "Don't worry about it, Emilie. It doesn't make sense for you to visit me after a day at the mill. We'll have Sundays, right?"

"Right," Emilie repeated, her voice breaking as tears started to fall.

All Angeline wanted to do was to hold Emilie and cry with her for a few hours, but that wasn't what they both needed, so she took a deep breath and took both of Emilie's hands, shaking her gently. "That's right, and we're not going to spend it crying. We've got better things to do, my dear friend. Like talk about how Arthur just proposed to Louise, for example." Angeline was relieved when she saw a smile on Emilie's face. Her diversion seemed to work.

"No! Your sister is really going to get married to that idiot?"

"That idiot just inherited a farm in the region of *Estrie* so yes, she's going to marry him."

"I can't believe it. What do your parents think about it?"

"Believe it or not, my mother is thrilled about it. My father is just disappointed the farm is in *Estrie* instead of the *Bas-du-fleuve*, where we come from. He says it's the most beautiful region in Canada."

"He's probably right about that, Angeline. It really is beautiful."

Angeline was surprised to hear a nostalgic tone in Emilie's voice when she talked about their homeland. Emilie rarely even talked about Rimouski, unlike her brother Joseph who couldn't stop talking about it. She'd never seemed to miss it at all.

Emilie added, "Maybe Louise is doing the right thing, after all."

"You can't really think that way, Emilie. One should marry for love, not for a situation. You've told me that so many times. Remember? You can't be telling me you approve of my sister's decision now. I don't believe you." The cotton mill had to be even worse than Angeline had thought if her friend was ready to reconsider all the romantic notions she'd read about in her books and had shared with Angeline over the years.

"No, no, of course not," Emilie replied, as if Angeline's words had brought back convictions she'd temporarily forgotten. "I don't approve of her decision, Angeline. I'm just saying it can be understandable. Real life is not like books, after all."

"Maybe not, but promise me that if I ever consider getting married for any other reason than love, you won't let me." Emilie didn't answer quickly enough for Angeline so she insisted. "Promise me, Emilie."

Emilie smiled at Angeline and appeared to be weighing her words very carefully before she spoke. "I promise I won't let my best friend get married to anyone unless I'm thoroughly convinced that marrying that person will make her happy. Satisfied?"

Angeline smiled and nodded but at the same time she tried to decide if Emilie had just manipulated words to sound like she'd said one thing while she meant another, an art Angeline knew her friend mastered all too well.

CHAPTER SEVEN

September 1893

After lunch on the first Sunday of September, fourteen-year-old Emilie took Pleasant Street and started walking west toward Main Street. The Levesques rarely ventured outside of Flint Village but Emilie was determined. Her parents wouldn't approve if they knew where she was really going; they thought she was meeting with Angeline as usual. Sundays with Angeline had been sacred for the past two years but Angeline too was now working as a spinner at the mill and Emilie saw her every day, so she didn't feel guilty about doing something different on this specific Sunday. Her destination: Fall River's town hall, where she'd recently learned from a conversation overheard at work that a library was open to the public.

Emilie craved books. She needed to learn something new. Her life was stagnant. It had not taken her long to learn her job as a spinner. It was repetitive, boring, stultifying. For two years Angeline had shared what she'd learned in school with Emilie. They'd gone over every topic discussed in class, Emilie's questions making Angeline dig deep in her memory and notes, sometimes even forcing her to ask questions of her own during class so she could satisfy Emilie's thirst for knowledge. They had even done Angeline's homework together. Emilie had almost felt like she was still going to school. She was grateful to Angeline for sharing that part of her life with her. Now that Angeline wasn't going back to school, Emilie had to find a new source of knowledge. The idea of a space where books were available to the public was exhilarating and gave her steps lightness and speed that her walks to and from the mill could never duplicate.

Unlike the streets of Flint that were nothing but wide dirt paths, Pleasant Street and Main Street were bordered with sidewalks. Streetcars were circulating on the tracks laid in the middle of the road while horse-drawn carriages traveled on either side. The architecture was also a lot more interesting than the triple-deckers of Flint. It seemed every building had been built with a lot of thought. Emilie slowed down when she reached Borden Block and walked in front of the Academy of Music, where she knew live concerts were held. She was happy to be reminded that there was more to Fall River than cotton dust and machine oil, despite the fact that her access to those other activities was limited if not entirely blocked.

Emilie finally arrived at the town hall and stopped in front of the stone building, suddenly intimidated. Did she even belong here? She'd never seen a building this beautiful other than churches. The town hall even had a bell tower. Instead of being topped with a cross, however, this bell tower was decorated with large clocks on each of its four sides. Fall River had no excuse not to be on time for everything, Emilie mused.

She took a deep breath and looked down to evaluate her appearance. She was wearing a white Sunday dress with blue stripes Angeline had given to her because it had become too small for her. At fourteen, Angeline was a fully grown woman and had all the necessary curves. Emilie had finally grown up too and she was now only two inches shorter than Angeline, but she still had the shape of a young girl, a shape she was beginning to fear she would keep all of her life. She didn't fill Angeline's dress as well as Angeline had two years ago, but she still looked clean and decent.

She took another breath, made sure the pale blue ribbon added to her simple sailor straw hat was in place, and started walking toward the building. She pulled on the door handle, pushed, pulled again, but the large door didn't move.

"May I help you, miss?"

Emilie turned toward the low-pitched, soft but distinctively female voice and came face-to-face with the most elegant woman she'd ever seen. Her features were delicate, modest, a stage for piercing blue eyes that demanded attention. She was probably ten years older than Emilie, and obviously from a higher social standing, judging by the rich fabric of her fashionable dress and the undoubtedly expensive black hat heavily decorated with chiffon and feathers.

Emilie hesitated. She was intimidated, and not just because of the woman's higher social and financial class. She had learned English and could speak it very well but had never been able to rid herself of a heavy French Canadian accent that betrayed her origins as soon as she opened her mouth. The woman would know she came straight out of Flint Village's little Canada as soon as she spoke and for some reason she didn't want her to know. She sighed and finally answered. "I was looking for the public library."

"Oh dear. It's closed on Sundays," the woman answered with a compassionate smile.

Emilie's shoulders fell forward and she sighed again, this time with frustration. "What? When are people supposed to use it, then?" As she asked the question Emilie realized she'd been an idiot to think a public library could be open to factory workers like her.

"People come during the week," the woman answered, then paused. Emilie knew she'd come to the same realization. "But you work during the week, don't you?" Emilie nodded. "Did you walk all the way here from Flint?"

Emilie nodded again, and noted for the first time that her feet hurt. There was no point trying to hide now. She'd been exposed.

"Oh, my poor child," the woman said with genuine empathy. "My name is Helen Banville," she started as she extended her hand to Emilie. "My husband, Doctor Maurice Banville, is from Canada, just like you."

Emilie shook Helen's hand but didn't reply, shocked that a doctor's wife was taking the time to introduce herself to her.

"You're from Canada, aren't you?" Helen insisted.

"Yes," Emilie finally answered. "Emilie Levesque. Nice to meet you."

"Nice to meet you too, Emilie. You know what? I'm sure my husband would be very happy to meet you too. Why don't you join us for tea? Our house is just a couple blocks away and it would give your feet some much needed rest."

Emilie was surprised by Helen's invitation and really wanted to accept but she knew her place and it was not in a doctor's house. "That's very kind of you, Mrs. Banville, but I can't impose," she protested.

"You're not imposing, dear, I'm inviting you. Please, follow me." Before Emilie could say anything else, Helen took her hand and gently pulled her into motion until Emilie obediently followed her the two blocks that separated the town hall from the Banville's residence.

And what a residence it was. The pale yellow Victorian home immediately impressed Emilie with its turret and a large covered porch that occupied its entire facade. Emilie imagined her parents sitting in the wooden rocking chairs on the porch and she smiled thinking of how much they would enjoy it. With two stories plus a basement, Dr. Banville's home was probably as big as one of the triple-deckers of Flint Village, except unlike the triple-deckers, which six families called home, this house was inhabited by one single family: the Banvilles.

A lady wearing a white apron met them at the door and took a bag Helen had been carrying as well as her hat. She offered to take Emilie's as well but Emilie preferred to keep her hat firmly in her hands, holding it against her stomach. Helen asked the lady, whose name was Rose—a lovely name for a domestic, Emilie thought—to bring their tea to the parlor, and Emilie followed Helen, continuing to marvel at the beauty of the house, especially the extensive woodwork of the dark staircase that curved up until it disappeared toward the second floor.

A beautiful wool rug covered the center of the parlor with rich red and gold patterns of rose bouquets and decorative swirls. Emilie hesitated when Helen invited her to sit next to her on a sofa upholstered with a similar rose bouquet pattern but in softer pinks on a lighter cream fabric. The sofa was framed in dark wood with curved legs and carved details that Emilie studied with admiration. She'd almost forgotten about her host until Helen laughed and urged, "Please, join me Emilie. I don't usually keep my guests standing up while I'm sitting down. You're making me feel guilty."

Emilie smiled politely and finally sat next to Helen. "I'm sorry. It's just that everything in your home is so beautiful."

"Thank you, Emilie. My husband and I chose everything we own with care."

"It shows."

Rose brought a tray holding a teapot and three cups and put it down on the round table in front of them. Emilie automatically started to move toward the table but stopped herself and watched in silence as Rose poured tea. She wondered how letting someone else serve her could seem so natural to Helen. It made her feel so uncomfortable.

Just as Rose finished serving the tea, a handsome man walked in wearing a three-piece suit and an ascot tie. He had dark hair and a dark trimmed beard that reminded her of the rare pictures she'd seen of her father when he was much younger. The leather doctor bag the man handed to Rose before she left the room confirmed the man's identity as Dr. Banville even before Helen stood up to introduce her husband to Emilie, who immediately got to her feet as well. "Maurice, there you are. I met this nice young lady outside of the city hall and I wanted you to meet her as well. Emilie Levesque, meet my husband, Dr. Maurice Banville."

"Pleased to meet you, Dr. Banville," Emilie said timidly.

"All the pleasure's mine, Emilie. And please, call me Maurice. *Tu habites à Flint, j'imagine?*"

"*Oui,*" Emilie started before Helen interrupted.

"Wait. English, please. I knew you'd be happy to have tea with a fellow Canadian, Maurice, but please don't forget I don't understand French."

"Of course, dear," Maurice said. He rolled his eyes and looked at Emilie with a mocking smile that made her laugh and put her at ease. She had a strange, instantaneous feeling of kinship with Dr. Banville. Maurice. Something she hadn't felt before. "Please sit down, ladies. Let's enjoy this tea before it gets cold." Maurice sat across from them in an armchair with the same wooden frame and light upholstery as the sofa on which she and Helen sat.

They shared tea and Maurice asked Emilie all about Flint, the mill, her family and Rimouski. His interest seemed genuine. The more Emilie talked, the more comfortable she became and the more she liked the Banvilles. She'd liked Helen right away because she admired her elegance and appreciated her kindness and generosity. But Maurice struck a different chord in Emilie. There was a familiarity with Maurice that went beyond the fact that they were both Canadians and Maurice was a nice person. He had a curious, inquiring mind that bled through intense green eyes and that Emilie recognized all too well. "All right, young lady, we've been interrogating you for close to an hour now. Is there anything you'd like to know about us?"

Emilie hesitated only briefly before she jumped at the chance to ask questions. There were a million things she wanted to know about the Banvilles. "Yes, of course. Where in Canada are you from? How long have you lived in Fall River? How did you two meet?"

Maurice laughed a deep, contagious laughter that made Helen and Emilie chuckle in their turn. "Wait a minute, Emilie. One at a time. I'm from Montreal but I was sent to a Catholic boarding school in Boston when I was twelve. I went to medical school in Boston and when I graduated five years ago I started working here in Fall River. That's when Helen and I met."

"He came to my parents' house when my father fell ill," Helen continued. "He accompanied us until Dad passed away and then he continued to visit. We talked and he made me laugh. He made me feel better. Less than a year later we were married."

Emilie watched as Helen spoke and she saw the same kind of love in her eyes as she'd seen a few times in her mother's eyes when she spoke of her father, especially of their first years on the farm. It was a mix of admiration and tenderness she would always associate with true love. "Do you have children?" Emilie was compelled to ask.

Helen's eyes met Maurice's and Emilie caught sadness in that brief moment before Maurice turned to her and answered. "No, we haven't been blessed with a child yet, but we would love that very much." He swallowed and forced a smile and Emilie knew she should not push further. "But tell me, Emilie, what possessed you to walk to the town hall all the way from Flint on a Sunday?"

Emilie welcomed the change of subject. "I wanted to go to the library."

"Hmm. Were you looking for anything in particular?"

"Not really. Just something I haven't read before."

"Hmm," he repeated with one of his mischievous smiles Emilie was already growing fond of. "I may be able to help with that. Will you follow me?" Emilie turned to Helen who simply smiled as if she knew what was about to happen. Emilie stood up and followed Maurice, who seemed even taller now that they were standing side by side. Maurice opened heavy wooden pocket doors that led to a smaller room that left Emilie breathless as soon as she entered. She could hear Maurice laugh quietly behind her as she took in the tall bookcases that covered the walls of the small room Emilie could only describe as a private library. "Are these all…"

"Mine. Yes. Why don't you choose a few? Then come back for more when you're done reading them."

Emilie turned to face Maurice, not certain she'd heard him correctly. Helen was standing beside him and he'd put his arm around her waist. They made a striking couple. "Are you saying I can borrow any of these books?"

Maurice laughed again. "That's what I'm saying. But there's one condition." Emilie held her breath. "Whenever you come back for more, you have to stay with us for tea so we can discuss what you've read. Do we have a deal?"

"Yes," Emilie answered enthusiastically. "Thank you so much."

"You're welcome, Emilie. We enjoyed your visit and if we can help feed a young hungry mind like yours, I believe it's our duty to do so. You're a special young woman, Emilie Levesque. Don't forget it."

Emilie smiled with gratitude and started studying the leather-bound books on the shelves. Overwhelmed, she decided to focus on one particular shelf, knowing she could come back later. Emilie didn't think Maurice and Helen realized the magnitude of the gift they were offering her. It was by far the best day of her life and as she browsed the titles in front of her she couldn't wait to share all of it with Angeline. She first chose Jane Austen's *Pride and Prejudice* and Mark Twain's *Adventures of Huckleberry Finn*. Then she smiled when she found a French section and picked Victor Hugo's *Les Misérables* and Honoré de Balzac's *Les Chouans*. Helen gave her an old brown leather mailbag to carry the books.

Maurice took her home on his horse-drawn buggy. He understood when Emilie asked him to drop her off just before they got to Flint, and was even amused by the necessary secrecy of their encounter.

Emilie left the leather mailbag concealed under old wood planks behind the triple-decker until the rest of her family was in bed. When she was certain everyone, especially Joseph, was asleep, she went to retrieve the bag and carefully laid the four books and the empty bag under her mattress. She would have to tell Joseph about her meeting with the Banvilles if she wanted to read the precious books in bed in the faint light of the moon, but it would have to wait until tomorrow. That night, despite a lumpy and somewhat hard mattress, she slept like a log.

CHAPTER EIGHT

September 1893

As she walked with Joseph and Angeline to the mill the next morning, Emilie told them about her hike to the city hall, her encounter with the Banvilles, and the books hiding under her mattress. They'd made a habit of strolling together to the mill a few minutes before the rest of their families in the morning and back home a few minutes after their families every night. It was a much shorter stretch than when they walked to and from school together but it still gave them some time to talk, time they had so little of now.

Angeline already knew about the walk to the town hall but everyone else, including Joseph, had thought she'd spent the day with Angeline. When he found out the truth, he was furious. "Are you crazy, walking alone all the way to Main Street? All kinds of things could have happened to you, Emilie! If you'd told me about it I could have gone with you. It would have been safer."

"If I'd told you Maman and Papa would have found out, Joseph. You know you never get away with anything."

Joseph grunted and turned his attention to Angeline, "And you, you should have known better too. You should have told me." He kicked a small rock with all the energy of his frustration and Emilie was relieved it didn't hit the small group walking in front of them.

"Joseph," Angeline started calmly, "you know as well as I do that when your sister has something in mind, there's no stopping her. And she's right. If we'd told you someone else would have found out. You're cursed that way." She smiled impishly at Joseph and he started laughing.

Emilie was both fascinated and annoyed with the effect Angeline had on Joseph, with her pretty curved up nose, big blue eyes and long curly light brown hair. Emilie could say something that got Joseph angry but when Angeline repeated the exact same thing two minutes later he thought it was the funniest thing he'd ever heard. Of course, she didn't say it the same way. Angeline had a talent for finding humor in any situation and to deliver the most horrible truth with remarkable charm. Emilie admired Angeline's technique, but lately it also aggravated her. She loved having all of Angeline's humor and charm addressed to her, but didn't like it as much when it made Joseph or other boys laugh the way Joseph was laughing now. That happened more and more and Emilie hated it. She didn't tell Angeline, of course. She knew she couldn't be so selfish. She was Angeline's best friend and Angeline was hers, but sooner or later a boy would steal much more of her best friend's attention and she tried to prepare for that moment. Her heart clenched at the thought.

"Besides, you should be happy for your sister," Angeline continued as she grabbed Emilie's arm and walked closer to her, bringing peace back to Emilie's mind and heart. "All Emilie wanted was a library so she could read all the books she wants and she found one. I, for one, can't wait for her to share these new stories with me." Angeline smiled at Emilie and Emilie could only smile back. Her friend really understood her need to learn. Better than her own brother.

"All right," Joseph finally conceded, "but next time you visit the doctor and his wife, I'll walk you there. I won't stay and wait for you since the doctor is kind enough to bring you back, but I'll walk you there."

"Don't be silly, Joseph. It's far."

"I said I'll walk you, Emilie," Joseph added with a sternness that surprised Emilie. She witnessed a smile and a nod of approval from Angeline to Joseph, who squared his shoulders, accepting her silent endorsement with pride as they entered the mill.

Angeline had tried to find a minute to talk to Emilie alone all day. Of course there was never a minute to talk at the mill. Maybe if Emilie hadn't worked at the other end of the spinning room she would have found a way. But even then, with the ruckus of the machines, it would have been impossible to talk. Yet she needed to talk to Emilie alone, without Joseph around.

What she'd told Joseph that morning was true: she was happy Emilie had found a way to read all the books she wanted. She knew how important that was to Emilie. The whole truth, however, was that she feared Emilie would spend all of her Sundays with the Banvilles and the little time they had together would be reduced to nothing. She'd missed Emilie that Sunday. She'd spent the day with her family listening to them talk about important adult stuff while she disappeared in the decor just like she used to before she'd met Emilie. She lived for her Sundays with Emilie and she couldn't bear the thought of losing them. So after work she met Emilie and Joseph outside of the mill as usual and gently asked Joseph, "Would you mind walking ahead of us tonight, Joseph? There are some things I need to discuss with your sister in private." When Joseph hesitated with a puzzled look, she simply added, "Girl things."

"Oh, I see. Of course. I'll go ahead, but I won't be far. Just call if you need me."

She smiled at him and he blushed as he often did when he responded to her smiles nowadays, which she found strange but endearing. She'd smiled at Joseph a thousand times over the years, but the blushing had only begun recently.

Joseph was not the only one. Many boys blushed when she smiled at them and Angeline found it quite amusing. She was in no hurry to find a *prétendant*, as her mother called the suitors that courted her older sisters. All she wanted was more time with her best friend, to talk about the books she was reading, to see the world through her eyes, a world that went beyond Flint, the mill, suitors, marriage and children. When she was with Emilie everything seemed possible and she needed to keep believing in that world a little longer. More than anything, she simply needed to be with Emilie.

Angeline grabbed Emilie's arm as she liked to do when they walked together, and giggled when she saw the familiar crease between her friend's eyebrows. "Don't worry, it's nothing horrible. It's not really a girl thing, but more an *us* thing."

"What do you mean, Angeline?" The furrow on Emilie's forehead deepened.

"I mean I'm very happy you met the Banvilles, but I'm also afraid that we won't see each other on Sundays anymore. Yesterday was such a bore, Emilie. I don't think I could stand it if you told me you'll be going to the Banvilles every Sunday."

Emilie sighed with what appeared to be relief and smiled as she rested her fingers on the hand Angeline had placed on her forearm. Emilie's hands were always so warm, the contact soothed Angeline instantly, even before Emilie started to speak. "Oh Angeline, I couldn't stand it either. I do want to visit the Banvilles often but I promise you I will find time for you, for us. Our time together is precious to me too. Please tell me you know that."

"I do," Angeline answered. A small part of her was still scared she might lose her friend but she was mostly reassured when they arrived at the triple-deckers and went their separate ways to have dinner with their families and get some rest.

When Angeline went to bed that night she couldn't go to sleep right away. She thought of the way Emilie's face lit up when she spoke of the Banvilles and she wondered, not for the first time, what she had to offer Emilie in their friendship. She took and learned so much from Emilie and she feared she didn't have much to give in return. Not since she'd stopped going to school and joined Emilie at the mill. Then she thought of Emilie's laughter and she smiled. She could always make Emilie laugh. She turned onto her side and stared at the window, then closed her eyes and drifted to sleep thinking of Emilie's warm hand on hers.

CHAPTER NINE

February 1895

"I don't understand why you don't ask Marcella to the dance, Joseph. Everyone is expecting you to. Especially Marcella."

The dance was planned for the following Saturday and as Joseph walked Emilie to the Banvilles on a sunny and unusually warm Sunday in late February, she was determined to find out more about her brother's intentions with Marcella Paquette, a girl who lived on their street in Flint. After all, if you believed Marcella, she and Joseph were surely going to get married someday. Joseph, however, had never even mentioned Marcella's name in Emilie's presence.

Joseph had kept his promise to escort Emilie to the Banvilles on each of her trips to Maurice's private library. It had given them time to talk and share their thoughts the way they did when they lived in Rimouski. Emilie was pleased they'd grown closer again and she was certain that if Joseph had been interested in courting Marcella she would have known about it. Then again, it was quite strange that her brother was not courting anyone, she thought as she observed him walking with a confident stride by her side.

Joseph had just turned seventeen and was undeniably handsome. His shoulders were wide under his dark gray overcoat. His square jaw was covered with a short beard, just a shade or two darker than his dark blond hair, which he wore a little longer and feathered over his ears. His eyes were still blue but the summer sky blue had become darker, closer to the color of the river at dusk. The color gave him an intense stare that Marcella couldn't stop talking about.

"Marcella? What are you talking about?"

Emilie laughed, not surprised by her brother's stupefaction. It only confirmed what she'd thought. "Marcella Paquette, Joseph. She's certain you're about to ask her to the dance."

"I don't know why she'd think that. We've barely shared ten words besides hello and goodbye."

"Well, she's certainly made a lot of those ten words. I think she may have chosen her wedding dress by now," Emilie said and she burst out laughing.

Joseph joined her in her laughter but soon went back to staring straight in front of him as they walked, deep in his thoughts. Emilie waited two blocks before she dared asking, "So, Joseph, if you're not interested in Marcella, who are you interested in? There must be a girl somewhere in Flint that's caught your eye."

"Sure there is, Emilie. I'm sure some fellow's caught your eye too, no?"

"Don't be ridiculous, Joseph. I still look like a little girl," Emilie answered as she swept her hand from her shoulders to her hips, indicating her svelte physique. "No boy's going to look at this broomstick. Besides, I'm quite content with my books. But don't change the subject. Tell me who's the lucky girl."

"I can't," Joseph answered and he sighed.

"Why not? Do I know her?"

"Of course you know her, Emilie. We know everyone in Flint. In fact, you know her too well, that's why I can't tell you."

Emilie felt her stomach instantly churn. Angeline. Of course Joseph would be interested in Angeline. Every young and not so young man in Flint was interested in Angeline. She should have seen it. She should not be surprised. She should even be happy Angeline might become a member of her family. Yet her stomach kept churning and she had to stop walking and close her eyes for a minute to compose herself.

Emilie had despised every boy that looked at her best friend. They were never good enough for Angeline. Too stupid, too childish, too unrefined. No suitor seemed adequate for Angeline. And Angeline agreed. Joseph was different. Joseph was a good man and logically Emilie had to admit he was quite probably the perfect suitor for Angeline. So why was she feeling worse about Joseph potentially courting Angeline than she'd felt about any other boy? Why was she sweating outside in February and why was she about to vomit her lunch on the sidewalk? She took a deep breath and opened her eyes to a concerned Joseph standing by her side, holding her arm. She stared into his dark blue eyes and asked, because she had to know for sure, "It's Angeline, isn't it? The girl who caught your eye?"

Joseph sighed and nodded slowly, hesitant. He tried to talk a few times and finally managed, "I think I fell in love with her that day she saved me from those Irish bastards." His confession was delivered in a swift, low voice. Then he took a deep breath and started walking again, appearing relieved that the truth was finally out.

Emilie was surprised she found the strength to follow him. She focused on taking deep, even breaths as she listened to her brother. "If I had it my way, Emilie, I'd marry Angeline and take her back with me to Rimouski. I'd buy Papa's farm, or maybe I'd work in that sawmill Angeline's father keeps talking about. The Price Company. We'd have lots of children and be happy. I can see it so clearly in my mind."

Emilie felt compassion for her brother. Like him, she could see his dreams clearly. Perhaps a little too clearly. She didn't like them. She was torn between doing what she could to help her brother and putting every effort into keeping Angeline all to herself. Her mind knew the latter option was not fair to any of them, but it seemed fair to her heart. "Does Angeline know how you feel?"

Joseph snorted a laugh. "No, Emilie. And I don't think I'll ever find the courage to tell her. She rejected so many boys already. Why would it be different for me, Emilie?"

It would have been so easy to tell Joseph that he was right. That Angeline would reject him and that he was better off keeping quiet to protect his own heart. It would have been so easy. But it was not the right thing to do and Emilie knew it. Women didn't grow up to live happily with their best friend. They grew up to marry and have children. And if they were lucky, they grew up to marry a good man like Joseph. She wanted that for Angeline, and she wanted her brother to be happy. She had to accept the fact that she would lose Angeline to a man someday and if that man was Joseph, at least they'd be family.

Emilie took a deep breath and mentally jumped on her heart with both feet to keep it quiet while she forced herself to do the right thing. "It's different because Angeline already likes you, Joseph. She knows you and you're great friends. If any Flint boy has any chance of winning her heart, it's you, my dear brother." She smiled as she imagined herself squeezing her heart between her heels.

She was rewarded with a smile from Joseph. "You think so?"

"I'm sure of it." Emilie had an idea but wondered whether she really wanted to push her desire to do the right thing that far. She might as well, now that she'd started mashing her heart with both feet. "Would you like me to test the waters for you? Ask a few questions and see if I can find out how she feels about you?"

Joseph smiled broadly and sighed with relief. "You would do that for me? That would be great, Emilie. I'd be very grateful."

"Of course I'll do that for you, Joseph. What are sisters for? Besides, you've been walking me to this house for a year and a half already. I owe you," Emilie added as they arrived in front of the Banvilles' home.

"No, Emilie. If you do this for me, I'm the one who'll owe you. Forever."

Emilie was touched by his candor and vulnerability. She lightly punched him on the chest and sent him on his way back to Flint with reassuring words: "I'll talk to Angeline, I promise. I'll ask Dr. Banville to take me home early and I'll talk to her before dinnertime. Now go and think of those beautiful dreams of yours, Joseph. And believe me when I say that there's a very good chance they'll come true."

She smiled and as soon as Joseph turned around to walk back home, she wiped the tears from her eyes and she climbed the stairs to the Banville's porch and knocked on the door.

Rose answered the door and took Emilie's long wool coat and hat. Emilie had learned that it was the way things were done at the Banvilles' but the only thing that made her feel less uncomfortable about it was the way Rose smiled at her when she greeted her at the door. It was a genuine smile, not a forced ripped-out-of-her-pride smile as Emilie would have imagined.

"Thank you, Rose."

She would usually exchange a few pleasantries with Rose but she was too distracted by her talk with Joseph to find anything to say about the weather or what she may have seen in the neighborhood that day. Rose simply left with a nod when Helen arrived to greet her guest.

"Emilie, you're here at last. I'm so happy to see you."

"Hello, Helen."

They kissed on the cheek and Helen turned toward the parlor. Helen was always delighted to see Emilie and the feeling was mutual but today Emilie's heart was not really into the mundane conversations she usually had with Helen and as she followed her she hoped Maurice would arrive soon. Helen was still as elegant and fundamentally good-hearted as Emilie had found her the first time they'd met, but she'd also discovered that she was a very proper lady who very much cared about things Emilie couldn't be bothered with.

Fashion was one of those things and Emilie was reminded of this as she followed Helen, wondering how she would possibly make it through the doorframe with those gigantic puffy sleeves. Every year it seemed these leg-o'mutton sleeves got fuller and puffier and most ladies like Helen wore them with pride. Emilie thought they were ridiculous. Her mother had shown her how to sew her own clothes and she was quite content with the same type of full sleeves extending from the shoulder and gathered at the wrist that she'd worn most of her life. She knew her beloved bishop sleeves were not stylish or fashionable, but at least her sensible gray skirt and simple dark blue bodice and functional sleeves would get through every door.

Emilie took a deep breath and closed her eyes. She had a tendency to criticize everything around her when she was upset with one particular thing, a habit she was not proud of and found overdramatic, a habit that was difficult to control.

Helen and her sleeves made it through the door to the parlor although Emilie distinctly heard the fabric rub against the wood of the frame. Emilie's mood improved as soon as she saw Maurice there, already sitting in his usual armchair. He stood to greet Emilie with an embrace and a kiss on the cheek. The greeting might have made people talk if they'd known; but Maurice had slowly come to think of Emilie as a daughter and he'd confessed as much during one of her visits. Their hopes of having a family of their own were dwindling.

Emilie didn't see Maurice as a father. She already had a father. She saw him as a friend first, one that shared her eagerness to learn and her analytic abilities. And she saw him as a teacher, someone who pushed her further in her thoughts about the books she read but also about life in general.

Rose served them tea and they talked about Helen's charity activities since their last visit, what had happened in their respective neighborhoods, as well as events in Emilie's family. Emilie didn't mention the still-too-recent news of Joseph's love for Angeline. Then Helen excused herself and Emilie took the last book she'd read out of her leather mailbag and placed it on the round table in front of her. It was their ritual. First all three of them would catch up on each other's life since their last visit, then Helen would leave her and Maurice alone to discuss the last book Emilie had read.

Maurice glanced at the book on the table and grinned. "Ah, *Madame Bovary*. So, what did you think of Flaubert's controversial novel, my dear?" His grin intensified and Emilie couldn't help but smile back. He knew she would identify with Emma Bovary, a woman who wanted so much more than what her life had in store for her.

"What I don't understand is why Flaubert had to make her kill herself. Can't a woman want more than a boring little married life?"

Maurice laughed, obviously satisfied with Emilie's reaction to the book. Emilie waited for him to do what she both hated and craved: shake her convictions to the core and make her see the other side of the coin. "Do you think Madame Bovary's life was that extraordinarily boring? If you compare it with your mother's life, for example, or even with Helen's."

There it was. Emilie sighed with frustration. "Well, no. But life in novels is not supposed to be like that. Characters are supposed to want more, aren't they?"

"Yes, I suppose so. But do you think there was something out there that would have satisfied Madame Bovary's need for more? Didn't she get bored or disappointed with everything? Her husband, her daughter, her lovers. Everything."

"Yes, she did," Emilie admitted with a sigh. A lump lodged in her throat at the realization. She'd identified with Madame Bovary on so many levels. She didn't want the married life women around her extolled as their entire purpose in life. She didn't want to work in the cotton mill all her life either. She didn't want children crying under her skirts at all times. She didn't want anything she knew—but what else was out there for her? Was she condemned to accept the life she, just like all the other Flint girls, was meant to live, or end her life like Emma Bovary?

"So that's it, then?" she finally asked Maurice. "Women like Emma, like me, who want more out of life, are condemned to live and die unhappy?"

Maurice's earlier grin became a smile of compassion. Then his green stare focused on Emilie as if it could pierce a hole through her and force her to listen carefully to what he was about to say. "That's not what I think, Emilie. There's a difference between wanting something different and reaching out for it, and just wanting more all your life and never being satisfied. There are women who are married or unmarried who become journalists, for example. There are even a few female doctors nowadays. These women wanted more, Emilie, but they knew what they wanted. You have the mind to do anything you want, young lady, but the fact that you're a woman will make it a lot more difficult. So you need to decide what it is you want and put all of your determination and stubbornness into it."

He winked at her and she had to smile. He knew her so well. "There's nothing wrong with wanting more, Emilie. You just have to know what you want."

Emilie sighed again. "Right now all I know is what I don't want."

"I know. But it'll come."

Maurice's smile was so reassuring and comforting that Emilie wanted to believe him. She was terrified she'd be the same kind of eternal unsatisfied woman Emma Bovary had been and in that moment she wished nothing more than being able to find happiness in marriage with a good Flint boy and half a dozen children. She found the idea as laughable as repugnant. She didn't know what she wanted, but there was no possible way she could be satisfied with the life she was expected to live. It was already too late for her. Then she suddenly thought of Joseph's revelation and of Angeline. It was too late for her but it may not be too late for Angeline.

As soon as Maurice dropped her off at the entrance of Flint, Emilie ran to Angeline's with new books in her old leather mailbag. She often visited Angeline right after her trips to the Banvilles' and sometimes even left her books at Angeline's house until she was ready to read them. Before she left the Banvilles' that day, she'd picked up Voltaire's *Candide* and Jonathan Swift's *Gulliver's Travels*. The last thing she wanted to read at the time was a romance and she was sure to avoid it with these titles.

Pierre Fournier opened the door of the apartment and Emilie greeted the family gathered in the kitchen. Angeline was already aunt to six young children and she was busy playing on the floor with them. Emilie's older half-brothers also had children, but she didn't feel like an aunt. She didn't see them as often as Angeline saw her nieces and nephews and she didn't get involved in their lives. Emilie often thought she'd make a horrible mother. She couldn't even imagine it. Angeline, on the other hand, was clearly made to be a mother.

Angeline got up from the floor and wiped her dark brown dress. While the enormous puffs on Helen's sleeves had seemed pretentious, the smaller puffs of Angeline's own dress made her look like a princess. Angeline's beauty truly was stunning and when she smiled at Emilie as she passed by her on the way to her bedroom, Emilie stopped breathing for a second, as she did every time Angeline smiled at her.

How could she blame Joseph when Angeline had this kind of effect on her? She wasn't even a boy and she couldn't resist Angeline's charms. How could Joseph? Emilie followed Angeline to her bedroom where they often talked when it was too cold outside to meet at their buttonwood tree.

Emilie put her bag down by Angeline's bed and sat by her friend, smiling when the small brass bed frame made the familiar squeaking sound when they sat on it together. Angeline laughed. "I don't think it'll survive many more years of our friendship."

The thought of the small bed collapsing under their weight instantly brought sadness to Emilie's throat and her smile vanished. It seemed their friendship was suddenly both threatened and threatening in so many ways. She knew she couldn't stop the changes that were happening, yet that was exactly what she wanted. All she wanted. For time to stop and let them be on this bed together forever.

Her sorrow must have shown when she turned to face Angeline because she saw her friend's wide smile disappear and the light in her beautiful blue eyes was replaced with concern. Angeline grabbed Emilie's hands in hers and asked, "What's wrong, Emilie? Did something happen during your visit with the Banvilles?"

Emilie looked down at the adorably pudgy yet elegant hands covering hers and felt the skin of her own hands under them tingle. She smiled at the sensation and looked up at Angeline again. "No, nothing happened. I just see all those changes around us and I can't help wishing the bed and everything else could just let our friendship be the way it is forever."

"The bed won't really stop us from being friends, Emilie. We could drag a chair next to it and share the weight, you know." Angeline laughed but the humor didn't reach her eyes and Emilie knew she understood her anguish. She continued more seriously. "We can't let anything come between us, Emilie. We just can't."

"Easier said than done, Angeline." Emilie took one hand out of Angeline's grip and slowly caressed one of her friend's naturally pink cheeks as she spoke. "Eventually you'll meet a boy you really like and you'll have less time for me. It's the way it goes."

Emilie followed the movement of her hand down Angeline's cheek to her long neck and stopped, hesitating long enough before she removed her hand for Angeline to trap it between her cheek and her shoulder instead.

Their eyes locked and they stayed like that for a moment that seemed to last a lifetime. Then Angeline broke the silence. "I don't think I'll ever meet a boy I really like, Emilie. I haven't found one yet I enjoy spending time with as much as I enjoy spending time with you."

"Not even Joseph?"

Angeline quickly raised her head in surprise at Emilie's mention of Joseph's name and Emilie immediately freed her hand from the nook of Angeline's neck and rested it on her own thigh. It seemed her hand was impregnated with Angeline's pulse.

"Joseph? We're friends, Emilie. It's different."

Angeline's puzzled look forced Emilie to take a deep breath and continue. "Joseph spoke to me today on our walk to Main Street. He likes you more than a friend, Angeline. He's in love with you. He dreams of marrying you and taking you to

Rimouski with him. He wants to be your husband and have children with you."

Although Emilie spoke solemnly and without even a trace of a smile, Angeline exploded into laughter. Emilie remained serious and stared at Angeline. "I'm not kidding, Angeline. He's too scared you'll reject him to talk to you, so I told him I would do it for him."

Slowly, Angeline stopped laughing and didn't seem as enthusiastic at the news as Emilie had both thought and feared. In fact, she looked more saddened than anything else. "So are you asking me to accept your brother as a suitor, Emilie?"

No! Emilie wanted to scream. Instead she remained calm. "I'm not asking you to do anything you don't want to do, Angeline. I'm doing my brother a favor, that's all. And let's face it, if you're going to have any suitor at all, Joseph is the best you could ever find," she added as her voice caught and she wiped tears at the corner of her eye.

"If, Emilie. That's a big 'if.' I don't need a suitor at all. Not even Joseph. All I need is our friendship." Angeline moved to hug her but Emilie stood up. She had to keep her distance from Angeline if she wanted to finish what she'd come to do. She couldn't keep thinking that life without a suitor, a husband, was conceivable.

"Of course you do, Angeline. You can't spend your life discussing books and gossiping about the neighborhood with your best friend. That's not what your life should be. You should get married with a good man who can take care of you, give you children and a comfortable life you deserve. Joseph can do that for you, Angeline. You know that's true as well as I do. I know you like him. You like the way he talks about Rimouski, the way he makes you laugh. Maybe you can fall in love with him too. Just think about it, that's all I ask."

"But, Emilie…"

Before Angeline could continue, Emilie took her leather mailbag and left her friend's bedroom and the Fourniers' apartment.

The temperature had dropped with the setting of the sun and Emilie walked briskly toward her apartment. The tears that fell to her cheeks briefly warmed them up before she wiped them away with determination, whispering between her clenched teeth, "Angeline Fournier will never be another Emma Bovary. Never."

CHAPTER TEN

February 1895

The next morning Emilie woke up with burning eyes. She'd been crying for a large portion of the night. She hurried to get dressed and waited outside for the others. If the day before had been unusually mild, this morning marked the return of February in all of its freezing glory, which Emilie welcomed. The cold air soothed her eyes, insuring that Joseph or anyone else wouldn't notice she'd been crying. Mathilde and Henri were the first outside, followed by Edouard. Jean-Baptiste had married a year ago and had left the Levesque apartment. Emilie's parents and her older brother greeted her with a sleepy nod and left toward the mill. Emilie wanted to start walking behind them but she waited for Joseph instead. If she didn't walk to the mill with Joseph and Angeline as she did every morning, they'd know she was upset. Joseph came out of the triple-decker and Emilie started walking toward their meeting spot but Joseph held her arm, forcing her to stop and face him.

"Did you talk to Angeline?" he asked with an expression of excitement mixed with apprehension that touched Emilie and left her no other choice but to smile.

"Yes, I talked to her."

"And?"

"And she was surprised. She sees you as a friend and she didn't suspect you had any deeper feelings. She's fond of you, though, Joseph. And she knows you're a decent man. That I am certain of, and I think if you approach her slowly you have good reasons to hope. Ask her to the dance. I'd be willing to bet she'll say yes."

"Really?"

"Really."

"I might do that, then. Thank you Emilie." He squeezed her shoulder to show his gratitude. Emilie stopped smiling as soon as he turned around to start walking, as if the smile she'd plastered on her face actually hurt. She followed Joseph but kept a distance between them, a space large enough to accommodate her brother's hopes and her own clashing desperation.

Angeline took a deep breath of fresh air as she walked out of the mill after the siren announced the end of her thirteen-hour shift. She heard some of her coworkers cough. The humidity and thick cotton dust of the mill were slow killers. Angeline had already lost two friends to brown lung disease since she'd started as a spinner. The lung infection started with a cough and breathing difficulties that got better for some, but much worse for others. Fortunately, Angeline had never been that affected by the thick wet air of the mill. It was not pleasant, of course, and she always enjoyed her first breath of fresh air after work, but she'd never had so much as a tickle in her throat.

She knew the air of the mill had nothing to do with her current difficulty to breathe. No, the awkwardness of her morning walk to the mill with Emilie and Joseph was entirely to blame. The dynamics of their trio had undeniably changed, and there was no turning back. Angeline did like Joseph very much, but she'd never thought of him as a suitor. At fifteen, she still felt too young to think of suitors. Joseph was a good friend. One who'd been there for her since the first day they'd met, just like his sister.

After Emilie had left her family's apartment the night before, however, Angeline has started to imagine Joseph as more than a friend. It was true that Joseph was by far the best prospect any young woman could dream of in Flint Village. Choosing him as a suitor would mean she would be respected and would also protect her from the multiple annoying propositions and requests she received from other boys. Yet she hesitated.

She hesitated because what she felt for Joseph was not the all-consuming love Emilie had told her about when they discussed the novels she read. She hesitated because her best friend, the one person on whom she thought she could always rely, seemed to push her toward a marriage of reason rather than love, and that made no sense to Angeline. The more she thought about it, the more she felt hurt by the way Emilie had presented Joseph as a perfect provider for Angeline. Didn't Emilie think Angeline was deserving of the same kind of love she wanted for herself? She wished she had the courage to ask Emilie.

Then again, sometimes it seemed like Emilie had given up on love entirely. Love was an afterthought in her discussions of the books she read recently and she never talked about her ideal romance anymore. She talked about more serious topics like women's right to vote and the corruption of American politics. Angeline was often lost, at sea in Emilie's speeches. Perhaps that was the real reason why Emilie was pushing her away toward her brother. Perhaps Angeline was no longer interesting enough as a friend. Angeline gasped at the thought and tears fell to her cheeks. That's what really hurt. She felt like Emilie was pushing her away when she wanted nothing more than to spend all of her time with Emilie. Learn from her, make her laugh.

When Emilie laughed, her face went through a complete metamorphosis. First the crease between her thick eyebrows that gave her that permanent serious look disappeared as her eyebrows lifted up. Almost at the same time, her black eyes took a sparkling shine that lit up her entire face. Then her thin-lipped mouth opened in loud laughter, showing two rows of perfectly straight and white teeth, a sight that was rare in their community. It was beautiful to see such solemn features, similar to those of a nun, transform to a childlike expression of complete abandon. Angeline could never get tired of making Emilie laugh.

Angeline's thoughts were interrupted when Joseph and Emilie approached. They smiled timidly at one another and Joseph took a deep breath before he spoke. "Angeline, I was hoping I could have a moment alone with you, if you don't mind."

Before Angeline could agree or disagree, Emilie took the lead. "Of course, the two of you go ahead and talk. I'll catch up with you later on."

Angeline considered the arm Joseph was offering and since Emilie had already disappeared when she looked up again, she accepted the offer. She held Joseph's arm as they walked, something she'd done so naturally with Emilie many times before, but it felt so much more formal and artificial now. Angeline felt the tension in Joseph's muscles through his overcoat. Under different circumstances she would have found a way to make him laugh to release some of that tension, but she just waited for him to talk instead. When he finally did, he was so proper Angeline barely recognized the boy she'd been friends with. "Angeline, I was hoping you would do me the honor of going to the dance with me this Saturday."

This was ridiculous, Angeline thought. This was Joseph, one of her best friends. She couldn't stand seeing him so nervous. "Relax. Joseph, it's just me you're talking to. And I'll be happy to go to the dance with you."

"You will?" he asked in a voice that was already much closer to the voice of the boy she knew and cared so much about.

"I will, Joseph." Angeline watched him sigh with relief and smile with pride before she added, "But it's just a dance, Joseph. I'm not ready to discuss anything more serious than that. I would really like us to continue being friends and see where this leads us in a year or two. That means I'll go to dances with you, and other such events if you want me to, but we need to take things very slowly. Can you deal with that?"

Angeline thought Joseph might be disappointed but instead his smile extended even further. "Yes, I can deal with that,

Angeline. I promise I will respect your wishes. All I want is a chance to spend time with you and show you that we could be really good together. Thank you for giving me that chance." As if his joy were contagious, Angeline couldn't help but smile. She kept holding his arm as they walked in the cold and Angeline tried to ignore the fact that Emilie never caught up with them. Joseph walked Angeline all the way to her door like a perfect gentleman and said good night.

Angeline entered the Fourniers' apartment and smiled as she imagined her mother's reaction when she told her about the dance. She would be overjoyed and excited to help Angeline choose the perfect dress. Emilie wouldn't be at the dance and that was unfortunate, but as Angeline chased that dark thought away, a new thought came to her mind and made her smile even more. If she ever ended up marrying Joseph, she would always be close to Emilie. She wondered if Emilie had considered that fact when she'd pushed her toward her brother. Of course she had. Emilie always considered every side to any situation. Maybe Emilie didn't want to drive Angeline away after all. Maybe she wanted to keep her close to her the only way she could. The thought comforted Angeline to the point where she almost got excited about going to the dance with Joseph.

CHAPTER ELEVEN

July 1896

Emilie turned seventeen on July fifth, a Sunday. Joseph had gone to the Fourth of July dance with Angeline the night before and was so tired the next morning he'd almost fallen asleep in church, so Emilie didn't have to work too hard to convince him to stay home and rest instead of walking her to the Banvilles'. It was not the first time she'd attempted to assure him she could make the trip by herself and be safe, but it was the first time she succeeded. Emilie knew Joseph would regret it as soon as he was rested enough but she'd already be at the Banville residence by then. She wanted to walk alone because she needed to think a little more about the book she planned on discussing with Maurice.

For several months now, Emilie's favorite author had been Emile Zola. She felt she could trust his portrait of France during the Second Empire in his series of novels focusing on two families of that period from 1852 to 1870, when France was ruled by Emperor Napoleon III. Zola was part of the French Naturalism movement and to Emilie that meant that everything he wrote was realistic and could actually happen in the context of his story. Through Zola she was learning about France and even more about French people and she couldn't get enough. The novels she'd read so far had inspired great conversations with Maurice, who'd been to Paris on two occasions in more recent years. He explained how things had changed or not changed that much since the Second Empire and she hung on every word he said.

The last book she'd read was *Nana* and Emilie didn't know how she could articulate her questions about very specific passages of the book that weren't really related to the main story. Nana Coupeau was a performer at the *Théâtre des Variétés* who ruined every man who was unfortunate enough to fall for her or develop any kind of carnal relationship with her. She took all of their money and even drove one to commit suicide. Nana ended up dying of smallpox, Zola's way of punishing her for her sins, Emilie thought. Nana's unscrupulous nature and the fact that she was a high-class prostitute were not what troubled Emilie so much though. At seventeen she'd already read about so many things other Flint girls her age knew nothing about. It took more and more to shake her.

Yet the brief relationship between Nana and another prostitute named Satin had raised all kinds of questions and emotions in Emilie. The two women started out as friends but then kissed on the lips and Zola hinted at more intimate caresses that created a relationship made of feelings Emilie attributed to couples: possessiveness, jealousy, love. Yes, Emilie was certain the two women had been in love.

But how could that be? Were there really women out there who were in love with other women? And if so, were there women who were in love exclusively with women? Those were the questions she didn't know how to ask Maurice. Not to mention other questions, even more perverse, she couldn't even ask herself yet. She blushed every time she tried to think of them or put them into words. Just imagining the kind of caress Zola had suggested sent an unfamiliar heat through her and left her cheeks flushed and lower parts of her body tingling in a way she couldn't remember feeling before. It was an exciting sensation, perhaps, but it was even more disturbing because she couldn't help thinking it was wrong. Especially when thoughts of Angeline popped into her mind at the same time.

"Whoa! You plan on going far like that?"

Maurice's voice startled Emilie and she stopped walking to turn toward him. She was so absorbed in her musings she would have walked right past the Banvilles' Victorian home if Maurice hadn't stopped her. She worried that her unsettling thoughts were visible on her face as she walked up the stairs that led to the porch. "I guess I was distracted."

"I guess you were," he said, and let out the deep, comforting laughter that never failed to pacify Emilie's stormy thoughts. She laughed and hugged Maurice. On warm summer days like today, they sat on the porch instead of staying in the parlor. "Helen had somewhere else to be but will join us later, so we can start talking about your book first if you want."

Maurice sat in his favorite wooden rocking chair and Emilie seated herself on a small wooden stool facing him. The one time Helen was not there to chat about her charity work and mundane events was the one time Emilie would have welcomed it. It would have given her more time to pull her thoughts together. Fortunately, Rose gave her a little of that much needed time when she came out on the porch to serve them tea.

"How are you doing on such a beautiful day, Rose?"

"I can't complain, Miss Levesque," was all Rose answered before she went back inside, leaving the teapot on the low square table that separated Maurice's rocking chair and another that looked just the same—even though Maurice swore it was different—from the two stools Emilie preferred. Emilie reached for her leather mailbag and timidly placed *Nana* next to the teapot on the table.

Maurice read the title and laughed again. Emilie looked at him and thought she could see him blush through his beard. "Oh, my dear Emilie, you can really pick them, can't you? Sometimes I wonder if giving you full access to my library is such a good idea. You do realize you couldn't find some of the books you read in the public library, don't you?"

"I do. And I'm very grateful for the opportunity."

He kept laughing, embarrassed as much as amused. Emilie knew he would never keep her from reading any book she wanted, though, even if discussing certain books sometimes put him in an awkward position. Like today.

After Maurice finally stopped laughing, they managed to talk as seriously as they could about prostitution and about how Emilie saw Nana's death as a way for Zola to show that Nana's actions could only be punished by a horrible death. They always found a way to tackle any subject, Emilie realized with relief. Yet she still hesitated to ask about the one aspect of the book that most intrigued her. And since Maurice read her like an open book, he knew it. "Something else in that book got you raddled up, young lady. What is it?" He smiled at her but the smile was inviting, different from his usual mocking grin.

Emilie opened her mouth and nothing came out. Finally she took a deep breath and found the courage to speak. "You're right. There's something else. I was wondering about the relationship between Nana and Satin."

Maurice shifted positions uncomfortably in his chair. "Hmm. What about it?"

Emilie hesitated again when she realized the question caused Maurice some discomfort, but it was too late to back out, so she continued. "I was wondering if it's something that really happens in France. Two women who have the same kind of relationship a man and a woman would have."

After a long silence, Maurice cleared his throat. "It happens, Emilie. But not only in France. It happens everywhere. A few doctors have even written books about it recently. They call it homosexuality, or Sapphism when they're referring to two women. It's a disease many great minds of the world are trying to understand these days. I'm afraid I don't know much about it myself."

"A disease?" Emilie asked with disappointment. She was not sure why she was disappointed but she was. Perhaps she was hoping to learn about a way of life she'd never heard of before. But a disease was not a way of life. It was an affliction. The excitement she felt when she thought about it was therefore even more disturbing than she'd imagined.

"Yes, a disease. That's what these doctors think anyway."

"And what about you? Do you think it's a disease?"

"Oh, I don't know enough about it to have a real opinion, my dear. I'm sorry. I imagine if they say it is, then it must be."

"Hmm, I see. And do you have any of those books those doctors wrote?"

"No, I don't, Emilie. I'm sorry. But what makes you so curious about this?"

Emilie couldn't help but note accusation in Maurice's question so she quickly brushed it off. "Oh, it's just that I'd never read anything like that before. You know me; I'm always trying to understand new things."

Maurice smiled but his piercing eyes were still questioning. Emilie was released from his inquisitive stare when Helen arrived with a carefully wrapped box. "I heard it was someone's birthday today," she said as she took *Nana* off the table and handed it to Emilie so she could place the mysterious box in its place on the table.

"Oh, yes, that's right," Emilie admitted as she felt her cheeks flush again. Emilie welcomed the much more familiar embarrassment.

"Happy birthday, my dear Emilie," Maurice said calmly as he stood up to hug her.

"Happy birthday Emilie!" Helen added with more excitement. "We wanted to spoil you a little. Please, go ahead and open it," she said as she tapped her index finger on the white cardboard of the box.

Emilie did open it and her eyes opened wide as she found three miniature fruit tarts. She'd seen the delicate pastries in the bakery's window many times on her way to Maurice and Helen's house, but she'd never dared enter the bakery, knowing she couldn't afford the luxury. One of these fruit tarts would probably cost as much as she earned in a day at the mill. She started salivating as she realized she was about to get the chance to finally taste one of these fabulous tarts. "Oh, thank you so much. You shouldn't have."

"Of course we should," Maurice said as he took a tart out of the box and handed it to Emilie. Maurice and Helen sat side by side on the rocking chairs with their own tarts but didn't take a bite, staring at Emilie.

She understood that they wanted to watch as she tasted her first fruit tart so she smiled and went for her first bite. She chewed on that first morsel for as long as she could, savoring every explosion of each small fruit, identifying each individual flavor first, then enjoying them as one. The taste was rich, sweet, and a little bitter all at once. "It's perfection," she finally said when she swallowed. Satisfied, Maurice and Helen laughed and started eating their own pastries.

After they enjoyed their dessert and talked with Helen for about an hour, Maurice took Emilie back to Flint. The ride was mostly in silence as it was often the case, which gave Emilie the opportunity to come back down from the emotion of her unexpected birthday celebration. She went back to the brief conversation she had with Maurice regarding homosexuality and Sapphism—two words she'd learned today—and she couldn't help but feel disillusioned.

For the first time since she'd met Maurice, she was disappointed in him. Not because he didn't know much about the subject. At an earlier time Emilie might have thought Maurice knew everything but she knew enough about the world now to understand that was impossible. What was disappointing was the complete disinterest he had for the subject. He obviously didn't care if he ever learned more about the question and certainly didn't want to talk about it. That much was clear. It was a disease and that was the end of it.

The problem was that it couldn't be the end of it for Emilie. The relationship between Nana and Satin had piqued her curiosity and she wanted, needed to learn more about it. She didn't know how she would go about it but she was glad she'd learned two new words from Maurice. Homosexuality and

Sapphism. That's all Maurice had given her but she would hold on to these words until she found a way to research them.

Emilie had been bitterly reminded today that she couldn't learn everything from one person. She loved Maurice and had kept nothing from him until now. This research she would have to do without him. On her own. For the first time in the three years since she'd met the Banvilles, Emilie felt alone in her thirst for knowledge.

Emilie hadn't even stopped by home before she went to the buttonwood tree where she was to meet Angeline later that afternoon. She'd spent the last hour sitting alone under the tree, leaning against its trunk. She hadn't taken a book out of her mailbag to read. She wasn't even sure which books she'd picked out of Maurice's library before she'd left. He didn't have the books she wanted to read, so it didn't matter.

She stared at the Quequechan River flowing in front of her. The way the water sparkled on such a sunny day almost allowed her to forget how soiled it was, saturated with debris from the several cotton mills that used its strong flow to power their machines. "Men take what they need and don't care about the consequences," Emilie grumbled as she tried to focus on the beautiful dancing diamonds the light of the sun created on the surface of the river. That was the problem with knowledge. Once you knew what was hiding under the surface, it was almost impossible to appreciate superficial beauty.

Emilie felt corrupted. The books she'd read had exposed her to realities Angeline, Joseph and most other people in Flint knew nothing about. That's what she'd wanted. More knowledge. But everyone around her seemed so happy in their absence of knowledge. They were in love, they went to dances, they swam in the river without a care in the world. She remained alone with all of her knowledge, sitting miserably under a tree. Yet she still needed to know more. Even though she already knew what she wanted to learn about now would only corrupt her further.

Love between women. Disease or not, Emilie had to know more about it. It was personal. There was a reason why this kind of love provoked such a visceral reaction in her while the love she'd read about all of her life, the love between a man and a woman, had been nothing but an ideal she could formulate without any emotion. She feared the reason, but still needed to know it. She might never be able to look at herself the same way. Might see nothing but garbage inside, just like when she looked at the river. But she still needed to know.

"Hi, have you been waiting for long?" Angeline asked as she arrived and sat by Emilie.

She wore a green skirt with a light beige bodice decorated with pink flowers. The same pink as the ribbon on her straw hat. Her thick mass of light brown hair was gathered in a chignon under her hat, with a few curls escaping and highlighting her long exposed neck. Emilie tried to visualize how Satin might have caressed that neck. She wondered if it was the same way she'd wanted to caress it for as long as she could remember. A way she'd thought innocent. She'd never imagined darker needs might hide behind that simple desire to touch Angeline until now. "I came early. I needed some time to think. You look lovely."

"Thank you."

"Did you enjoy the dance last night?"

"Yes, it was very pleasant. Your brother was a perfect gentleman, as always. Marcella came with Tony Berardi. Can you believe it?" Angeline giggled but not with the same contagious lightness as usual. Something was bothering her.

"Actually yes, I can believe it. Those two idiots deserve each other."

Angeline's laughter was a little more sincere this time but something in her expression didn't sit well with Emilie. She looked sad. Emilie couldn't stand seeing Angeline sad and if her brother was responsible for that cloudy veil in her pretty blue eyes, he would pay for it. "Are you sure nothing happened, Angeline? You look upset."

Angeline sighed. "I can't hide anything from you, can I?" Emilie shook her head to confirm Angeline's suspicion that she couldn't keep secrets from her and was grateful that it was not reciprocal. If Angeline could see the dark secrets Emilie was hiding from her now, she'd probably run away.

Angeline smiled briefly and continued, "I'm upset, but it has nothing to do with last night. My parents are going back to Rimouski. They told us after church. My father's been trying to get a job with The Price Company for a couple of years and something finally opened up."

"That's the sawmill, right?"

"Yes. The pay's good and it's the perfect occasion for them to finally go back home."

Emilie could hear the distress in Angeline's voice but she had to appease her own worries before she could begin to properly comfort her friend. The knots were multiplying in her throat and soon she wouldn't be able to breathe if she didn't ask. "Are you going with them, Angeline?"

"No," Angeline said as she looked at Emilie. She must have seen the anxiety her news had caused in Emilie because the sadness in her own eyes was temporarily replaced with tenderness as she reassured her friend, "Oh no, Emilie. I'm not leaving, don't worry. I'll be staying with my older sister and her husband. She could use help with the younger children and besides, my wages will help them too until..."

"Until you get married."

"Right. In a few years."

"Right."

They never talked about Angeline's eventual marriage to Joseph. They knew it would happen but talking about it always made them uncomfortable. It was almost like death. Everyone knew it would happen, but no one wanted to talk about it.

"I'll miss them so much, Emilie," Angeline said as she started crying. She lay down on her side and placed her head on Emilie's lap, her hat falling to the ground. Emilie instinctively started rubbing her friend's back.

"I know, Angeline, I know. But think about it. In a couple of years you might join them in Rimouski. That's still Joseph's plan, isn't it?"

"Yes."

Instead of helping, Emilie's words made Angeline cry even harder. In a panic, Emilie rubbed Angeline's back more vigorously. "What? Isn't that what you want?"

"I don't know, Emilie," Angeline managed to say through sobs. "I'll miss my parents while I'm still here, but I think I'll miss you even more if I'm there with them."

Angeline cried against Emilie's skirt and Emilie kept rubbing her back. "I'll miss you too, my dear Angeline, but I don't think I'll be staying in Fall River either, so you can't stay for me."

"Will you be going back to Rimouski?"

Angeline asked the question with such hope in her sweet little voice that Emilie's heart broke knowing her answer would crush that hope to pieces.

"No. There's nothing in Canada for me, Angeline. I don't know where I'll be going yet, but Fall River has nothing to teach me anymore."

They stayed like that in silence for a long time. Emilie's hand caressed slowly the length of Angeline's back, sometimes venturing to her side. Emilie felt the weight of Angeline's head press onto her thighs and she feared the skin under the weight would burn a hole through her skirt. She looked at her hand traveling over Angeline's back and side and fantasized about what it might be like to slide her hand under the fabric of Angeline's bodice and touch her tender skin. It would be warm and soft, Emilie knew it. She studied the curls on Angeline's neck and she imagined putting her lips right there, just under the curly hair.

Emilie's mouth was dry. She licked her lips and tried to ignore the tingling in her body. The same tingling she'd felt reading and thinking about Nana and Satin.

Sapphism, she repeated to herself. If it was a disease, she was sick with it. There was no doubt about it. For the first time she wished Joseph would hurry and ask for Angeline's hand in marriage. She wished he would take her away, safe from her and her perversion. At least until she could learn more about her disease and hopefully find a cure. She didn't know if such a cure existed but she knew she wouldn't find it in Fall River. What she'd told Angeline was true: Fall River had nothing to teach her anymore. She needed to find her own direction. Maurice had told her once that it was good to want more as long as she knew what she wanted. She didn't have a clear path yet, but she'd just made an important decision: when Joseph and Angeline got married and left for Rimouski, she would leave too. She'd use the time she had left to make plans. Perhaps Maurice would help her. He had connections everywhere, after all.

Emilie was forced out of her thoughts by the sound of light snoring coming from her lap. Emilie stretched out her arm to pick up Angeline's straw hat and delicately placed it on her friend's neck to save the pale skin from sunburn. She leaned her own head against the buttonwood tree and closed her eyes, trying to focus on anything but the sensations moving through her body.

When Angeline got back to the Fourniers' apartment just before dinner, Joseph was waiting for her in front of the triple-decker. "Can we go for a short walk?" he asked timidly. Angeline accepted Joseph's offered arm and walked with him back in the direction of the river. "I just spoke to your father. He told me about his decision. How do you feel about it?"

"Oh, it's sad, but I know it's what they want." Angeline had a lot more to say about her parents leaving Fall River, but she'd already talked about her feelings with Emilie and she didn't want to talk about them again so soon. Not with Joseph.

"You know it's what I want too, Angeline, don't you? It's what I want for us."

"Yes, I know," Angeline acknowledged without much enthusiasm. Joseph stopped walking and extended his arm toward an old wooden bench facing the river, silently asking Angeline to sit down. He sat next to her. Angeline immediately tensed up.

The last time they'd sat on this bench a few weeks ago, Joseph had kissed her on the lips. Their first kiss. It hadn't been unpleasant but it hadn't been what Angeline had imagined a first kiss should be either, what she'd hoped her first kiss with

Joseph would be. Some kind of deep revelation that she was meant for him and that he was meant for her. An answer to all of her questions. And last but not least, something she'd want to do again and again, something she'd never get enough of. A few weeks later, there had been no second kiss yet and as Angeline realized it was probably about to happen, she sadly had to admit she wasn't looking forward to it. Joseph seemed just as nervous as she was, and she wasn't sure if that comforted her or exacerbated her own nerves.

Joseph cleared his throat before he spoke, "Your father thinks there's a good chance once he starts at Price he could get me in too. That means our dreams could happen very soon, Angeline."

Angeline shifted in her seat. What was about to happen was a lot bigger than a second kiss. She closed her eyes and prayed for Joseph to stop talking but he continued.

"Your father and I think you and I could be in Rimouski as early as next winter, Angeline. And it might be a good idea to make things official before then."

"Official?" Angeline asked in a low voice. She wasn't ready for Joseph to propose, but could that even be considered as a proposal?

She didn't have time to question Joseph's motives any longer as he stepped up from the bench and dropped to one knee, facing her with a newfound bravery. He grabbed her hand and with his free hand, he searched the deep pocket of his trousers until he took out a gold ring that looked minuscule resting between his index finger and his thumb. "Yes, official. Angeline Fournier, will you marry me?"

And there it was. The proposal. What had been implied since the first dance they'd attended together but always remained distant, at least in Angeline's mind, was being dropped in her lap the same day she'd found out about her parents leaving town. The same day she'd run not to Joseph but to his sister Emilie to cry out her emotions. The same day she'd learned the moment she'd leave Fall River with Joseph might be the last time she'd see Emilie. It was all too much, yet she couldn't say no to Joseph. She'd always known she'd have to say yes. "Yes, Joseph, I'll marry you."

Joseph kissed Angeline's hand and looked at her with that wide smile that reminded her of the boy she'd met, a smile that filled her heart with tenderness. "You're making me the happiest man on earth, Angeline," he said as he placed the gold band on her ring finger. "Would you like a fall wedding? Or maybe a Christmas wedding?"

Angeline couldn't help but smile at Joseph's enthusiasm. Joseph would make a good husband and a wonderful father, she was convinced of it. So why was she digging through her mind for a way to delay the wedding? "I don't want to decide yet. Once my father gets you a job at The Price Company, I'll go back to Rimouski with you and we can get married there. That's what I really want, Joseph. Can you wait until then?"

"I'll wait as long as it takes, Angeline," Joseph answered as he got up from the ground and sat down next to her. "It makes perfect sense for us to get married in Rimouski. I should have thought of that myself. That's where our life will be, after all. It won't take long, you'll see."

Angeline looked at the simple gold band textured with a subtle flower motif, and felt slightly guilty for letting Joseph believe her reasons for wanting to get married in Rimouski were sentimental and romantic. The truth was that she was simply buying time. Her father had waited two years to finally get a job at Price. Maybe it would take Joseph just as long.

"Do you like it?"

At Joseph's question, Angeline realized she'd been staring at the ring on her finger. "Yes, of course. It's beautiful."

"It was my grandmother's. My father gave it to me when I told him about my intentions. It's been in my pocket for a while, you know."

Angeline smiled at Joseph, and her smile was genuine. She vowed to make every effort to become as excited about their wedding as he was. She just needed more time. Her resolution compelled her to kiss him on the cheek. As she moved away from his face, he turned to her and she recognized the way his eyes had looked just before he'd kissed her on the lips for the first time. They were so dark. Angeline could have imagined they were Emilie's eyes if his hadn't been rimmed with just a tiny circle of blue. Emilie's eyelashes were also longer, although Joseph's were quite long for a boy. For a man, she corrected herself as Joseph brought his lips closer to hers. She closed her eyes just before their lips met. His mouth was soft. She could have imagined it was Emilie's mouth, if his hadn't been covered with a somewhat prickly beard. He pressed his mouth harder against hers and she let him, wondering why she was thinking of Emilie in this moment, why she still felt Emilie's hand on her back and on her side, where it had been earlier. Why now, while Joseph was kissing her, she was enjoying this kiss so much more than the first one.

CHAPTER TWELVE

September 1897

Emilie sat in the same wooden chair she'd sat in for every meal she'd shared with her family since their arrival in Fall River more than nine years ago. Her father and Joseph were sitting in their usual chairs too, except they were not around the table. They were around her parents' bed, staring at her mother as she labored for every breath.

Her mother was dying.

Emilie watched as Joseph cried, holding her hand as he sat by her side. On the other side, her father shook his head with anger. "Damn cotton," he kept whispering. "Damn mill," he repeated as tears fell to his bearded cheeks.

Emilie sat at the foot of the bed, watching quietly. She hadn't cried yet. She felt like she wasn't really there, not really part of the scene. It was almost like a scene out of a book. Like Fantine's death in Hugo's *Les Misérables*. It wasn't really happening to her and her family.

Her mother had been coughing for about a month. They'd all heard her cough, but the sound of coughing was so common in Flint that they didn't pay much attention to it. When she complained she couldn't breathe right and they finally all thought it might be brown lung disease, Emilie asked Maurice to come and examine her mother. He came, of course, and Emilie saw in her father's expression that he wondered how his daughter knew a doctor, but he didn't ask questions. He was just grateful a real doctor had come to see his wife. Unfortunately, Maurice couldn't do anything for her. It was already too late.

Emilie watched as her mother took her hand out of Joseph's and wiggled her finger weakly, asking Emilie to come closer. Joseph wiped the tears from his eyes and got up from his chair to let Emilie sit by their mother. She wasn't talking much anymore and when she tried to speak, her voice was nothing but a low, scratchy whisper. Emilie brought her ear directly over her mother's mouth while making sure the frail woman could still get enough air.

She spoke in brief sentences, with long pauses to catch her breath. "Emilie, you're different...I know...Could do anything...So proud of you...Get out...Out of the mill..."

Emilie's first tears fell down to her mother's face. As more tears threatened to follow, she looked into her mother's eyes and managed to say, "I promise, Maman." Then she dropped her forehead to her mother's shoulder and started sobbing. The woman dying in her bed was not Fantine or any other character from any book. This woman was her own mother, and she was losing her. This was really happening, and it was happening to her. Emilie kept sobbing harder and felt her brother's hand in her back, shaking with his own grief as he tried to comfort her. It was happening to him too, and to their father. Their family would never be the same.

Later that day, the priest came to administer the last rites and Mathilde Levesque took her last breath.

For the next four days Emilie went back to being nothing but a spectator to her own life. She couldn't cope with actually being there as people filled their small apartment for three days of wake, then came back on the fourth day to share a meal in honor of her mother after the funeral and burial. She'd had enough of the good people of Flint, of their prayers, food and good intentions. Yet she almost missed them the minute they all left, including her older half-brothers and their families, when she found herself alone with Joseph and their father. The worst of the pain her mother's death had caused was on their shoulders, and the void she'd left was suddenly all too obvious. They stood in the kitchen and looked at each other almost as strangers, as if the only thing that had kept them together was Mathilde Levesque.

Joseph was the first to move, and he made it toward Emilie. He hugged her and Emilie understood her brother needed to be held so she held him. As she felt his strong arms around her small body she remembered. Joseph was her big brother, her first friend, her only human friend until she'd met Angeline. Joseph would always be there for her. She was certain of that. Their bond was strong and their mother's death could only make it stronger. Emilie and Joseph held on to each other in silence until they heard their father's voice. "She didn't want to come here."

The voice came from their parents' bedroom. Emilie hadn't even noticed her father leave the kitchen. When Joseph and Emilie entered the bedroom, he was staring at the empty bed where his wife had died. He kept staring as he talked. "It was my idea. She didn't want to come here. Did you know that?" Only then did he look at Emilie and Joseph. They both nodded and the way Joseph grabbed her hand, the same way he'd held it the night they'd sat on the top step of the wooden stairs and listened to their parents discussing their upcoming move to Fall River, she knew he was remembering it too. Yes, they knew coming to Fall River was their father's idea and their mother hadn't really wanted to come.

"I promised her we'd go back to Canada," her father continued. "I promised her. If I'd kept my promise..." His voice broke and he wiped tears from his eyes.

Her father's pain and guilt were tangible and Emilie felt powerless to comfort him. He'd always been the strong one.

What did she have to give the man who'd always been the strongest person in her life? If he fell apart, they would all break to pieces.

Emilie watched as he squared his jaw and approached her. He looked straight into her eyes, and then looked at Joseph, who was standing by her side. "I made your mother another promise. Just before she died. I promised her I'd get you out of that mill. I will keep that promise if it kills me, you hear me?" He spoke with a determination that was almost threatening. "You," he continued as he spoke to Joseph, "you marry that girl of yours and go back to Canada. If Price doesn't have a job for you, you'll find something else. Her father will help you any way he can. Pierre Fournier is a good man and he'll guide you better than I ever could."

Joseph simply nodded. He seemed frightened by their father.

"And you," her father said as he turned to Emilie, "I wish you'd find a good fellow to marry and take care of you, but that doesn't seem to be your calling. I don't know what it is you're meant for, my sweet girl, but I know it's not the cotton mill. I worry about you, but I figure if you can find a way to make friends with a doctor, you can find a way out of here. Am I wrong, Emilie? Do you want me to keep worrying?"

Emilie shook her head. "No, Papa, I made the same promise to Maman and I'll keep it. I'll find a way. You don't need to worry."

"Good. That's what I want to hear." He smiled briefly before he squared his jaw again and turned his back to them to resume staring at the empty bed in the room.

"What about you, Papa? Will you come back to Canada with me and Angeline?" Joseph asked.

Their father didn't turn around to face Joseph when he answered. "It's too late for me, son. I brought your mother here and she died here. The least I can do is stay here until I can finally join her."

Without another word, he knelt by the bed, joined his hands together, and leaned his forehead against the mattress. Joseph and Emilie exchanged a look and exited the room in silent agreement to leave their father alone with his prayers.

When they got back to the kitchen, they whispered so they wouldn't disturb their father. "So what will you do, Emilie? You know you can come to Canada with me and Angeline. We'll be happy to have you."

Emilie smiled at her brother. He'd placed his hands on the back of a chair and was leaning on it the same way their father so often did. "Thank you, but no. Dr. Banville and his wife are helping me figure things out. I'll have a definite plan soon, but it won't take me to Canada. What about you? Are you really going to work for The Price Company?"

"That's the plan. Mr. Fournier likes the work and in his last letter to Angeline he told her it wouldn't be long before he could get me a job there. He said they're expanding."

"I see. Angeline hadn't mentioned that to me." Emilie wondered why Angeline had kept that information from her. It was an important piece of information, after all; one that meant Angeline and Joseph would leave for Canada and get married in the near future. Emilie had thought she'd cried her eyes out over her mother's death, but thinking Angeline's departure could be imminent brought fresh tears to her eyes.

"I wish you'd reconsider your decision, Emilie. Your place is in Canada, with us."

"You have no idea where my place is, Joseph." Emilie's anger surprised her as much as it surprised her brother, but she was unable to contain it. "You go ahead and trade in cotton dust for sawdust if you want, but I want something better for myself."

Joseph sighed with exasperation. "I know you think you're better than the rest of us, Emilie, but don't forget who your family is." With that, he pushed away the chair he'd been leaning against and left the apartment, but not before Emilie could see his eyes glisten with tears.

She hated herself instantly for causing those tears. She hadn't meant to hurt him. She wished she could run after him and tell him the truth. That she was jealous of him, for he was the one who'd get to leave with Angeline and therefore would have the better life. No matter where he was or what job he worked.

Of course, Emilie knew she couldn't tell her brother any of that, so she sat at the kitchen table and cried until she couldn't cry anymore. Then she took a deep breath, stood up, and prepared to make her way to the Banville residence. The plan they'd started to formulate would be finalized today.

Angeline waited at the buttonwood tree. She wanted to be there before Emilie arrived. She hadn't seen her much since Mrs. Levesque's death and she knew her friend was suffering in silence. Emilie had been keeping most of her feelings to herself for the past year, since around the same time Angeline had become engaged to Joseph. Angeline figured it was the knowledge that they would soon be taking separate roads that had made Emilie close up like a clam. Even to her best friend. Perhaps she was upset they wouldn't see each other anymore, or perhaps she was just focused on her own plans, on her own road. Either way she'd become secretive, almost distant, and Angeline couldn't find a way in.

Joseph, however, had told her all about his pain. He'd even talked about his father's outburst and his plea for Joseph and Emilie to leave the cotton mill. When Angeline had asked about Emilie's reaction, Joseph had tensed up and avoided answering the question. He urged Angeline to pack up and follow him to Rimouski before December so they could settle in and have a Christmas wedding. Angeline had managed to convince him to wait until after the Christmas holiday, when, according to her father, The Price Company would begin its expansion plans. She needed time, more time with Emilie. She needed to get through to her, perhaps even convince her to come to Canada.

When Angeline spotted Emilie walking toward her, she was shocked at her appearance. Her friend looked like a ghost. The black skirt and bodice made her skin look even paler than usual. Her face always seemed a little emaciated, but dark circles under her eyes made it look thinner yet. The black hair tied into a tight chignon made her look older. Even the way she walked was different, as if she'd lost the usual drive in her step. "Am I late?" Emilie asked softly. "I thought I'd make it here before you."

"No, you're not late. I didn't want to miss a minute with you," Angeline said as she patted her hand on the ground beside her, asking Emilie to sit down. "How are you holding up?"

Emilie sat on the ground but not quite as close as Angeline had hoped for. Without so much as a glance in Angeline's direction, she shrugged with a nonchalance Angeline didn't believe. "I'm doing fine."

"Emilie, it's me you're talking to. I know you're in pain. You can tell me the truth." Angeline spoke in a voice she wanted to be soft, comforting and inviting, but the effect was not what she'd expected.

Emilie straightened up and sat solid as a wall, impenetrable. "I'm telling you the truth, Angeline. I can't waste any more time crying. That's not what my mother would want. I promised her I'd get out of the mill and that's what I'm working on. Now is time for action, Angeline, not for tears. You hear me?"

Angeline's heart broke. Emilie was so defensive. She'd shut everyone out, including her. Since she was getting nowhere trying to get Emilie to talk about her feelings, she figured she'd make her talk about her plans. She just wanted Emilie to talk. About something, about anything, as long as she finally opened up. "Yes, Emilie, I hear you. So tell me how you're going to do it, then. How are you going to get out of the mill?"

Emilie had been staring at the river. She made eye contact with Angeline at last, as if the question had surprised her. "Do you really want to know? Even if it's not what you want to hear? Even if I'm not going back to Canada?"

Angeline swallowed. She knew she had to hear her friend's plans and be supportive even if it tore her apart, but she still hesitated to give up all hopes of having Emilie in Canada with her. She took a deep breath before she said what she had to say to keep Emilie talking. "Yes, of course, I want to hear all about it." She swallowed again, this time with more difficulty, braced her hands on the grass and offered Emilie an encouraging smile.

Emilie relaxed ever so slightly and leaned on one hand toward Angeline, ready to reveal her intentions. "Maurice has a friend who owns a small bookstore in Boston. The man also owns the space just above the bookstore, which he turned into a lodging house. Maurice will write to ask if he could rent me a room and hire me as a clerk for his bookstore. Maurice says he might object to hiring a woman at first but he owes Maurice a favor so there's a good chance it will work out in the end. Can you imagine, Angeline? I'd be surrounded with books all the time, in the middle of a large city buzzing with possibilities. It's what I've always wanted."

Yes, it was what Emilie had always wanted. Yet she looked like she was trying to convince herself that she was truly excited about the opportunity. The light that should have been in her eyes as she spoke about the job that was indeed made for her, the life she was most likely meant to live, remained absent.

"Yes, I know it is, Emilie. You must be so happy," Angeline finally said without much conviction. Her attempt at cheering sounded more like a question and her answer was Emilie's eyes quickly filling with tears before her forced smiled vanished and she let Angeline do what her instinct compelled her to do: pull her into a tight embrace.

Angeline felt her skin instantly become wet as Emilie sobbed, her face tightly cradled in the nook of Angeline's neck. She felt her friend's frail body shake in her arms, defenseless. The vulnerability contrasted with the strength of Emilie's arms around Angeline's shoulders. Her grip was so tight Angeline could hardly breathe, but she was not going to complain. It was too good to have Emilie so close to her again, to be the strong one for her the way she'd wanted to be.

Slowly, Emilie's crying subsided but her grip remained strong and her face stayed against Angeline's neck. As she gently rubbed her friend's back, Angeline could feel Emilie breathe against her and the contact of warm breath on her skin, still damp with tears, gave her chills. Emilie was breathing heavily, probably from crying so hard.

There was something so intimate about Emilie's panting into her neck it sent a jolt of pleasure through Angeline's veins. It was almost like another chill, but ran deeper into her. She had never known this sensation before. It was not just the satisfaction of being a source of comfort for her friend. That felt wonderful, of course, but this new sensation was much more concrete than that, much more tangible. She found physical satisfaction in holding Emilie, in feeling her tight grip around her and her breath against her skin. The closeness they were sharing in that moment was both emotional and physical. It was complete. It was the kind of closeness she knew she could only find with Emilie. The kind of closeness she would have to live without once they went their separate ways.

"You don't have to go with him, Angeline. You don't have to get married," Emilie said in a raspy whisper.

Angeline could have imagined she'd simply thought the words in her own mind if she hadn't felt Emilie's lips move against her skin, sending another deep chill through her body.

Angeline forced her friend out of the safety of the nook of her neck so she could see her face. She was surprised to see fresh tears in the dark eyes as she held her at arm's length. "What? What are you saying, Emilie?"

Emilie blinked and let the tears fall freely to her cheeks as a timid but genuine smile appeared on her mouth. Angeline felt the familiar caress of Emilie's hand on her face and leaned into it. Emilie's thumb brushed over Angeline's bottom lip in a less familiar but pleasant touch and Angeline watched nervously as Emilie's eyes paused on her mouth for a few seconds.

Emilie blinked slowly and when she opened her eyes again she focused on Angeline's. "I'm saying you could come with me, Angeline. There's no rule that says you have to go to Rimouski with Joseph. If I can live as an unmarried woman in Boston, so could you. Maurice says there are many unmarried women living in lodging houses and working in Boston. We could both do it, Angeline. Together. Can you imagine? We could be so…"

"Happy," Angeline finished.

"Yes." Emilie's smile widened and Angeline smiled too. Her Emilie was back. The one who made her believe everything was possible. The one who didn't let obstacles or conventions stop her. She thought she'd lost her forever.

Angeline was glad Emilie was back, but she couldn't help but wonder what had happened to the more serious and cautious Emilie of the past two years, the Emilie who'd pushed Angeline toward her brother.

"But wait, Emilie. I thought you wanted me to marry your brother. You're the one who convinced me to accept him as a suitor, remember? You said I couldn't spend my life discussing books and gossiping with my best friend. Do you remember?"

Her own tears took her by surprise. She wasn't sure if they were tears of sadness from remembering the moment she'd felt rejected by her best friend, tears of joy from Emilie's change of heart, or tears of frustration from knowing that it might be too late for that change. How was she supposed to break her engagement with Joseph now? It would break his heart, and he didn't deserve that after being nothing but good to her.

"I remember, my sweet Angeline. I just wanted you to be happy. I still do. But I don't think you have to get married to Joseph to be happy. Not anymore. And more than anything I know I can't be happy if you're not with me."

Angeline kept crying but these new tears were from a heart filled with happiness at Emilie's declaration. "Oh, Emilie, I can't be happy without you either."

Emilie pulled Angeline into her arms. She was back to being the strong one, holding Angeline as she dried her tears on the black fabric covering Emilie's shoulder.

"I'm not asking you to make any decision right now, Angeline," Emilie whispered tenderly into Angeline's ear. "I know you have a lot to think about. Just promise me you realize that you have more than one option and that you will consider all of your options carefully."

"I promise," Angeline answered without hesitation. Her mind was already overwhelmed with thoughts but she let Emilie rock her gently before dusk fell on them much too soon and they had to go back to their respective triple-deckers for the night.

That night over dinner, Joseph told Emilie and their father he would be leaving for Rimouski after the Christmas holiday with Angeline. Their father was pleased with the decision. Then Emilie told both men about Maurice's friend in Boston, the bookstore, and the lodging house. Joseph said with genuine concern that it couldn't be safe for a woman to live by herself in a large city like Boston. Their father ended the conversation stating it had to be safer than the cotton mill and left the dining table to go pray in the bedroom he'd shared with their mother.

Emilie was now in bed but she couldn't sleep. Ever since her older half-brothers had left the apartment, she'd taken their room while Joseph remained in the parlor. She had her own bedroom and she was happy about that, but she often suffered from insomnia and sometimes it felt like there was now too much space for her never-ending profusion of thoughts within these four walls. She massaged the wrinkle between her eyebrows with her thumb, as if the pressure could make the worries that caused it to go away.

She worried about her father. She wondered if he would ever leave his bedroom once she and Joseph were gone. She knew he would keep going to work, at least, as a form of self-punishment for her mother's death. He would endure the cotton mill's damp, deadly air until his last breath. That's what she knew her father was convinced he had to pay for bringing his wife to Fall River and making her work in the cotton mill that eventually killed her.

Outside of work, however, he would probably stay in his bedroom, forgetting to eat, bathe, take care of himself in any way. Emilie wished he would accept Edouard's invitation to stay with him and his family. Realistically, he couldn't afford to live in this apartment by himself and would sooner or later be evicted. The fact that her father, who'd been so proud, would be forced out of yet another home, broke Emilie's heart.

He'd been forced out of Rimouski by circumstances out of his control but ultimately it had been his choice to leave and take his family to the United States. This time it would be different. He would be kicked out like a worthless old man. It was painful to think about it but Emilie couldn't stay to take care of him. He wouldn't let her even if she begged him.

Emilie turned to her left side as if the new position could chase her thoughts away. All she achieved was to replace thoughts of her father with thoughts of Angeline. What had gotten into her that afternoon, asking Angeline to break her engagement to Joseph and follow her to Boston? When she cried into the nook of Angeline's neck and breathed in the delicate scent of her skin, she couldn't control herself, it had just happened. She'd become intoxicated, excited by the proximity of Angeline's body, and the only clarity in her mind at that moment had been that she couldn't live without Angeline. She had to have Angeline close to her at all times, in Boston or anywhere else.

She would have to learn to keep her physical reactions under control, of course. She didn't know much more about the disease that was Sapphism than the day she'd learned it existed beside the fact that she was undeniably affected. She hoped she would find out more about her condition in Boston, where she would have access to so much more knowledge. She hoped she would also learn to control it and keep Angeline safe from it. She was willing to do anything she needed to do to keep Angeline safe, but staying away from her could no longer be the only solution. She wasn't willing to accept or live with that solution. She needed Angeline in her life. As a friend and as the person she loved more than anyone else in the world. There was nothing wrong with loving Angeline as long as that love remained chaste. Was there?

"No, there's nothing wrong with loving her," Emilie whispered, trying to convince herself as she attempted to block any thought of shortcomings her love for Angeline may have, like the lack of physical intimacy and the impossibility of giving her children. Other than those deficiencies, she could give Angeline everything else her brother had to offer.

She would find a way to provide for her, to protect her, to cherish her. They would be together and that was all that really mattered, she repeated to herself. And since Joseph didn't plan to leave before Christmas, she still had time to convince Angeline to believe the same.

She let her mind go back to the way Angeline's blue eyes had lit up when Emilie had admitted she couldn't live without her. She grinned. It was clear Angeline wanted to be with her as much as she wanted to be with Angeline. All she needed to do was convince Angeline to put her desires before her duty. It would be difficult, certainly, but not impossible.

CHAPTER THIRTEEN

February 1898

Angeline still spent most Sunday afternoons with Emilie, under their buttonwood tree when the weather allowed it. When it was cold and windy like today, however, the time they used to spend in Angeline's bedroom was now spent at the Levesque apartment instead of the home Angeline shared with her sister's family. It gave Angeline a little time away from the children. She loved her nieces and nephews, but they were not her children.

Angeline found lately that she craved a home of her own and her own family to take care of. So much so that she would have married Joseph without hesitation even though she knew what she felt for him was not the kind of love she'd learned about in Emilie's books. But she hadn't been able to take that step yet, and the one and only reason was Emilie.

The other reason why they met at the Levesque apartment was because they were most often alone, or almost alone. Emilie's father remained locked up in his bedroom and Joseph busied himself elsewhere, giving them what he called "ladies time." They took full advantage of this time. Emilie made tea and they sat sometimes at the kitchen table and other times, like today, on Emilie's bed. Then they talked. But they didn't talk about books or Flint gossips. Their conversations had changed drastically ever since Emilie had asked Angeline not to marry her brother and follow her to Boston instead, taking a direction Angeline and Emilie had never dared before. The future. A future they would share together.

Emilie did most of the talking. She spoke of the room they'd share and how Emilie would work and take care of Angeline. They didn't need much, she said. God knows they weren't used to much. At night they would discover Boston together and perhaps meet with other single women who chose to live outside of the norms, women who refused the married life society tried to force upon them, or even married women who questioned the place of women in conventional marriage and in society in general. Women like Susan B. Anthony who had been fighting for years to earn the right to vote. Someday, Emilie swore, women would earn every right men already had simply because they were born male. There were many women like them who wanted something different, she assured Angeline, and there was nothing wrong with it.

Yet Emilie always spoke in a low voice, making sure her father couldn't hear a single word of her promises. Angeline wasn't a fool. She knew the life Emilie painted with such pretty colors would be much harder in reality. Even in Boston, people would point fingers and judge, and without a man to open doors for them, they would find most doors would remain shut in their face. She knew the life Emilie described would be one of hardship, but Angeline listened anyway. She listened and somehow couldn't help but want that life with Emilie. She would be with Emilie, after all, and that's what she really wanted, wasn't it?

"Have you talked to Joseph yet?"

The question Emilie asked with such hope brought Angeline back to the dilemma she'd been both facing and avoiding for five months. "No, I haven't talked to him." She paused before adding, "I haven't made a decision yet, Emilie."

The deep and heavy sigh Emilie let out broke Angeline's heart. Emilie had been smiling a lot more lately as she planned their future and organized their life in Boston. Angeline had seen hope and happiness take root in her friend, and she liked the effect it had on her. Knowing that she had the power with just a few words to send Emilie back to a state of such deep sorrow and worry hurt her, but she couldn't lie to Emilie. She hadn't made any promises. She simply couldn't.

Emilie's description of their future excited her and tempted her, yes, but a part of her was unable to give up on living a more quiet life, with a husband and children. A life she might not have to fight for with every breath. A life she might just be able to live peacefully, day in and day out.

The truth was that she didn't have the courage Emilie had. She didn't have the same will or urge to fight. A part of her wanted to go ahead and do it so she could be with Emilie, but another part wanted the tranquillity she knew she'd have to give up forever to be with her.

She looked at Emilie's frail body kneeling on the bed, as if begging for Angeline to make a decision, the decision she was convinced was right. It would be easy to say yes at this very moment, just to see a smile come back to Emilie's lips, but she couldn't. Instead, Angeline pushed back a strand of black hair that had escaped Emilie's chignon and murmured, "I will decide soon, Emilie. I promise."

She'd hoped Emilie's features would soften at her commitment and they almost did before Emilie sighed again and stood up. She faced Angeline, who was still sitting on the edge of the bed, and took Angeline's hands in hers, slowly massaging her skin with her thumbs. Emilie looked down at their joined hands for several seconds as if gathering her thoughts. At last, Emilie fixed her black stare on Angeline's eyes and announced. "It will have to be very soon, Angeline."

Angeline swallowed. She knew an ultimatum would come eventually but she didn't expect it now. "How soon?" she asked in a barely audible voice.

"When I was at Maurice's earlier we read a letter he'd just received from his friend in Boston. He's expecting me at the bookstore in two weeks from today. His clerk is moving away and if I don't take the position now, I may never have another chance." Emilie's voice caught and she took a deep breath before she continued. "I want you to come with me more than anything, Angeline, but please understand that I have to go." After a moment of hesitation, Emilie added, "With or without you."

Angeline could have sworn her heart stopped beating and it might not have started again if she and Emilie hadn't been abruptly interrupted by the sound of a door slamming and Joseph's voice calling their names from the kitchen. Emilie quickly dropped Angeline's hands and Angeline stood up just as fast as if they'd been caught doing something wrong.

They exchanged a last glance and she hoped Emilie could see her own despair as well as Angeline could see hers. Then they joined Joseph in the kitchen.

Joseph had asked to talk to Angeline alone and since Emilie had to prepare dinner for their father, Angeline put on her long, heavy coat and followed Joseph outside for a walk in the February cold that penetrated through the wool all the way to her bones. She knew that the chill was not entirely due to the weather. She hated leaving Emilie after what she'd just learned, but quickly realized Joseph seemed just as perturbed as his sister. Reluctantly, she tried to put her unfinished conversation with Emilie in the back of her mind and focus on Joseph. As they walked briskly, she held Joseph's arm and stayed close to him in an effort to warm up.

They'd walked two blocks before Joseph finally spoke. "Angeline, I think you can agree that I've been patient," he started.

Angeline didn't let go of Joseph's arm but put more distance between them as they slowed their pace. Surely Joseph couldn't choose the same day for his own ultimatum, could he? She didn't like the way the conversation was beginning, but she couldn't disagree with him. Joseph had been more patient than she was entitled to ask any man to be. "Yes, you've been very patient, Joseph. And I truly appreciate it."

They reached their bench, the one where they'd shared their first kiss, and they sat, Angeline trembling in the cold. He put his strong arm around her shoulders and started rubbing her arm in an effort to keep her warm. He sighed before he spoke again. "I'd keep being patient forever if I could. I think you know that. But…"

He stopped talking and Angeline surprised herself worrying more about the expression she saw in his face than about what he was trying to say. The same profile that always seemed so impassible was marked with concern, perhaps even fear. She'd never seen that crease between his eyebrows before, the same kind that had almost become a permanent feature on Emilie's face. Something was most definitely wrong. "But what, Joseph? Please say what you have to say. You're scaring me."

He turned slightly on the bench so he could look at her in the eye when he finally explained what was troubling him. "I don't think we can wait anymore, Angeline. We should be going to Rimouski and get married right away. I think we'll be safer there."

Yes, it seemed to be the ultimatum Angeline had feared, but Joseph also appeared to have a good reason. "Why now? Did something happen?"

He hesitated. "I don't want to trouble your mind with news you don't need to worry about, Angeline, but yes, something happened. I know it's my job to protect you from the craziness that happens in this world but in this case I think you need to know."

Angeline was both touched and annoyed by Joseph's consideration. Mostly annoyed. "You don't have to protect me from anything, Joseph. I can take the truth. Tell me."

"All right, then. A few days ago a ship, the USS Maine, mysteriously exploded off the coast of Havana. I've been talking with other men and they think this may force the United States to get involved in the Cuban war for independence from Spain. And I'm beginning to think the same."

Angeline hoped her expression was not quite as puzzled as she felt, but she'd asked for the truth so she had to make the effort to understand it. "I'm sorry, Joseph, but I don't see what that has to do with us rushing to Rimouski now."

Joseph's smile was tender but almost condescending, as if he'd expected she wouldn't see how both events were linked. "If the United States gets involved, Angeline, it means they will declare war against Spain. And they will need men to fight that war. Do you understand now?"

Angeline gasped. "Oh no, Joseph." She understood all too well. Joseph wanted to go back to Canada before he was forced to go to war. It made perfect sense.

"I don't want to fight a war that has nothing to do with me, with us and with our plans. If I'd had it my way we'd be in Canada already and the possibility would not even exist. Even if we'd left right after Christmas like we were supposed to…" He stopped himself but Angeline knew how frustrated he'd been when she'd asked him to wait a little longer. Again. "But the threat is here now, Angeline, and it's real. I know I'm rushing you and that's not what I want but I don't have any other choice. We have to leave before it's too late. You understand?"

"Yes. Yes, of course I understand." Thoughts of Joseph being killed in a war she hadn't even known was threatening them filled Angeline's mind. It made no sense for Joseph to stay in this country and die for a cause they knew nothing about. He had to go back to Canada now. If he stayed for her and something happened to him, she couldn't live with the guilt. And she really didn't want anything to happen to Joseph. She loved him. As a friend, as a companion, as family. So she had to go with him and get married, didn't she? It was her duty, wasn't it?

Her brain screamed an unequivocal yes but her heart whispered Emilie's name. A whisper so loud it interfered with all of her noble thoughts. As much as she wanted to tell Joseph she'd go with him right now she was incapable of doing so. She needed time alone to think it through, so she made the only promise she could make. "Twenty-four hours."

"What?" Joseph asked, baffled.

"I know you've been very patient and we must act quickly, Joseph, but I just need a little time to organize my thoughts and talk this through with my family. Please meet me here in just twenty-four hours, and we'll make definite plans then." *Or I'll break your heart and send you back to Canada by yourself,* she added to herself.

Joseph readily agreed and he walked her back to her sister's apartment for dinner. She wouldn't talk about anything with her family. She just needed to think and to come up with her own decision. Rimouski with Joseph or Boston with Emilie. By tomorrow evening, she would have decided which path she'd follow. She was panicked but also strangely relieved at the thought.

Emilie didn't intend to walk toward Angeline's apartment when she first came outside. She just needed to breathe in some fresh air to calm down after her brother had announced over dinner that he and Angeline would be leaving for Canada very soon to avoid the imminent war. They were going to meet tomorrow after their workday at the mill to make plans. He thought they'd leave next week.

Outside, Emilie knew it had to be cold because she could see the condensation of her breath in the air, but she didn't feel cold. In fact, she was hot. She was so angry she could swear her blood was boiling and soon she had to open up the top button of her wool coat so she could keep breathing as she paced back and forth in front of their triple-decker.

Who did Joseph think he was? How dare he put Angeline in such a situation? How dare he force her to marry him when she was not ready yet? She hadn't told her brother any of that, of course. Even she knew he'd been more than patient with Angeline. She couldn't keep quiet though. In that moment over dinner she wanted to hurt her brother because he was threatening her own happiness and as always she knew exactly what would hurt him the most.

"Don't you think perhaps it is your duty to fight for this country? Are you really such a coward, Joseph?" she said sternly and then stalked away from the table. She knew she hit his pride and that had been what she was going for at that moment.

Now, however, as the frigid air finally permeated her senses and her temper cooled, she regretted her words. What she had really wanted was not to hurt her brother; it was to convince Angeline not to go with him. Angeline was the one Emilie's happiness depended on, and if she was really ready to make plans with Joseph to go to Rimouski, Emilie hadn't succeeded in getting through to her as well as she thought she had. She needed to talk to her tonight. She needed to talk to her before she met Joseph tomorrow. Before it was too late. She needed to make one last plea. So she started walking.

When Emilie knocked on the door, Angeline came to open it with a dishcloth in her hand. "I'm sorry to interrupt your evening," Emilie said to her startled face, "but I need to talk to you. It's about my brother."

Angeline quickly put on her coat as her sister implored her to be careful outside in the frigid evening. Angeline promised she wouldn't be long and joined Emilie outside. They automatically started walking toward their buttonwood tree. Night had fallen but the sky was well lit by a full moon that allowed them to see where they were stepping.

"Will you say what's on your mind at last, Emilie? You're scaring me."

Angeline was out of breath and searching for air between every word she spoke, and Emilie realized they'd almost run to the tree. She'd kept a few steps ahead of Angeline, not looking at her until now, when she turned around and saw an expression of panic on her beautiful face. She was really scared.

Emilie grabbed Angeline's hands, covered with thick mittens, and smiled in an attempt to reassure her. "I'm sorry. I didn't want to scare you. I just had to talk to you. Joseph told us about the possible war and your meeting tomorrow to discuss the details of your departure for Canada. Is it true, Angeline? Are you really going to do it?"

Angeline took her hands out of Emilie's and sighed. "I don't know, Emilie. I wanted the evening to make my own decision. I needed to think things through."

Emilie felt her heart shrink inside her chest and every nerve in her raised a terrified alarm. For the first time since she'd asked Angeline to follow her to Boston instead of marrying her brother, she realized she might lose the fight. She was out of control, desperate, and her voice showed it. "I don't understand what there is to think through, Angeline. Haven't you heard a word I said in the past months? We can be together. We can be happy together. I have a way. Isn't that what you want?"

"It's not as easy as you make it sound, Emilie. I do want to be with you, but I also want a family, a home of my own. If I go with you I'll never have that. Your brother is a good man. You know that. He can give me what I always thought I wanted before…"

"Before what?" Emilie asked as tears started flowing down her cheeks.

"Before you put other thoughts in my mind, Emilie. Before you made me believe something else might be possible."

"So it's all my fault?" Emilie asked incredulously. "I put thoughts in your head, Angeline? You can't really believe that. It's not true. You want to be with me as much as I want to be with you and you know it. I didn't put any thoughts in your mind that you didn't already have. I just gave you solutions you couldn't think of yourself."

"Because they're not real solutions at all, Emilie. Don't you see how difficult it would be for both of us? Our life would be nothing but fights and obstacles and it might even ruin our friendship eventually. Women aren't meant to live together. Without men. It's not the way things are done. Even you must know that, don't you?"

Emilie could hardly recognize Angeline through her tear-filled eyes. She was not the woman she loved. Her face was in distress, yes, but her eyes remained dry. She almost appeared cold. Their connection was broken and Emilie panicked, clueless as to how to fix it. Her appeal of the last five months, logical and calculated, had failed. What else was left to do but to let her heart cry out and beg?

"Angeline, please. I know it will be hard. But I can't live without you. You said you couldn't live without me either. Don't you remember?" Emilie hated her voice. It was small and shrill and ugly, punctuated with weak sobs. But there was no time for control. No place for pride.

"I know, Emilie. I just don't see how it's possible," Angeline answered as her voice broke for the first time and her blue eyes welled up with tears at last.

Angeline was losing her resolve. She just didn't understand. She had to make her understand, had to let her heart speak. She stepped closer to Angeline, under the protection of their tree, and lowered her voice. "Please, Angeline. I love you. I love you so much."

Emilie didn't try to stop herself and she pressed her lips to Angeline's with all the desperation that inhabited her. She just had to make her understand how deep were her love and her need to be with her.

Angeline gasped at the contact but didn't pull away. Emilie even thought she might have felt her press harder against her mouth. Emilie's lips parted with an unexplainable desire to taste Angeline, and to her surprise Angeline allowed the timid exploration of Emilie's tongue. Angeline's mouth was salty and sweet at the same time. She gently sucked in the full bottom lip and when in return she felt Angeline's tongue on her own upper lip, the tender, wet caress made her moan softly. Angeline responded with a small whimper and moved her tongue until it met with Emilie's.

The union of their tongues made their mouths hungrier and their kiss deepened until Angeline abruptly pushed Emilie away with strong arms and screamed, "No!"

Angeline's strength easily forced Emilie to her knees and when she looked up she saw a glimpse of shame in Angeline's face as she labored to catch her breath, a shame that was quickly replaced with anger and disgust.

Emilie stood back up with difficulty and didn't look at Angeline again before she ran away saying "I'm sorry" in a voice she knew was too weak and broken for Angeline to hear.

Angeline waited for Joseph by the bench. She hadn't walked with him before or after work because she didn't want to see

Emilie. She'd succeeded in avoiding her all day and she didn't want to see her before she saw Joseph, before she told him they needed to leave and get married right away. She feared that if she saw Emilie before she spoke to Joseph, she might change her mind. She couldn't change her mind. What she'd felt with Emilie the night before when they'd kissed couldn't happen again.

Angeline had spent the night awake, thinking about Emilie's desperate plea, her declaration of love and most of all her soft lips pressed against hers. The way they felt, the way they tasted, the way their touch had awakened Angeline's entire body. Joseph's kisses had never had that effect on her. It was as if Emilie's lips had sent a violent whirlpool of desires inside her that left every inch of her skin wanting more. More contact, more sensation, more of Emilie.

In a way, what had happened explained so much. How she had needed to be close to Emilie all those years, how she couldn't help thinking of Emilie when she got close to Joseph, how she'd even wanted to believe it was possible for her to live with Emilie.

But most of all, what had happened proved that Angeline needed to get away from Emilie as soon as possible. These feelings she had for Emilie, and that Emilie obviously had for her, she had no words for them, but she knew they were wrong. They were unhealthy, unacceptable, and if she had to leave the country and get married to Joseph to forget about them once and for all, that was exactly what she'd do. She'd save both Emilie and herself from something so evil she had never even heard of it before.

Joseph arrived and she hugged him tightly, as if clinging to a savior. "I packed everything that's mine, Joseph. I'll be ready to leave whenever you are." At Joseph's disconcerted smile, she added "What? Is there something wrong?"

Joseph laughed and gave her another hug, holding her tighter. "No, nothing's wrong. You're just surprising me, that's all. I was coming here halfway expecting you to ask me to wait a little longer, or even worse, break off our engagement. I was certainly not expecting you to tell me you were all packed."

She giggled nervously at his excitement. "I didn't have much to pack, Joseph. It's not that shocking. We have to leave the country as soon as possible. You said it yourself."

Because of the war, but mostly because I have to get away from your sister.

"I know. I do have money saved up for train tickets and the bare necessities once we get there. We won't be rich, Angeline."

"I know, but my parents will be there to help us and I trust you, Joseph. We'll be fine, I know it."

"So this is really happening, Angeline? We're going to Rimouski to get married?"

His childish grin was most endearing and helped her keep threatening tears at bay. She even managed a smile to answer, "Yes, Joseph, it's really happening."

She would be happy with Joseph. She knew she would be.

MEANDERS

1898-1905

CHAPTER FOURTEEN

Boston, November 1898

Emilie sat at the small round table placed in a corner of her room, trying to read an article in a medical journal she'd borrowed from the bookstore. She plunged her fingers through her long black hair and massaged her scalp. Mr. Flaherty required that she wore the most complicated and sophisticated hairstyles when she worked in his store. They made her look a little older, he claimed, and gave her more credibility. The bouffant, pompadour and other hairstyles she'd so carefully avoided before she moved to Boston were now part of her daily routine.

Fortunately, Mrs. Flaherty had been able to teach her how to accomplish such hairstyles popularized by the Gibson Girl, a character created by Charles Dana Gibson that inspired all young American women when it came to style and fashion. A character made up by a man, of course, Emilie repeated to herself every time she let her hair loose at the end of the day and attempted to massage the pain out of her scalp.

She couldn't complain, though, as the hairstyles she had to wear were the only aspect of her work she didn't enjoy.

Flaherty Books was located in a three-story house on Bromfield Street. It was a red brick building, like so many buildings in Boston. The second and third floors had regular-sized windows, but on the first floor, the front door was flanked by two enormous windows where new books were displayed to tempt passersby inside the store which occupied the entire first floor of the building. The light through the front windows faded as it moved along the dark wooden shelves toward the back of the deep and narrow space. Emilie had quickly realized that the books, just like the store, became more obscure the farther she walked toward the back. That was where she found the medical journals and books Mr. Flaherty let her borrow as long as she didn't bend or crease any of the pages. Emilie was grateful he never kept track or paid any kind of attention to what she borrowed.

She was grateful to Mr. and Mrs. Flaherty for many reasons. The couple, both in their forties, had been nothing but kind and generous to Emilie. Michael Flaherty, with his large belly and his red mustache, had trusted her with his store from the very first day. He never talked to her about books the way his friend Maurice had because, Emilie suspected, he still wasn't convinced women had much to say about books, but he'd taken her under his protective wing and helped Emilie feel safe in her new surroundings.

Margaret Flaherty had been nothing short of a second mother. On one hand it made Emilie miss her own mother even more and she'd often cried herself to sleep when she'd first moved in, thinking of her. On the other hand, it made her life in Boston so much easier. She couldn't help but smile every time she thought of the corpulent, rosy-cheeked woman who couldn't be caught without a smile on her face. Showing Emilie how to do her hair every morning was just one of the many things Margaret had done for her. She also washed her clothes, even her sheets, and she fed her. While most lodging houses in Boston didn't include meals, Mrs. Flaherty cooked both breakfast and dinner for her four lodgers every day.

Emilie was definitely grateful to Mr. and Mrs. Flaherty, who had also successfully reconciled her with Irish people after the horrors she'd lived during her childhood in Fall River. Mr. and Mrs. Flaherty didn't go out much. He would go to business meetings once in a while but she never left the house. Emilie would have liked to explore the city with them. She didn't dare go too far on her own. She'd walked two blocks on a sidewalk made of red bricks that resembled the bricks of the bookstore to a nearby eatery a few times, but that was the extent of her solitary exploration thus far. It would have been easier with Angeline, she often mused before she forced herself to think of something else. She didn't have much time to wander off anyway. She worked all day long and read every night. On Sundays, she went to church with Mr. and Mrs. Flaherty and helped Margaret clean the lodging house. She didn't have time to get bored.

Emilie straightened up to stretch her back, often sore from bending over the table to read, and hit her head on a nail in the wall. She gasped and started massaging her head again. Her room was just that: a room. It was smaller than her bedroom in Flint but the walls had been recently painted in white which gave it a much cleaner look. There was a small bed in one corner with no space to put anything else at the foot of the bed, and a small rounded wooden table with a wooden chair in the other corner. A narrow window separated the bed from the table and a few nails in the wall allowed her to hang her clothes. Or hit her head.

One big advantage over the triple-decker of Fall River was an interior bathroom with fully functioning plumbing. There was also electricity, but Emilie didn't like its flickering light. It seemed more dangerous than the flickering candlelight she was used to so she preferred lighting a candle at night to read. Her room and the other three lodgers' were on the third floor while the second floor hosted the bathroom, a small and comfortably furnished parlor, the Flahertys' bedroom, and Mrs. Flaherty's kitchen.

Once the pain subsided, Emilie returned to her reading, frustrated. She'd found information about Sapphism and homosexuality in medical journals, but not what she was looking for. The articles all agreed that homosexuality was a disease, but no cure seemed to exist. It could be caused by a variety of factors from climate and excessive masturbation to fear of pregnancy or simple curiosity.

They used complicated words like sexual inversion, which meant that someone who desired their own sex was somehow reversed. A woman who desired another woman, for example, would essentially be a man inside a woman's body. According to these articles, women with such feelings had deep voices and big muscles and liked sports. They even suggested that such women smoked and could spit, whistle and curse like no other woman. Emilie was lost. She couldn't recognize herself in the doctors' descriptions, although she was very tempted to spit on their articles and curse them out. But she knew her feelings were real. She most certainly had desire for Angeline. She'd always been skinny and short and didn't care anything for sports. She'd never been tempted to smoke either but her love for Angeline was real. The articles and books she read didn't talk much about that love or desire.

They didn't do much better when it came to potential cures, especially for women, the gist of which could be summarized as "get married and have children, woman." No pills, no drops, no medicine of any kind. Just forget about all of these unnatural feelings and do the right thing. Socially, morally and religiously, the right thing was to get married and have children. Emilie couldn't accept that.

Only one article had given her hope. It was an article published in 1891, written by Albert Moll, a young German. According to him, homosexuality was not learned like a bad habit but appeared in early childhood, perhaps even at birth. It was not a disease, and therefore searching for a cure was futile. The reason homosexuals suffered was society, not their homosexuality. He even went as far as claiming that homosexuality was natural.

Emilie kept reading, hoping she'd find more articles that might support Moll's theory and extrapolate on it, but nothing else made sense to her. The more she read about these other doctors' theories, the more she thought that even if there had been a pill or a drop she could have taken to be cured from homosexuality, she wouldn't have taken it. She didn't want to forget the way she'd felt every time she saw Angeline, the way her body roused when she touched her in the most innocent way, the way all of her senses had melted into liquid desire the night she'd kissed her.

Emilie closed the medical journal with a sigh. She blew out the candle and slipped under the covers to do what she allowed herself to do every night: thinking of Angeline. Trying not to think of her was useless. When she was alone at night in the darkness of her small room, Emilie couldn't fall asleep until she let her mind draw a perfect portrait of Angeline and she imagined her own hands caressing that heavy curly hair or cupping those wide hips. Until she kissed those full lips…

She hadn't seen Angeline again after the kiss. When her father and Joseph went to work the next morning, she left a note for them on the kitchen table. Packed her clothes in a small suitcase Helen had bought for her and the few books she owned in her precious leather mailbag. She stayed with the Banvilles for a few days before she took the train to Boston to start her new life. Since then she wrote her father every week. He had apparently forgiven her; he wrote back about once a month and she knew from him that Joseph and Angeline had made their way to Rimouski. They were married and Angeline was expecting their first child.

But those were not the thoughts Emilie let enter her mind at night. She preferred the Angeline who'd kissed her back, just for a few unforgettable seconds, and in her musings she didn't let Angeline push her away. She didn't let the kiss end. It continued and she let her lips and her hands explore other parts of Angeline's body. She heard over and over again the small whimper that had escaped Angeline in response to her own moan, transformed it into louder or softer sounds as she willed.

Lying on her back, Emilie moved her hand up and down her own thigh before wandering to the wetness between her legs. She often touched herself in that particular spot when thoughts of Angeline escalated. She couldn't resist the throbbing of her own sex and didn't see why she should. According to the doctors she read, too much masturbation might be the cause of homosexuality, but since she was already an incurable Sapphist, it couldn't do much harm, could it?

CHAPTER FIFTEEN

Rimouski, January 1899

Angeline had a hard time putting the baby down, even when he slept peacefully as he did now, comfortably wrapped in a soft blanket and held closely to his mother's bosom. She kept the movement of the rocking chair slow and steady. She knew she should put him in the crib Joseph had built and placed in their bedroom. She had to go take care of the chickens among other numerous chores that were waiting for her in and outside the house. But she couldn't move, her eyes fixed on the beautiful boy in her arms.

She still had trouble believing she was a mother; yet felt deeply inside like she was meant to be nothing else. Her son briefly opened his eyes and closed them again with an adorable yawn. He was six weeks old today. The day he was born was the day Angeline had finally been able to feel comfortable in Rimouski, in this house Joseph and her father had built for them on Tessier Road. Before then, she'd been restless, often sad. She'd even lost her usual sense of humor. Joseph and her parents were worried but kept hope that becoming a mother would change everything. They were right.

When Joseph and Angeline first arrived in Rimouski, they lived with her father and mother. They shared the Fourniers' modest home for a few months while Joseph and her father built an even smaller home for the young couple just next door. The first floor of the house had a small bedroom for Joseph and Angeline and a larger room for the kitchen and parlor where she'd placed the old rocking chair her parents had offered her when she became pregnant. The woodstove was at the center of the house, keeping them warm. It was set against a central wall that separated the kitchen from the narrow wooden stairs leading to the attic where livable space was limited but could eventually fit a couple of beds for their children. She'd liked her home right away. It was small but it was hers. She liked its simple wood board exterior walls, its crisp white door and window trim, its front porch, and its single dorm popping out of the high-pitched metal sheet roof. It had charm and character.

Angeline wasn't so sure about Rimouski. It didn't fit the image she'd dreamed of in her childhood. The Saint-Laurent River was as magnificent as she'd imagined but they'd only been to its shore once, soon after they'd moved, and they couldn't see it from their house. Instead they lived by the Rimouski River, which didn't look much better than the Quequechan River, in Angeline's opinion.

She was also surprised at how rural Rimouski truly was. She'd laughed when Joseph had told her he couldn't believe how much the town had grown in the ten years he'd been gone. With less than two thousand people, Rimouski was still far short of the population of Fall River, which counted more than eighty thousand people. In Angeline's eyes, Rimouski was not a town at all. It was as country as country could get. As country as she'd ever experienced. She missed the city more than she ever thought she would. She missed sidewalks, eateries, shops of all kinds she didn't frequent often but at least knew existed. Rimouski had a church, a train station, a general store, and that was about it. She knew that was all they really needed but she couldn't help but feel limited in her options.

She was lonely. The Price Company hadn't expanded yet as her father had hoped, but he'd still managed to find Joseph work at the mill. He didn't have a proper position or salary yet, but he did have a foot in the door doing whatever odd jobs they had to give him. He did all he could to make a good impression so he could earn the first stable job that opened up, which meant he worked at all hours of the day or night doing whatever they needed done, whenever they needed it. Angeline spent a lot of time alone and if it hadn't been for her mother, her state of mind would have been even worse.

Her mother kept her company and also kept her busy with the farm animals she and her father kept in a small barn and chicken coop just behind their house. They didn't have many, just a few chickens for eggs and a couple of cows for milk and butter. They also had cats to keep the rodents away, and a large garden in the summer. It was not a real farm, but it was close enough. Their life was quiet, peaceful, the kind of life Angeline had always thought she wanted. But something was inexplicably missing. Until she gave birth to her son.

Angeline watched him sleep in her arms. He was almost smiling. His skin was pale and he had the thickest hair she'd ever seen on a baby. Fluffy black hair she couldn't stop caressing. She delicately moved her little finger inside his tiny hand and he immediately took hold of it. She enjoyed feeling his grip as she watched his fragile yet perfectly shaped hand. "You're just as strong as your papa, aren't you, Paul-Emile?"

Joseph and Angeline had determined while she was pregnant that if they had a girl, they would name her Mathilde in honor of Joseph's mother. They hadn't decided on a name for a baby boy until the day Paul-Emile was born. Joseph had suggested Paul-Emile without referring to his sister Emilie, but Angeline knew how much he really missed her and that the name was his way to make room for her in their own, new family. Angeline agreed with her husband and their son was baptized Paul-Emile Joseph Levesque.

Angeline breathed in her son's hair and thought that even with a different name, Paul-Emile would have reminded her of Emilie. His hair, his dark eyes, that serious expression he had sometimes, everything about him reminded her of Emilie. Angeline sighed heavily. Since the birth of her son, she was able to think of Emilie in a new, positive light. She was nostalgic for their friendship, for the laughter and the discussions they'd shared. She rarely thought of the kiss that had made her rush to move to Rimouski and get married. The kiss that had made her question her own nature and was at least partially responsible for her pre-motherhood melancholy when they'd moved here.

Things were different now. She didn't question her nature anymore. How could she? Her nature was sleeping in her arms. It was being a mother to this little boy and the brothers and sisters he would have soon. What had happened with Emilie was just a brief lapse of judgment. Emilie was nothing more than the best friend she'd lost. She would miss her, yes, but the loss of Emilie couldn't keep her from her own happiness. Not anymore.

Later that night, Angeline laid Paul-Emile in his crib and joined Joseph in their bed. The wood frame Joseph had built was rustic but the mattress was comfortable. Angeline thought Joseph was already sleeping so she slipped into bed quietly and snuffed the flame of the oil lamp that had been slowly burning on her nightstand.

When she finally lay down, Joseph turned to face her. The room was dark and the faint moonlight from the window behind Joseph to light up her face only allowed her to see his strong silhouette. He touched her face with his callused hand and whispered, "You're so beautiful."

Angeline smiled. She didn't need light to know what was on his face. There was not one single brief moment since they'd been married that she hadn't seen love in Joseph's eyes. Even in her darkest times, when he could easily have shown frustration, he'd been patient, loving and hopeful for their future. Joseph loved her unconditionally and she was touched by his devotion. She couldn't imagine a better husband or a better father for Paul-Emile and the children that were still to come. "Do you think we waited long enough?" he asked nervously.

Angeline knew he wanted to make love. He loved touching her, moving inside her, taking her. Angeline didn't find making love as pleasurable as he did, but she liked giving him pleasure. She knew it was her duty as his wife, but she didn't see it as a chore. She also knew she hadn't been bleeding in over a week and the six weeks the doctor had asked them to wait after their son's birth had passed. "I think it's safe, yes," she said as she turned on her back and let him settle between her legs.

As he began moving into her and kissed her neck tenderly, she focused on the smell of sawdust that permeated his skin. She loved that scent, found it comforting. She inhaled it loudly knowing the sound of her breathing excited him. She listened to his increasingly ragged respiration and felt the rhythm of his hips gain momentum. She whimpered then, softly, knowing it would send him over the edge, knowing she would soon hear the familiar grunt of satisfaction and feel the intimate sticky liquid between her legs. And then he collapsed next to her on the bed and laid his head on her breast, still covered by the light fabric of her nightgown. She caressed the blond hair on the back of his neck. It was always so soft. Angeline sighed with contentment and smiled.

The first night they were married, Angeline had feared making love with Joseph. She didn't know what to expect and she was afraid she'd disappoint him. Of course he'd taken his time and had been tender. She hadn't expected anything less from him, but his gentleness had helped her get through their first night as man and wife even more than she'd thought. She hadn't felt much pain that first time, and she'd never felt pain at all since then. Joseph would never hurt her. She'd quickly realized she would never take as much gratification as he did in the conjugal act. She would never crave it as she'd once hoped. She also knew that she would never refuse her husband.

Angeline caressed Joseph's hair even after his breathing deepened and she knew he was asleep. She would never refuse him this satisfaction because it made him happy and because it alleviated some of her guilt. Giving him her body, her core, temporarily made up, she hoped, for the fact that Joseph would never see in her own eyes the same kind of love she saw in his eyes every day. He would see gratitude, friendship, respect, admiration and trust. Of course, that was a given. He might even see glimpses of love. But the deep, unconditional love that he truly deserved would never be there in her eyes because it would never be in her heart. But she would gladly keep offering anything else she had to give. Letting her husband make love to her was not a chore, it was a temporary relief from her endless culpability.

Joseph soon left her breast and turned his back to Angeline as he slept. Angeline turned onto her side and fixed her gaze on the crib that held the only person who had her unconditional love, the tiny person who was named after another one Angeline had loved in a way she would never love again. She didn't need that kind of love, she thought as she drifted to sleep. That love had been unhealthy and much too dangerous. The love she had for her son, pure and boundless, was the only kind of love any woman truly needed. It certainly met all of her needs.

CHAPTER SIXTEEN

Boston, December 1899

Emilie didn't mind working on New Year's Eve. She often worked on holidays at the cotton mill. She took a deep breath and revelled as she always did in the air that filled the bookstore. The smell of ink and paper infused her lungs and she found it exhilarating, such a deep contrast from the stifling wet air of the mill. She didn't think she'd ever lose that complete gratitude and satisfaction she felt when she was in Mr. Flaherty's bookstore, in her bookstore as she liked to think of it. New Year's Eve was quiet and she'd already dusted the bookshelves with care. She was sitting behind the counter that held a massive cast-iron cash register, reading her favorite Jane Austen novel, *Sense and Sensibility*. She couldn't believe she was being paid to sit and read. She felt guilty.

She glanced at the front door, then looked down at the dress Margaret had made for her and felt sorry no one would see her beautiful new outfit and her particularly successful bouffant hairstyle. Although sleeves had gotten narrower in the past couple of years, a small round puff was still common at the shoulder and Margaret had argued with Emilie that her deep purple dress would be much more fashionable with the addition of such a puff, but Emilie had insisted on bishop sleeves. The argument was solved when Emilie stated she would sew the sleeves herself and Margaret refused, reluctantly mumbling that she would give Emilie her same boring old bishop sleeves if she had to, but she wouldn't let Emilie touch the dress that was meant as a Christmas present. Emilie giggled as she remembered Margaret's expression when she'd finally tried on the dress. "Exquisite," she'd said, "even without proper sleeves." They'd laughed about their silly dispute over sleeves, but Emilie knew she could never have worn the dress if it had been ruined with those ridiculous puffs.

Emilie's thoughts were interrupted by an unexpected customer entering the store. Unexpected in more than one way, Emilie noted as she greeted the customer with a timid "Hello, welcome to Flaherty Books."

Not only was it surprising that anyone would shop for books on New Year's Eve, but it was rare for women to enter the bookstore, and this particular woman was not a type of woman Emilie had ever seen before. Her wavy brown hair had as much volume as any hairstyle popularized by the Gibson Girl, but it wasn't pulled up in any particular style. It was cut above the shoulders and seemed to naturally, freely create the fullness she herself spent so much time trying to re-create every morning.

Emilie already had trouble not staring at this strange woman who had dared cutting her hair, but when she took off her coat Emilie found the way she was dressed even more fascinating than her hairstyle. She wore a simple enough black skirt, but the man's shirt and the silk plaid waistcoat she wore with it gave her a style Emilie had never seen. She was already thinking of the descriptions of female inverts she'd read in medical journals when the woman did the unthinkable. She reached into the breast pocket of her waistcoat and took out a cigarette and a matchbox. She shamelessly lit her cigarette and started walking toward the back of the store, but not before she glanced at Emilie and nodded.

That brief eye contact before the woman disappeared behind a bookshelf left Emilie breathless. Who was this woman? No, what was she? When she started feeling pain in her fingertips Emilie realized she'd been digging her nails into the wood of the counter. She moved directly behind the cash register, hoping to disappear.

She held her breath as the woman reappeared and started walking toward her, looking straight into her eyes as she kept smoking. "Hello," she said when she finally stopped on the other side of the counter. Emilie stupidly looked behind her, which made the woman laugh with a deep, throaty laughter. "Yes, you, with the French accent. I was hoping you could help me."

"Of course," Emilie finally managed. From the way she talked the woman might be British, Emilie thought. She guessed she was probably in her early thirties. Her hazel eyes were almond-shaped, giving her an air of mystery, and her pointy nose made her look mischievous. "Are you looking for something in particular?"

The woman smiled and took another puff of her cigarette before she spoke again. "Your accent really is lovely. Yes, I was hoping you might carry French books. I'm looking for something very specific. A book by Emile Zola called *Nana*."

Emilie's heart fluttered as the woman carefully observed her reaction. She knew she was blushing. How could she not be? This strange woman was standing just on the other side of the counter, looking like no other woman she'd ever met yet so familiar at the same time, asking for the book that had completely changed Emilie's life. Sapphist, she couldn't help thinking. This woman could very well be an actual Sapphist. In the flesh. A kindred spirit. Emilie had to clear her throat before she could answer the customer in a voice barely louder than a whisper. "We don't sell French books, unfortunately."

The woman put one hand on the counter and kept looking into Emilie's eyes as if she were searching her very soul. "But you do know the book, don't you?"

Emilie instinctively knew that admitting to knowing Zola's novel was admitting to much more. She swallowed and nodded discreetly while everything inside her wanted to scream yes. *Yes, I'm like you.*

"I thought so," the woman said with another smile. Then she extended her hand and added, "My name is Kathleen. Kathleen Pierce, but please call me Kate."

Emilie shook Kate's offered hand, speechless, wondering how Kate might have known that she'd recognize that particular title.

"And what's your name, darling?"

"Oh, sorry," Emilie mumbled, remembering her manners. "My name is Emilie Levesque. I'm sorry we don't have the book you're looking for, madam—Kate," she corrected herself.

"Don't worry about it, Emilie. I know exactly how you can make up for it."

The way Kate smiled was not the way any other woman had smiled at Emilie before. The way she looked at her was different too. Emilie was used to gentlemen smiling and looking at her that way when they paid for their books, as if she'd been an especially juicy piece of roast. It had always made Emilie feel uneasy, sometimes nauseated, but it was part of the job, as Mr. Flaherty had explained. Coming from Kate it made her feel different. Nervous, impure, somewhat guilty, but mostly excited. She certainly wanted to know what Kate had in mind. "How is that?"

"I'm hosting a New Year's Eve party tonight. Say you'll come, Emilie."

"I will," Emilie said without hesitation.

Emilie felt terrible about lying to Mr. and Mrs. Flaherty, but how else could she explain suddenly going out this night after being a hermit all that time? She'd told them she was going to spend New Year's Eve with a cousin of her mother's who lived in Boston and had stopped by the bookstore to invite her. The Flahertys were happy to learn Emilie had family in Boston and Mr. Flaherty had even offered to take her to her cousin's house, arguing that the address was too far for a young woman to walk alone at night. Emilie had barely managed to dissuade him.

Now, Emilie knocked on the door of the Queen Anne style home and waited, distractedly admiring the decorative details of the turret and the front porch. She was looking forward to seeing Kate again and was disappointed when a servant opened the door and took her coat and hat. Emilie wore the same dress as she had earlier that day. It was the most beautiful dress she owned and she hoped Kate would not remember it since she'd been partially hiding behind the cash register. She could barely control her nerves as she followed the servant. She was terrified, curious, anxious, but her feet kept following the servant. There was no going back.

Her trepidation reached its climax when the servant opened the door to an intimately lit parlor and Emilie saw nothing but women. There must have been at least twenty of them in this small room, sitting on sofas or chaise lounges, or standing by the fireplace or in a corner of the room. The servant disappeared, leaving Emilie alone at the door to observe the scene.

She soon realized that several of the women wore their hair short like Kate and were dressed in a mixture of men's and women's clothes. A couple of the women even wore trousers. Most, however, wore dresses, so Emilie didn't feel out of place. A few women smoked, creating a soft, cloudy atmosphere in the parlor. Emilie's pulse started racing when she spotted two women kissing in a darker corner. Her brain warned her she should leave, but her legs remained immobile, as if rooted into the wooden floor.

Emilie forced herself to look away and came face-to-face with Kate, who'd seemed to appear suddenly from a cloud of smoke. "There you are, my darling Emilie. I was beginning to think you might not come after all," she said as she took hold of Emilie's arm and pulled her into the room.

Emilie smiled. Kate exuded such confidence that she couldn't help but feel intimidated if not overpowered in her presence. She simply followed her around the room as she was introduced to the other women.

Some granted Kate a strangely congratulatory smile as they shook or kissed Emilie's hand, a kind of smile that left Emilie with little doubt about Kate's intentions. Part of her wanted to be insulted by the insinuation but a larger part was too curious to protest. She'd keep following Kate wherever she wanted to lead her tonight, learning in a way that took her out of the books she found so comfortable and into an unknown world. Kate, with her assurance, would be her experienced mentor. Emilie trusted her, even though she didn't quite understand why.

Kate guided Emilie to a quiet corner of the room where they stood until they finished a glass of champagne. Since she'd first taken her arm to lead her through to the room, Kate had never broken contact with Emilie until now. She took the empty flutes out of their hands and placed them on a nearby table only to come back and grab Emilie's hands, facing her. The touch was comforting and amicable. "What do you think of this little gathering of mine, my darling Emilie?" she asked with a low, soothing voice.

For the first time, Emilie realized that Kate cared about her feelings and knew just how foreign this event was to her. "It's all very new," she confirmed, "and I'm rather nervous, but I'm still very happy I came."

The relief she saw in Kate's smile betrayed a glimpse of self-doubt Emilie hadn't seen in her and she found it endearing. It made Kate more human, more approachable.

"I'm glad you came too, Emilie."

Kate took a step toward Emilie so that mere inches separated them and slowly ran one fingertip up Emilie's arm, from the inside of her wrist to the bend of her elbow. The caress seemed innocent yet felt so intimate that Emilie gasped. She knew Kate would kiss her soon and she would let her, but before that happened she had to ask, "How did you know? About me, I mean."

Kate laughed softly, as if she knew Emilie would ask. "I don't really know, my darling. Call it intuition, instinct, or simply call it hope. All I know is that never yet have I been wrong."

With that Emilie watched quietly as Kate's almond-shaped eyes closed and her fine lips closed the distance between them. She let Kate's expert mouth explore hers. Soon Kate's tongue probed inside and Emilie leaned back against the wall, taking pleasure in Kate's kiss but even more in knowing it wouldn't stop. Kate wouldn't push her away and look at her with hate and disgust like Angeline had. Kate would keep kissing her as long as she offered her mouth to be kissed.

Kate was not Angeline. Emilie shook her head, forcing Angeline out of her mind as Kate's lips traveled down to her exposed neck. She grabbed Kate's shoulders and pulled her closer yet. Kate groaned as her mouth was pressed hard against Emilie's skin. Emilie moaned, simply knowing this delight wouldn't be taken away from her until it reached the ultimate peak she was longing for.

Kate rose from her neck then and looked into Emilie's eyes. Emilie saw the lust in Kate's dark pupils and in her parted, reddened, breathless mouth. "Stay with me tonight," she said hoarsely.

Emilie simply nodded. Kate took her hand and led her to her bedroom on the second floor.

That night, Emilie let Kate teach her everything she'd imagined a Sapphist ought to know and even some things she'd never imagined. Mouths, flesh, sexes mixed together in such ecstasy Emilie no longer cared what kind of illness made it possible. Emilie made love with Kate all night and began the new century as a new woman.

She came back to Kate's house many more nights afterward. She never read another medical journal. If anyone ever came up with a cure, she didn't want to know about it.

CHAPTER SEVENTEEN

Rimouski, April 1900

April was a messy time of the year in Rimouski, Angeline was reminded again as she walked out of the barn with two pints of milk in two glass bottles. Little Paul-Emile followed her with difficulty, his small moose-leather boots catching in mud several times, causing him to fall on his behind. Everywhere, even on the roads, the ground was nothing but a mix of melting snow and mud.

She brought one of the bottles to her parents' house and left it on the porch then walked back to her own house, grabbing Paul-Emile into her free arm to make the trip a little faster.

Angeline milked the cows every evening and she'd usually go in to talk with her mother before going back home to finish getting dinner ready. Today she didn't feel like it and had managed to avoid her all day. She didn't feel like talking to anyone. She'd done her chores routinely all day long, her thoughts elsewhere, taking only a few minutes to play with Paul-Emile. He'd made her laugh almost despite herself when he'd fallen face first into mud and had gotten back up giggling, his face covered with wet dirt. She'd wiped his face but he desperately needed a bath.

Angeline barely had time to remove her boots and coat as well as Paul-Emile's before Joseph ran into the house and announced with an enthusiasm she hadn't seen in him since the birth of their son, "It's happening, Angeline! They're expanding the mill and guess who's becoming head of maintenance. That's right, little man! Your papa is the new head of maintenance at The Price Company." Joseph grabbed Paul-Emile and held him above his head, then threw him in the air before catching him.

The boy's unrestrained laughter and his father's joyous pride forced a smile onto Angeline's face. Joseph had slowly made a reputation for himself as the guy who could fix machines no one else seemed to know how to fix. No matter what was wrong with any kind of machinery at the sawmill, he always found a way to make it work again in a timely manner. He'd learned back at the cotton mill what stoppage meant. *Stoppage means loss! Stoppage means loss!* Angeline remembered it too. The phrase had been drilled into all of them with such forcefulness that they couldn't forget it even if they'd wanted to. It seemed like it was paying off for them now. Joseph's bosses at The Price Company appreciated his sense of urgency. They'd promised him a better position once they were ready to expand and it was finally happening.

"That's great news, Joseph," she said with as much excitement as she could muster, which was not enough to convince Joseph.

From the suddenly serious expression on his face when he turned from Paul-Emile to look at her, Angeline knew that he understood that something was wrong and one look at the hand she'd put on her stomach almost unconsciously was enough for him to know exactly what it was. She fought tears as Joseph put Paul-Emile down on the wide pine planks of floor and walked toward her with compassionate sadness in his dark blue eyes. When he wrapped his arms around her, she started sobbing uncontrollably into his chest, quickly making his working shirt damp.

She'd miscarried early that morning. It was the second baby she'd lost since Paul-Emile's birth, and she couldn't understand why it was so difficult for her to do the one thing she was convinced she'd been born to do. She couldn't help but think that perhaps she was being punished for her sins. For the feelings she'd had for Emilie, for that kiss she was so desperately trying to forget. For the dreams that crept up at night, rare but inescapable, in which she lay with her sister-in-law in her bed somewhere in Boston.

Joseph caressed her hair and held her close, comforting her. She squeezed his waist as tight as she could. She might deserve punishment, she admitted to herself, but Joseph didn't. *Please don't keep punishing him.*

CHAPTER EIGHTEEN

Boston, February 1901

Emilie kissed Kate's nude buttocks again and laid her head on her lover's lower back, admiring the roundness of her bottom as Kate slowly caught her breath after a long, particularly strong orgasm.

Emilie was filled with pride every time she brought Kate to climax, every time she felt her muscles tense up under the touch of her fingers or her mouth. It made her feel powerful and she couldn't get enough. She lay naked in Kate's bed like she did every Sunday, languorously caressing the round, soft, ivory bottom. It was her favorite part of Kate's body apart from the folds of flesh she knew so well after a little over a year of their strange, unnamed relationship.

Emilie felt Kate rise under her head and knew she was going to light a cigarette. She moved to her side so she could watch Kate smoke. Kate was still lying on her stomach but held herself up on her elbows.

"I wish I liked smoking," Emilie said with sincerity. She'd tried smoking a few times shortly after she'd met Kate but she couldn't get used to it. It burned her lungs and she hated doing it as much as she liked watching Kate do it.

Kate laughed as she exhaled, a white cloud escaping from her fine lips. "Why, my darling?"

"I don't know. Isn't it the lesbian thing to do?" Emilie had learned the word *lesbian* from Kate. She liked it better than Sapphist. She liked the idea of a community of women who loved other women living together on a small island called Lesbos. It was a nice, comforting thought.

Kate laughed even louder, choking on her most recent puff of cigarette. "You're mixing things up, my darling. I smoke because I love the taste of cigarettes. I'm a lesbian because I love the taste of twat. See? Two very separate things."

Emilie joined in Kate's laughter. Kate's sense of humor was one of the traits she most appreciated in her. The only other person who'd ever made her laugh that much was Angeline, but Kate's humor was much more salacious than Angeline's. It was difficult not to compare the two women although Emilie tried hard not to. She came to Kate every Sunday with the firm intention to leave all thoughts of Angeline in her room on Bromfield Street, but she didn't always succeed.

After lying to Mr. and Mrs. Flaherty about spending New Year's Eve with her mother's cousin, Emilie told them that moving forward she would spend Sundays with that same cousin's family, even going to Mass with them. Of course, Emilie had not gone to Mass in more than a year.

Her new church was Kate's body. Her sins were beyond saving by now anyway, she was sure of it, and there was no room in church for someone like her. Not only did she sleep with a woman, but she was also an adulterer. Kate's husband lived in London and had a life of his own, Kate assured her, but what they did remained adultery nonetheless.

Kate called herself a new woman and being a new woman apparently meant living guilt free, among other things. Emilie tried to follow her older lover's footsteps and become a new woman but she still battled with guilt. She felt most guilty about her new life when she received a letter from her father and she was forced to think of her old life, her family, and what they would think if they knew about the way she was living now.

Emilie turned her back to Kate and closed her eyes, pretending to sleep. Kate put her arm around Emilie's waist and snuggled up to her, accepting a restful pause from their frolics. Thinking of her family always made Emilie nostalgic.

Joseph had turned twenty-three last week. She hadn't spoken to him since she'd accused him of being a coward three years ago. They'd been so close when they were children, inseparable. It was difficult to accept that the harsh words she'd told him out of jealousy could be the last words she'd speak to him. She kept telling herself she would write to him, but she never did. She had no excuse. Her father had given her the address on Tessier Road as soon and he and Angeline had moved to their own house.

She didn't know what to tell Joseph. She had no news that would make him proud of her, she figured, no stories he could relate to in any way. He was probably better off not knowing more than the superficial bits and pieces she wrote in letters to their father. She assumed he shared those with Joseph. He surely shared everything about Joseph's life with her.

She often wished he wouldn't. Knowing everything about Joseph's happy married life made her sad and bitter, and then she felt guilty about her inability to simply be happy for her brother. Knowing about Angeline's life was even worse. How could she put the woman she'd loved out of her mind when she kept being informed of every event in her life? A life Angeline had chosen to live with Emilie's brother despite Emilie's efforts.

When she'd learned they'd named their first son Paul-Emile she'd cried herself to sleep for one full week. She'd cried because she couldn't believe Joseph and Angeline still thought enough of her to name their first child after her. She'd cried most of all because she might never know the boy who shared her hair color, her own nephew. Then she'd learned about Angeline's miscarriages and she'd cried for her friend, feeling her pain as her own.

But more recently, she'd learned of the birth of Victor Henri Levesque, their second son. Emilie's father wrote that Victor looked exactly like Joseph when he was a baby, with blond hair and clear blue eyes. Emilie wanted to be happy for Joseph and Angeline and she was, in a way. She was truly happy for her father, who seemed to be such a proud grandfather, even from a distance. But she couldn't help but feel sorry for herself. And she couldn't help but wonder whether Victor was named after Victor Hugo. She remembered Angeline's appreciation for *Les Misérables* and wondered if Angeline, when she named her son Victor, had thought of the hours they'd spent reading and discussing the novel together under their buttonwood tree in Flint. She ached thinking she might never know.

Emilie slowly came out of her reflections when she felt the soft kisses Kate had started to place on the back of her neck. There was no point losing any more time on Joseph, Angeline and their children. They weren't part of her life anymore. They had nothing in common but blood and memories. They would never understand what she'd become. She forced her attention back to the woman behind her, who did understand who she was, who was in fact in part responsible for what she'd become. Kate had helped her and accepted her in ways her family never could. More importantly, she'd made it possible for Emilie to accept herself. Acceptance was still a work in progress but that progress wouldn't have been possible without Kate, *her* new woman.

Emilie chased all of her nostalgic thoughts away to replace them with the concrete, immediate sensation of Kate's nipples hardening against her back and Kate's hand slowly going down her side to her hip. When the same hand moved to the front of her thigh and made its way to Emilie's sex just as Kate's kisses became more insistent and her breathing irregular, Emilie found herself wanting her again. It was a need that was tangible and could be fulfilled so easily, right in this moment. They'd rested enough and there wasn't much of this Sunday left to take advantage of, so Emilie turned on her back and let Kate cover her body with her skin and her mouth.

Working in the bookstore surrounded with the books she loved, Sundays in Kate's bed taking the pleasure she wanted—it was her life and it was the life she'd chosen. Why should she care whether they understood it or not?

CHAPTER NINETEEN

Rimouski, July 1901

Angeline rocked Victor on the porch as she watched Paul-Emile play in the yard. The rustic chair Joseph had made from leftover lumber he'd gotten from the mill didn't rock as smoothly as the one her father had built and that remained inside, safe from bad weather, but Angeline liked having the option to sit with the baby outside. It gave her a chance to enjoy sunny days like today and keep an eye on Paul-Emile who, like all two-year-olds, always found trouble to get into.

She looked down at Victor and marveled yet again at how different two brothers could be. In every way. Of course what other people saw was the contrast between Victor's fine blond hair and Paul-Emile's thick black mane or Victor's blue eyes compared to his older brother's dark gaze. Some even noticed that Victor seemed stronger and heavier than Paul-Emile had been at the same age, a fact Angeline could confirm as she held Victor.

Angeline knew, however, that the differences between her sons went beyond their physique. Paul-Emilie had been inquisitive from a very young age, fighting sleep as long as he could at night, waking up with the chickens every morning, as if he were afraid he'd miss something. Victor had slept through the night very shortly after his birth and once he was asleep nothing could disturb him. Another difference Angeline noticed was in their respective relationship with their father. Joseph liked to rock his sons to sleep when he had the chance, which didn't happen often. Their oldest son had never seemed comfortable in his father's arms, refusing to sleep as long as Angeline wasn't the one holding him. Victor, however, fell asleep faster and deeper in his father's arms than in his mother's. Sometimes when he cried, Angeline asked Joseph to take Victor because he always stopped crying as soon as Joseph held him. Angeline wondered what kind of divergence she would keep observing in her sons and hoped their differences wouldn't keep them from getting along.

Victor started whining. "Be good, Victor. Papa is at work so you're stuck with me," Angeline said as she started rocking her chair faster.

It was Sunday afternoon but Joseph had to fix a piece of machinery before the early shift tomorrow. His new position paid a little better but unfortunately his schedule was still as unpredictable as ever and would always be by nature. Machinery needed to be fixed when it stopped, whenever that was. They'd gone to the Saint-Laurent's shore a couple more times and had talked about taking a trip to Quebec City, which they could afford now, but Joseph's schedule made it impossible to plan outings. Angeline understood. She would have loved to see Quebec City but she was lucky her husband had a good job and they had a good home where they could raise their children.

Victor finally stopped whining and fell asleep. Angeline glanced at Paul-Emile who was exploring the garden and decided to quickly go inside the house to put Victor in the crib, knowing he wouldn't wake up now that he was sleeping. She was on her way back outside to grab Paul-Emile when she heard him scream, "Puppy! Puppy!" She ran back to the porch where she saw Paul-Emilie playing with a puppy and Joseph watching them, laughing at their antics. The scene made her smile. "What's that, Joseph?"

"That's a puppy," he said sarcastically as he approached her and kissed her cheek.

"I see that, Joseph, but where did he come from?"

"Fat Pineau from the mill said he had eight pups he was trying to get rid of, so I stopped by his house on my way home. I figured the boys would like a puppy."

"Well this one sure does," Angeline said and she started laughing as she watched Paul-Emile try to pick up a puppy that was already too heavy for him. "How old is he?"

"Fat Pineau said he's nine weeks old. I met his mama when I picked him up and she weighs about seventy pounds so he should be a big fellow. Do you think it was a bad idea?"

Angeline looked as the dog licked Paul-Emilie's face. His coat was golden in color and a little thicker around the neck. She bent down and extended a hand toward the puppy. "You think you're some kind of lion with that hair, little one?" she asked the dog quietly. He immediately started walking awkwardly toward her, his wide paws appearing disproportionately large for his body. He licked her hand and she laughed. He was a bizarre-looking little dog, but he was theirs now. She'd never had a dog before, and she liked the idea of her sons growing up with one. "It was a great idea, Joseph," she declared as she stood up. She squeezed Joseph's arm and smiled at him in silent gratitude, then turned back to Paul-Emile and his new best friend. "So what should we call him?"

Paul-Emile looked down at the puppy and grabbed two fistfuls of the thick golden hair. "Yellow!" he exclaimed.

Angeline and Joseph laughed. "All right, Yellow it is," Angeline agreed. It was a simple name but it suited him. Besides, what else was she expecting? At two years and seven months of age, Paul-Emile didn't have many words in his vocabulary yet and she'd been teaching him colors for a few weeks. Yellow made perfect sense. "What do you think, Yellow? You like your new name?"

The dog wagged his tail and Angeline took that as her answer.

CHAPTER TWENTY

Boston, March 1902

Emilie stood alone in a corner of the parlor, observing the women gathered around the fireplace or the sofa and chaise lounge drinking champagne and discussing trivial events of their lives. She even spotted duos kissing in the less well-lit periphery of the room. She rarely came to Kate's Saturday night social affairs anymore. She'd grown bored with the scene. Most women were rich and disconnected from the reality of women like Emilie. They were married to rich men while they slept with women, more or less discreetly depending on the kind of marriage they had. They paraded around in these soirées making declarations of rebellion against society while they conveniently hid in conventional marriages with men. Nights like these reminded Emilie that Kate was one of them, and Emilie didn't really like Kate in such settings. She was different in the intimacy of their bedroom. Or perhaps it was just easier to forget that Kate was married when they were in bed together.

There was one couple Emilie enjoyed talking to once in a while, but they weren't there tonight. The Brothel Girls. That's what everyone called them because they prostituted themselves so they could afford to live together. They sold their bodies to men so they could remain in love under the same roof. It was tragic, perhaps, but wasn't it what these other women were doing too? At least the Brothel Girls were honest about the nature of their commerce. It was straightforward prostitution, not prostitution disguised as marriage. Emilie often thought that she would have preferred selling her body to men so she could live with Angeline rather than marrying a rich man who would own her. Then she reminded herself that she was no better than Kate. She worked at the bookstore and she had her own room, yes, but she still slept with a married woman in the safety of her Queen Anne style home every Sunday, something they couldn't do if Kate hadn't been married to a rich man who didn't mind whom his wife slept with on this continent because he was living his own extramarital affairs in London.

Emilie looked for Kate and found her in deep conversation with a couple of women by the fireplace. She looked so elegant in her black silk evening gown that one could almost miss its two thin black lace shoulder straps because of the two other decorative straps, made of silk purple flowers, that fell off her bare shoulders.

Emilie admired her lover's shoulders and waited until Kate looked at her to point her index finger up, indicating that she was ready to go upstairs. Then she went to wait by the door leading to the hallway, knowing Kate would come to say good night. When Emilie came to Kate's gatherings, she always excused herself early and waited for Kate in bed in tempting positions. Soon Kate approached with a seductive smile and embraced Emilie. "My poor darling, I know you hate these things. Go up and wait for me. I'll get rid of these brats."

Emilie leaned against the door and accepted Kate's promising kiss. That was the reason she kept coming once in a while, she reminded herself as she felt her body tingle. She'd felt the ground move under her feet before from the way Kate kissed her, but this time as she kept falling backward she realized it was the door she was leaning against that had opened. She gasped and started laughing nervously when she realized someone had caught her from behind, until Kate looked past her and asked sternly, "Who the hell are you and what are you doing in my home?"

"I'm sorry, Madam, I asked him to wait at the front door but…" The servant didn't finish her sentence.

Emilie had regained her balance and slowly turned around. Of course she recognized the man and his piercing green eyes before he introduced himself to Kate. "Dr. Maurice Banville, madam. I was looking for Miss Levesque. I won't take any more of your time. Good night."

Emilie wanted to disappear. To run upstairs or throw herself into the fireplace. More than anything she wished she could erase the expression of embarrassment and disgust she saw in Maurice's face before he turned around and walked away, but all she could do was say his name, and even then her voice caught.

"Who is that man, Emilie?" she heard Kate ask as she started running after Maurice.

Emilie caught up with Maurice just before he opened the front door. "Maurice, wait. What are you doing here?"

He turned to face her and she barely recognized him. She'd never seen Maurice angry before. His eyes were glacial and terrifying. She'd seen him hurt though, when she'd had the nerve to ask him if he and Helen had children the first day they'd met. She'd seen pain in his eyes then, and she recognized that pain now behind the anger. Pain she'd caused.

"I went to Michael's home to surprise you, Emilie. When he told me about a supposed cousin of your mother's I knew something was wrong. If you'd had a cousin in Boston you would have told me years ago. I don't know what kind of perversion you've fallen into, Emilie," he started, almost spitting his words before he had to pause to catch his breath. He looked down to his feet, as if he couldn't bear to look at her. "Maybe I should never have helped you move to this city," he continued. Then he took a deep breath and faced her again, pointing his finger toward something behind her.

Emilie turned around to see Kate, standing there with a defiant glare. Emilie didn't know she'd followed her and she wished she hadn't. When she turned back to Maurice he was brandishing a finger at her. "This, whatever it is, has to stop. I will find a suitable young man for you and you will get married, Emilie. Mark my words."

Before Emilie could answer, Maurice was gone. She couldn't move or say anything. She'd disappointed the man who'd been her mentor, who'd helped her make her way to Boston, to the bookstore, to the Flahertys' lodging house. She'd hurt him badly and she felt horrible about it, but the life he'd helped her make here in Boston was hers now, and there was no way she'd let him take it all away.

CHAPTER TWENTY-ONE

Rimouski, September 1902

"It's a girl, Madam Levesque," young Doctor Michaud announced.

The young doctor had taken over his father's practice the same year Angeline had moved to Rimouski. He was timid and didn't talk much but she trusted him. Angeline had heard her mother repeat with emotion, "A girl, Angeline, it's a girl," before she passed out from exhaustion.

When she opened her eyes again, she saw Joseph sitting in the rocking chair, in his arms the smallest baby she'd ever seen. Their daughter was wrapped up in a blanket and her papa looked at her with pride. Angeline smiled. Joseph must have moved the rocking chair to the bedroom while she was sleeping. Yellow was asleep by his feet on the floor. The dog had grown into his large paws. He was enormous and had kept his thick collar of fur that almost made him look like a lion. He was never far from Joseph.

Angeline suddenly realized the perfect family portrait was missing two very important faces. "Where are the boys?" she asked in a raspy voice. Her mouth was dry. Her hair was stuck to her forehead and her neck, still damp with sweat. Everything in her belly and between her thighs was sore.

Joseph stood up, the small bundle in one arm, and handed Angeline a glass of water from her bedside table. Yellow woke up only to lie back on the floor by the bed. "Your mother took them home with her when she left. They'll be back later."

Angeline sat up in bed with difficulty. She leaned against the headboard to take a sip of water and put the glass back on the bedside table. "Let me see her," she said softly.

Joseph carefully put the baby in her mother's arms and sat on the bed next to Angeline, leaning back against the headboard, an arm around his wife's shoulders so they could both admire their daughter. "She's a beauty, isn't she?"

"Oh yes," Angeline whispered, staring at the round pink face and the cutest button nose. "Mathilde?" she asked Joseph. They hadn't discussed names during her pregnancy but Angeline imagined Joseph would still want to name their first daughter in honor of his mother. For some reason she didn't think the name suited the baby girl she was holding, but she knew it was important to Joseph.

"No, she doesn't look like a Mathilde," Joseph answered, surprising her. "She looks just like you, Angeline. Look at her skin, her face, her nose. She is just as beautiful, like an angel. I was staring at her while you were sleeping and that's all I could think about. She's an angel. Our angel."

Angeline looked at her daughter more attentively, touched by Joseph's words. She did look like an angel, she had to admit. "I see what you mean. And did you think of any particular name we could call this angel while I was sleeping?" she asked teasingly.

Joseph kissed Angeline's forehead and smiled at her. "What would you think about Marie-Ange?"

"Marie-Ange," Angeline repeated as she observed her daughter. It did suit her perfectly. "I like it, Joseph." She turned to him and smiled her agreement before she added, "Marie-Ange Mathilde Levesque."

Joseph attempted to swallow his emotion but tears still welled up in his eyes. Angeline had not seen Joseph cry often. When she did, she imagined restless waves in the dark blue eyes. "That's perfect," he said with gratitude. Then he turned to their new baby and repeated softly, as if to himself, "Marie-Ange Mathilde Levesque."

CHAPTER TWENTY-TWO

Boston, April 1903

Emilie hadn't seen Maurice again after he'd showed up unannounced at Kate's house. After he'd seen them kiss. Yet she was reminded of his existence on a regular basis. "Dr. Banville's friend, Mr. Black, will be joining us for dinner this evening, Emilie. We expect you to show up early with your best behavior," Mr. Flaherty announced before he winked at her and left her alone in the bookstore. Emilie sighed with exasperation.

Mr. Black would be the fifth friend of Maurice's Mr. and Mrs. Flaherty would introduce to Emilie since Maurice had come to Boston a little more than a year ago. Poor Maurice. Emilie was certain he hadn't realized how difficult a task finding her a husband would be.

She wasn't exactly a catch for the young men of Boston, who had plenty of options. Three of the previous candidates had shown no interest whatsoever from their first glance in Emilie's direction. Emilie suspected the lack of interest came from her petite physique. Despite her vigorous appetite Emilie remained thin to the point of appearing unhealthy, and the fact that she refused to smile or show her usual high level of energy during those gruesome dinners made it worse. The woman she portrayed didn't exactly scream child bearer, which most men looked for in a wife.

Her age didn't help either. When asked, Emilie always answered that she was almost twenty-four years old rather than simply stating she was twenty-three. At almost twenty-four, she knew she was slightly over the ideal age for a good Catholic woman to start manufacturing babies.

The one man who hadn't seemed bothered by Emilie's physique or her age had lost interest the minute she'd started talking about literature and women's right to vote. No, Emilie wasn't really worried she'd ever be faced with having to refuse a marriage proposal. She knew no man would propose to her. These dinners were just an inconvenience she wished she didn't have to put these men, the Flahertys and herself through.

Mr. Flaherty played his part as he'd promised Maurice, Emilie imagined, but he knew the exercise was futile. He knew Emilie didn't want to get married, although she was certain Maurice hadn't told him about Kate and the nature of their relationship. She was grateful for the discretion even though she knew Maurice had remained quiet out of shame rather than out of respect for her.

The one thing Maurice had achieved with his plan was to limit the number of Saturday nights Emilie could spend at Kate's soirées since these dinners with potential fiancés were always on Saturdays. Not going to Kate's parties didn't bother Emilie too much since she didn't like them and often chose not to go anyway, but the fact that not going was not her choice on those specific nights infuriated her. She hated that she had to bend to a man's will, a man who was not her husband and certainly not her father. She was tempted not to show up to meet Mr. Black but she knew the consequences would make her life even more miserable.

As independant as she thought she was and wanted to be, Emilie was still depending on men. She had to play the game Maurice and Mr. Flaherty wanted her to play because they had power over her. She could lose her job and be thrown out on the street and then what? She might go live with Kate and depend on Kate's husband, but that would make her no less dependent, and she figured that meeting young men Maurice hoped would become her husband was the lesser of two evils. She would keep playing the game until she was too old to marry, hoping Maurice wouldn't get desperate enough to pay a man a small fortune just so he'd marry her.

"Are you going to marry this lad, my darling?" Kate asked as she watched Emilie undress in her bedroom the next day. Most of Kate's body was covered with the satin sheet but Emilie could see the shape of one perfectly tantalizing nipple under the fabric. Kate's head was propped up on one hand as she lay on her side and she looked at Emilie with seductively half-closed eyes and a teasing smile. Once she was completely nude, Emilie joined Kate in bed and grabbed the tempting nipple between her lips through the satin of the sheet. Kate gasped. "That's a no, I assume?"

"The lad won't propose, don't worry. One look at me and Mr. Black started talking politics with Mr. Flaherty. Their conversation lasted through dinner and he barely looked at me to say goodnight when he left. It was almost too easy." Emilie took the nipple back into her mouth, but this time she moved the sheet away first. Kate moaned in pleasure but then placed her hand under Emilie's chin and gently forced her to look into her eyes. Emilie recognized the familiar lust in Kate's hazel eyes, but she also saw something else: something she'd never seen there before. She'd shown tenderness several times, but this was deeper, and it almost scared Emilie.

"I don't know what's wrong with these men, Emilie. If I were a man I'd want you as a wife. As my wife." Kate's voice caught on that last part and she looked down as if she'd been embarrassed by her declaration. Tears sparkled in her eyes and her chin trembled. It was the first time Kate said anything that led Emilie to believe she wished their relationship could be more than what it was. Emilie didn't know how to answer so she kissed her with as much strength and passion as she could. Kate let herself fall to her back under the pressure of Emilie's kiss, and they made love.

CHAPTER TWENTY-THREE

Rimouski, December 1903

It was Christmas morning and Angeline sat at her parents'
kitchen table with her father, mother and the three children.
She heard steps on the outside stairs and went to open the front
door to Joseph and Yellow standing on the porch, covered with
snow. She took the bottles of milk out of Joseph's hands with a
smile and closed the door again to keep the heat in the house.
She handed the milk to her mother and through the small
window of the door she watched Joseph shake the snow off his
coat and boots.

He'd insisted on giving the women a break from milking the
cows that morning. Angeline opened the door again to let Joseph
inside. Yellow whined but lay down on the porch by the door.
He was not allowed in her parents' home. Her father always
said that animals were meant to live outside and that Yellow was
spoiled. She patted him on the head before she closed the door
again, giving her father enough time to say firmly, "Leave that
dog alone, you're letting all the cold wind inside." She smiled at
her father, who smiled back even as he shook his head. Joseph

took his coat and boots off at the door and the couple went back to the kitchen table where the children were getting impatient.

"Can we eat it now, Papa?" Paul-Emile asked, his eyes focused on the orange he'd received for Christmas.

"Yes, you can," Joseph said with a laugh. Five-year-old Paul-Emile didn't have any trouble peeling his orange but he did it meticulously, enjoying every bit of the experiment. Almost three-year-old Victor had more difficulty and became frustrated with the process so Angeline went to help him while her mother peeled Marie-Ange's fruit and fed the fifteen-month-old girl small pieces as she sat on her father's lap.

Angeline and Joseph watched in awe as their children ate the Christmas fruit. They were rarely that quiet so she enjoyed the moment. Paul-Emile and Victor often fought which was exhausting for Angeline. "Let them fight and settle it on their own," her mother would say, but Angeline had a hard time following her mother's advice.

Fortunately, Marie-Ange's name proved to be predestined and their baby girl was truly an angel. Angeline had miscarried earlier that fall but she hadn't reacted as badly as she had the two times she'd miscarried before she had Victor. She wanted a larger family, of course, but she was already blessed with three healthy and beautiful children. If nature wanted them to have more they would, but it wouldn't be the end of the world if they didn't. She no longer felt like God was trying to punish her for anything.

"Delphine told me you received a letter from your sister. How's life in Boston?"

Angeline tensed up at her father's question to Joseph. The letter had come a week before Christmas. Joseph had been so happy to hear from his sister, but Angeline didn't know how to react to this letter. She was hurt that the letter hadn't come with a second one or even a small note addressed to her. Emilie had barely mentioned her at all in her letter to Joseph, only to say she hoped his wife was doing well. She hadn't even bothered to write Angeline's name, just "your wife," as if Angeline wasn't anything more than Joseph's property. They hadn't heard from her in almost five years and Emilie obviously hadn't missed her. As painful as it was Angeline had to come to the conclusion that she didn't exist anymore in Emilie's eyes.

"She's doing well. She works in a bookstore and has made lots of friends. Her boss and his wife take good care of her. She made fun of me for running away from a war that lasted just a few months but she says she's happy I'm here now and she hopes she can meet our children someday. She knows their names, when they were born, what they like to do, everything. Our father's done a great job keeping her informed."

Angeline realized Joseph was becoming emotional and she put a hand on his to comfort him. What he wasn't saying was that Emilie had formally apologized for calling him a coward. She'd admitted she'd done it out of frustration because she was losing her brother and her best friend and she had no right to do so. She knew Joseph was brave and strong and she'd lived long enough with that guilt on her conscience.

Joseph looked at Angeline and smiled. Angeline smiled in return. As hurt as she was that Emilie had completely disregarded her in her letter to Joseph, she was grateful for the apology she'd made to him. It had been a huge relief for him and he deserved it.

"Is there no chance she might come back here to live? You were so close at one point, such good friends."

This time her father's question was addressed to Angeline. She dropped her husband's hand and answered more defensively than she intended to, "No, Papa. That was a long time ago. Emilie's life is in Boston now. And ours is here. I don't think we'd have anything to say to each other."

She went back to watching the children eat their oranges as she swallowed the lump in her throat. She felt her father's eyes on her, silently questioning her reaction, but she refused to look back in his direction.

CHAPTER TWENTY-FOUR

Boston, November 1904

Emilie was in Kate's bed, staring at the ceiling while her lover slept by her side. She'd been thinking about Emma Bovary lately, about that feeling of eternal dissatisfaction. The first time she'd read *Madame Bovary*, Maurice had told her it was acceptable to want more out of life as long as she knew what she wanted and put all of her energy in obtaining it. Emilie hadn't known what she wanted at the time but she'd thought she'd known when she moved to Boston. A job in a bookstore and a woman like Kate in her life should have been enough, she was certain of it. Of course she'd wanted Angeline more than anything else, but Angeline wasn't hers to have, so she'd made the best of her situation. Was she truly condemned to never be completely happy because she couldn't have Angeline?

At some point, not too long ago, she'd thought she was over Angeline and that old pain. She felt good when she was with Kate and she rarely thought of Angeline. She hadn't been forced to have dinner with one of Maurice's friends in several months and that also made her life easier. She wasn't sure if Maurice thought she was too old or if he'd run out of friends, but she was grateful he'd given up nonetheless. She was as happy as she'd ever been in Boston until she had the brilliant idea to write a letter to her brother to ask for his forgiveness, and he wrote back a couple of months later.

Not only was he forgiving her but he asked her to come live with them in Rimouski. He would add a room to their house and they could be together again. Angeline would love having her close, he'd said.

So would the children. He'd written details about her nephews' and her niece's activities and personalities that even her father couldn't have known. Emilie missed them. She missed her brother and Angeline, and she missed children she'd never even met. How was that possible?

Of course, going to live with them in Rimouski was out of the question. She could never be the good sister, friend and aunt they all wanted her to be. She was different from all of them. Rimouski had no room for someone like her. But the biggest obstacle, the one she was slowly admitting to herself, was that she was still in love with Angeline and would always be. It could never work, so she didn't write back.

"My gorgeous darling," Kate whispered in a sleepy voice. Emilie turned to her and smiled. She was beautiful when she woke up from a nap. She lay on her stomach, her head turned in Emilie's direction, one side of her face on the white satin of the pillow. Emilie could barely see the other side through the messy, short hair. "I just had the most fascinating dream."

"Oh really? What was it?" Emilie asked as she kissed Kate's shoulder and caressed her bare back.

"You were with me, like you are now, but not just on Sundays. You were in bed with me every night of the week and we lived happily."

Emilie stopped caressing Kate for a moment before she forced herself to resume her movement. Kate had made this kind of insinuation more often recently. She'd even asked Emilie to move in with her. She clearly wanted more out of their relationship, and Emilie wasn't sure she wanted to or could give her more. She didn't want to depend on Kate's money—or on her husband's money to be more accurate. She also knew with more certainty each day that passed that she would never be in love with Kate the way she was in love with Angeline. She knew she could probably be happy with Kate. They made great lovers and definitely knew how to have a good time together. But she wasn't sure how that could translate into living together as a couple. "That's a beautiful dream, Kate," she simply said before she turned to her back.

Kate propped herself up on her elbows so she could bring her face over Emilie's and force her to look into her eyes again. What Emilie saw was determination. She wouldn't let it go this time. "It doesn't have to be just a dream, Emilie. I want you to live with me."

"And I've told you before I don't want to live in this house with you, be your pretty little thing and help you plan your parties. That's not who I am."

Emilie started to sit up but Kate gently pushed her back and left one hand on her chest as she spoke. "I know, my darling. You're much better than that, and it's not what I want either. Don't you understand that I don't want all of these women in my house every Saturday night anymore either? All I want is you, Emilie. I love you."

Emilie gasped in surprise. In almost five years, they'd never said those three words to each other. Emilie had expected them at first but had finally accepted that their relationship was not a love story. It was a passionate tale, an erotic affair perhaps, but not a love story. Kate was changing the game on her and she didn't know how to react. "Kate," she simply murmured, closing her eyes.

"I'm tired of this scene, of this city. My sweet Emilie, we could move to New York together. No one would know who we are there. No one would care. We could start fresh, just the two of us."

"Kate," Emilie said again before Kate put a finger on her lips to keep her from talking.

"Don't say anything now, just think about it. It's what I want, my darling. I want to share a life with you and only you. I've been thinking about it, wanting it for months. Please take at least a few days to think about it too before you make up your mind."

Emilie nodded and Kate kissed her. The kiss was softer than usual yet seemed deeper at the same time. There were definitely new intentions behind Kate's lips and Emilie thought as she abandoned herself in Kate's physical declaration that there could be worse things than letting this woman love her.

CHAPTER TWENTY-FIVE

Rimouski, April 1905

The children were sleeping soundly in the attic. Joseph had placed three beds in the small space, creating a cozy bedroom for Paul-Emile, Victor and Marie-Ange. The boys had first objected to Marie-Ange getting the bed by the dormer window, but had accepted their faith because as much as they fought with each other, they both loved their sister very much.

Angeline sat alone in the rocking chair, worried, trying to focus on the sound of a loose plank creaking underneath one of the rockers. Joseph meant to fix that plank but he worked so much he never had time. Angeline usually moved the chair to avoid the noise when she sat at night to knit while she waited for her husband, but tonight the sound of the squeaky plank helped soothe her nerves.

Yellow stayed by the door, restless. He stood up at the slightest movement or sound of the wind, wagging his tail, then lay back down on the floor with a heavy sigh every time he realized Joseph wasn't home yet. The presence of the dog usually comforted Angeline, but it failed to reassure her tonight.

Joseph often worked on Sundays or late at night during the week, but he'd never worked after dark on a Sunday before. He'd left for the sawmill right after lunch and wasn't back yet at nine p.m. Angeline repeated to herself that once Joseph was focused on fixing a piece of machinery he didn't give up until it worked again and he'd probably just lost track of time, but she couldn't help but imagine the worst. A chill had passed through her spine around sunset and she couldn't shake the feeling that something was wrong. She'd finally gone to her parents' house around eight to ask for help and her father had gone to the sawmill right away, telling her he'd be back with her husband in no time. The fact that her father wasn't back yet made her worry even more.

Yellow stood up again and wagged his tail. This time he let out a deep, warning bark, and Angeline heard steps on the porch. She jumped out of the chair and hurried to the door. She opened it and couldn't hide her disappointment when she didn't see Joseph behind her father. "He's not done yet?" she asked.

"Angeline, my girl, let's go inside and sit down."

Her father's words, accompanied by his solemn tone and expression, made Angeline's heart tighten on the spot and another chill traveled through her body as she moved to the side to let her father inside. "What happened, Papa? Joseph had an accident, didn't he? Is he in the hospital?"

Her father walked into the house and sat in one of the wooden chairs at the kitchen table. He slowly put his gray wool cap on the table. Angeline remained at the door, powerless to move. Yellow stayed by her side. Her father extended a hand toward her as he asked, "Please sit down, Angeline."

She obeyed and sat in the chair next to her father, who took her hands in his. "I stopped by Fat Pineau's house on my way to the mill earlier and he came with me. When we arrived we saw Joseph on the ground."

"Oh no, Papa, was he hurt?" Angeline's voice broke and her father held her hands with more strength.

"His head was bleeding and he wasn't moving, Angeline." He paused to take a deep breath and Angeline shut her eyes as if it could keep her from hearing the news. "I sent Fat Pineau to get Doctor Michaud, but he wasn't breathing and he'd lost a lot of blood. He was next to the circular saw. Fat Pineau thinks a heavy piece of wood probably got stuck in the saw and when Joseph got it to work again, the piece of wood must have been thrown out of it and hit him right in the head."

Angeline opened her eyes again when her father took one of the hands that were holding hers to hit his own head with his finger, right on the temple, showing her where the piece of wood had hit Joseph.

"Did Doctor Michaud make it to the mill, Papa? What did he say?"

Her father sighed again, looking straight into his daughter's eyes, and had to swallow a lump in his throat before he spoke. He grimaced, trying to hold in the tears as he answered, "Doctor Michaud said Joseph probably didn't suffer, Angeline. The blow killed him instantly." Her father lost control then and started sobbing as Angeline violently pulled her hands out of his.

"You're lying, Papa. I don't believe you. I need to see him. Take me to my husband, Papa. Please."

She stood up and walked toward the door. Her father followed her and placed himself between her and the door. Yellow growled defensively but her father ignored him and forcefully grabbed Angeline and held her in his arms. Through his tears, he explained, "He's not at the mill anymore, Angeline. Doctor Michaud had his body taken to the hospital to confirm what happened. You can see him tomorrow, my girl."

Angeline struggled in vain in her father's embrace, protesting, "I can't wait until tomorrow, Papa, Joseph needs me."

Her father held her at arm's length and forced her to look into his eyes as he declared firmly, "He's dead, Angeline. Joseph is dead."

Only then did she finally start crying, collapsing into her father's arms. He held her tight and cried with her, gently caressing her hair and her back. "We've lost him, my dear girl," he added.

Yellow lay down at their feet and whimpered.

CHAPTER TWENTY-SIX

Boston, May 1905

Emilie had read her father's letter a dozen times, hoping she would read different words, the same way she'd often read the same book over and over again as a child, hoping it would end differently. But words, once they were written on paper, became truth. Joseph was dead. Reading the letter again wouldn't change that horrible truth, yet she kept it folded inside her suitcase, just in case she needed to read it again. She hadn't cried since Mrs. Flaherty had given her her father's letter earlier in the week, but when she arrived at the train station that Sunday afternoon and saw Kate waving at her, she sat on a bench and started sobbing.

Kate and Emilie had planned a trip to New York. Emilie had finally accepted to go with Kate just to visit the city and see if perhaps living there with Kate might be a possibility after all. She'd asked for a week of vacation which Mr. Flaherty was happy to grant her and she'd quickly become genuinely excited about visiting New York. Even after she'd read her father's letter she'd kept her focus on carefully packing her suitcase, the same suitcase she'd packed to move to Boston. Joseph hadn't been a part of her life in years and by the time she'd received the news he'd been buried for a few weeks already, so why should she change her plans?

Now, sitting on a bench in the middle of the train station, she knew she couldn't get on that train. She kept crying hysterically, her hands clenching the carefully packed suitcase on her lap.

Kate sat next to her on the bench and put a hand on her back to comfort her. Emilie couldn't look at her, but she imagined Kate must have had an expression of panic on her face when she heard her tone of voice. "What's wrong, my darling?"

"My brother died," she said softly before she started crying more quietly, this time on Kate's shoulder. She repeated the words to herself. Her brother was dead. She couldn't use his name anymore. Joseph was a man, a man who'd moved to Rimouski with the woman she loved. She might have been able to live through a man named Joseph's death as if nothing had happened, but the death of her brother was something else. The images rushing through her mind now were those of their childhood, their connection, the games they played together, the numerous times she had to jump to his defense, and the laughs they shared. Her brother was gone, and all she wanted to do was run back to her small room on Bromfield Street to mourn him.

"Oh my poor darling. I'm so sorry," Kate offered. "Why don't we go to our sleeping car so we can have more privacy?" She stood up and extended her hand to Emilie.

At the abrupt separation from Kate's shoulder, Emilie regained her composure and remained seated. She wiped away tears with the back of her hand and looked up into Kate's eyes. "I can't go to New York with you, Kate. I'm sorry," she said in a low, scratchy voice, afraid that if she attempted to speak louder tears would take over again.

Kate sat down next to her on the bench. "Of course. That was so insensitive of me. Please forgive me, my darling. We can postpone our trip."

Emilie turned sideways so she could face Kate on the bench. "No, Kate. I can't go to New York with you. Not now. Not ever."

She knew her tone was cold, but Emilie couldn't help the words that came out of her mouth. It was as if there was suddenly no room inside her for anything but her pain and the truth, as if she wanted to rid herself of all the complications of her life to go back to the simplicity of the childhood she'd shared with her brother.

Kate's expression showed she was hurt but her words were calm and understanding. "I know you're in pain, Emilie. Why don't we just go back to my house and talk about New York later, when you feel better? Let me just be there for you right now."

Emilie was glad they were in a public space. If Kate could have kissed her or touched her in a more intimate way Emilie might have warmed up to her comfort. Instead, she was able to maintain a glacial tone when she answered, "No. I want you to go, Kate. I don't love you." Nothing but the truth, perhaps, but even Emilie was shocked at her latest declaration.

Kate's compassion took an angry turn. She was clearly both hurt and humiliated. "Stop, Emilie. You don't mean what you're saying. You're hurting, I know, but stop before you say something you might regret."

Emilie turned her attention to the train in front of them. She motioned with her chin and repeated without any emotion showing in her voice, "Go, Kate. I want you to go now."

Kate stood up and faced Emilie. She held on to her pride with fire in her eyes, yet her voice caught when she pleaded, "Whatever you're feeling, Emilie, it doesn't give you the right to break my heart so shamelessly. You'll regret this."

This time Emilie managed to look into Kate's eyes yet stay completely detached from her. "You'll miss your train, my darling."

Kate's eyes filled with tears and she whispered through clenched teeth, "You ungrateful little bitch." Then she turned around and walked toward the train, her shoulders slightly moving up and down, just enough for Emilie to know she was crying.

Emilie stood up and left the station before she could see Kate climb on the train. She walked toward the lodging house at a fast pace and with a desperate energy. She'd been incredibly cruel and Kate was right, she already regretted it. But something inside her had told her she had to let go of Kate today.

When she got to her room she lay down on her small bed and cried furiously, putting all of her strength into every tear and every scream she poured into her pillow.

CHAPTER TWENTY-SEVEN

Rimouski, August 1905

Angeline put the children to bed and sat at the kitchen table with an oil lamp, paper and a fountain pen. She was determined to write that letter tonight. She'd waited too long already.

The months after Joseph's death had been a whirlwind of emotion. Marie-Ange was too young to realize exactly what was going on but the boys missed their papa every day, especially Victor. He had tantrums over everything and anything, and Angeline knew all of his rage boiled down to anger over losing his father. Paul-Emile had always been close to Angeline but he'd clung to her even tighter, as if he'd been afraid of losing her too. He was starting school in September and Angeline thought the forced daily hours of separation would be very beneficial to him. And to her.

She'd remained strong for her children, crying only at night when the children were sleeping and she retreated to the bedroom she'd shared with Joseph. She missed his companionship, his sweet, loving presence. She missed making him laugh and his scent of sawdust. She missed him all the time, but mostly at night, when she was alone in bed. She'd lost the head of their family and it was as if he'd taken her sense of direction with him, her ability to make adult decisions.

Her parents had been there for her and the children. They'd really stepped up, especially financially. Angeline was grateful for their help but sometimes felt crowded by their presence. Some days she even felt like she was her own children's older sister instead of their mother, as if she'd become one of the Fourniers' many children again. She hated that feeling yet wasn't ready or able to take control of her own house again. She didn't know how. She needed her parents.

Angeline put her hand to her stomach and felt the baby kick. She smiled for a brief moment before she was taken by the same sadness she felt every time she remembered Joseph didn't know about her pregnancy when he died. She wasn't sure herself at that time, but even if she'd been certain she was pregnant she would have waited to tell him. She'd had three miscarriages since the birth of Marie-Ange and she would have wanted to spare him from more disappointment.

She was glad this baby had found a way to grab on to her belly and keep growing. She often caught herself foolishly thinking his or her birth would in some way bring Joseph back. She'd never shared that thought with anyone, of course. In fact, no one else knew about her condition.

She knew she couldn't keep her secret much longer. She was five months pregnant and she was starting to show. The little weight she'd put on since the birth of Paul-Emile wouldn't help her hide this new baby much longer. She would have to tell her parents and the children before they found out on their own. She'd waited that long because she knew her pregnancy would make her even more of an invalid to her parents' eyes and would increase their protective presence. It made her feel powerless, almost invisible, and lonely.

Exactly the same way she'd felt as a child before she met Joseph and Emilie. She'd lost Joseph, but she couldn't get

Emilie out of her mind. Each day that passed convinced her more and more that she needed her best friend, that only Emilie could help her through the loss of Joseph and help her feel like a capable adult woman again. She'd decided she would write Emilie a couple of weeks ago but hadn't found the courage.

She didn't know what to tell Emilie. They hadn't parted on good terms, after all. Angeline refused to mull over the last time they'd seen each other, but she didn't know how to avoid it. She didn't know how to ask for help without apologizing for pushing Emilie away and she didn't want to apologize for rejecting a part of Emilie she still felt was bad. Even if she did apologize, she didn't know how Emilie would react.

Emilie might still be angry with her for all she knew. There had to be a reason why she'd written to Joseph without including a note for Angeline. She probably hated her, or worse, didn't even think about her anymore.

There was another reason why Angeline didn't want to think of that last time she'd seen her friend. She didn't want to revisit her own feelings, because they were just as wrong as Emilie's. It would be wiser to leave Emilie alone. Angeline knew it but she just wanted her friend back. She needed her.

Every letter she'd composed in her mind over the last two weeks had been dismissed. She'd thought that sitting with a pen and a piece of paper would help her find the right words to tell Emilie how much she needed her, but as she again sat in front of a blank page she realized it had been nothing more than wishful thinking. She sighed with frustration. The lamp had already burned most of its oil. She was running out of time, and she wouldn't wait one more day. She just needed to go straight to the point and hope for the best.

She brought her pen to the middle of the page and waited for a few seconds until her hand stopped shaking. She wrote three lines and quickly folded the page and put it in an envelope before she could change her mind. She wrote Emilie's address on the envelope. She'd known it by heart since they'd received the letter addressed to Joseph. She would take it to the post office tomorrow. She left the envelope on the table and went to her bedroom, trying to imagine Emilie's reaction when she read:

My dearest Emilie,
Please come.
Angeline

UNDERTOW

1905-1906

CHAPTER TWENTY-EIGHT

Rimouski, September 1905

Emilie had been admiring the fall colors of the Appalachian Mountains from the window until the train approached Rimouski and slowed down. Then she became so anxious she could hardly breathe. Looking at the beautiful countryside from a distance, its peaks and valleys in red, yellow and orange hues, had awakened a romantic nostalgia in her that she'd found appealing, almost reassuring. But the thought of physically being back in Rimouski, of stepping on the same ground and breathing the same air as Angeline, was too tangible and sent her into panic. When the train came to a complete halt, she took off the simple sailor hat she'd been wearing and ran her fingers through her short locks.

Before she'd left Boston she'd cut her black hair just below her ears, adopting a hairstyle similar to Kate's. She hadn't done it to copy Kate or as an homage to her—although she did owe a lot to Kate and still felt terrible about the way she'd treated her at the train station. The haircut was more like a physical guarantee, a way to hold on to the woman she'd become in

Boston. Even though she'd decided to temporarily come back to Rimouski, she would never go back to her old self, and cutting her hair was the best way she knew to make that statement. Every time she ran her fingers through it, she'd be reminded of who she truly was. It worked, to some extent, and with a deep breath Emilie found the courage to stand up and walk out of the train with her suitcase and her old leather mailbag. She started walking at a leisurely pace, gathering her thoughts as she took in familiar sights and scents mixed with completely new scenery.

In his only letter to Emilie, Joseph had mentioned that the place had changed and the population had grown in Rimouski since their departure in 1888, and Emilie was now realizing just how right he was. New streets, new buildings and new people made her feel like a complete stranger in the village where she'd grown up. She couldn't even call it a village anymore. Not a city yet, but perhaps a town. It was different and big enough that Emilie had to ask for directions to Tessier Road, yet small enough that the man who gave her directions looked at her suspiciously, as if he knew everyone who would usually venture in that direction.

As she walked away from the buzzing center of the growing town it didn't take Emilie long to recognize the Rimouski she'd known. After she'd met Kate, Emilie had found enough courage to explore more of Boston, often walking for hours without ever leaving the sidewalks of the city. But it took her just a few minutes in Rimouski to find herself on narrow dirt roads with nothing but small homes, farmland and forest.

Emilie was glad of her black leather high-top shoes. She knew they'd be comfortable and would be practical for walking in the dirt and mud. She'd left the boots Kate had given her behind, knowing their tan cloth tops wouldn't survive a simple walk in Rimouski. She'd also left behind the two fancier dresses she sometimes wore at Kate's soirées, knowing she wouldn't have the occasion to wear them in Rimouski. She'd only packed her most practical outfits, like the dark gray skirt that slightly flared around her feet, the white tucked shirtwaist, and dark gray double-breasted jacket she wore today.

Her fancy clothes would wait for her in Boston. She'd asked Mrs. Flaherty to hold on to them until her return. She'd emptied her room so the Flahertys could find another lodger while she was gone but they'd promised she would have a room to stay when she got back. Emilie didn't think she could have left Boston without the reassurance that she could come back when she was ready.

Emilie walked more slowly as she drew closer to her destination. Walking in dirt was not easy but she knew that was not the reason for dragging her feet. A part of her was looking forward to seeing Angeline again and meeting her nephews and her niece, but a bigger part of her was terrified. She hadn't seen Angeline in seven years, and she didn't know how their reunion would unfold.

When she received Angeline's brief letter she'd known right away she couldn't deny Angeline's request. Angeline needed her as a friend, as a sister-in-law, as family. Emilie's decision to come to Rimouski was not entirely selfless though. She needed to be here as much as Angeline needed her here.

Since Joseph's death, she'd thought about going to Rimouski every day. She needed to feel close to Joseph and she knew the only place where she could find that closeness was Rimouski where they'd grown up together, where his own family was now growing up. She'd thought about jumping on a train to Canada many times but didn't dare, not certain she'd be welcome. Angeline's invitation was the permission she needed. She hadn't replied to Angeline's letter, hadn't told her she was coming. That way, she could have changed her mind at any time. But she hadn't. And she hoped Angeline hadn't either.

Emilie stopped and put her suitcase down. She'd come to the top of a hill and stood approximately three hundred feet from two houses built close together in front of a small barn. She knew instinctively that she was looking at her brother's house, smaller than the Fournier home next to it.

She smiled at the sight of the simple home in the late afternoon light, so similar to the one where she and Joseph had grown up except for the addition of a dormer. She remembered how much their mother had wished for a dormer and she was certain Joseph had built this one as much for her as for Angeline. She also knew Joseph and her mother both watched over that little house every day and so, standing on top of the hill three hundred feet from it, she felt their presence more than she had in a long time.

Emilie saw two young boys run in front of the house. She knew the boy with dark hair was Paul-Emile and was surprised to see he was only slightly taller than the blond boy who had to be his younger brother, Victor. They were both running with a dog that was almost as tall as they were, with blond fur so thick around the neck that he reminded Emilie of a lion. Soon the boys ran to the side of the house where Emilie couldn't see them but the lion-dog remained immobile, his nose pointing in her direction.

Emilie didn't move, not sure he'd spotted her until he started running toward her at such a high speed that Emilie was tempted to turn around and start running from him. She quickly decided she couldn't outrun him even if she tried and stayed in place where the dog quickly joined her. She realized by his wagging tail that her fear had been unjustified and when he sat in front of her she bent down to pet his head. "That's at least one of you who's happy to see me, isn't it, big fellow?"

She smiled at the dog. She saw complete trust and recognition in his black eyes, as if he'd known her his whole life. When she stopped petting him he reached for her hand again, pushing his head to her palm, and she laughed quietly. "You and I are going to be good friends, I think." She caressed his head one more time. His friendly presence reassured her and gave her the courage to continue to walk all the way to the house.

When she straightened up, the dog moved to her side, ready to follow her. Only then did she look toward the house—and gasped when she discovered Angeline standing on the porch, looking at her with one hand on her heart.

Angeline had briefly gone inside to check on the barley soup slowly cooking on the woodstove and when she came back outside she saw Yellow take off running the way he used to every time he saw Joseph come home from work. He would join his master and calmly walk back to the house by his side.

Angeline's heart lurched when she saw the woman Yellow had run to, and then it started beating so fast she pressed a hand to her chest as if that might slow it down. She had no doubt the woman standing on top of the hill was Emilie. She couldn't see her face but she would have recognized the petite figure anywhere. Even if Emilie had gained weight to the point of being unrecognizable, the way Yellow had run to her and was now walking calmly by her side as they approached the house, the same exact way he'd done with Joseph so many times before, would have revealed Emilie's identity.

Angeline walked off her porch and then stopped, unable to move any farther as she watched Emilie come toward her, faster and faster as she got closer. When she was just a few feet in front of her, Angeline couldn't help but smile at the familiar wrinkle between the thick eyebrows. "You came," was all she could manage to say.

Emilie returned her smile and the wrinkle between her brows disappeared for a brief moment before she spoke. "I did. I'm sorry I didn't write to announce my visit."

Emilie took off her hat and nervously ran her fingers through her hair, and Angeline noticed it was short. Carefully combed back behind her ears, her hair had simply looked pulled back in a chignon like her own until she'd uncovered her head.

"You cut your hair," she stated with a smirk, recognizing her friend's rebellious streak. The haircut suited Emilie. Her black hair looked thicker and Emilie looked younger than the last time she'd seen her, reminding Angeline piercingly of the nine-year-old she'd met in Fall River. "Is that the way girls wear their hair in Boston?" she asked teasingly.

"No, it's the way I wear my hair. Do you have a problem with it?" Emilie answered defensively.

Angeline chuckled at her reaction. "Calm down, Emilie, I'm just teasing. Did you leave your sense of humor on the barber's floor with your hair?"

Emilie laughed this time, and Angeline smiled with satisfaction. It had been a long time since she'd made someone laugh and it felt good, even if she was using humor to cover up her nerves as she stood face-to-face with Emilie for the first time since that terrible night all those years ago.

Emilie's laughter subsided and her worried frown reappeared as she asked in a voice filled with concern, "Is it all right that I came, Angeline?"

Angeline was no longer able to cover up her emotions and her voice caught when she answered, "Of course, Emilie." Tears welled in her eyes as she walked the short distance that separated them to pull Emilie's small body into a desperate embrace. "I'm so glad you're here," she added softly in Emilie's ear.

She felt Emilie's arms hesitate around her waist and realized she'd probably noticed her belly. She broke the embrace long enough to look into Emilie's eyes and answer the wordless question in her expression. "Yes, I became pregnant just before Joseph..." She didn't finish her sentence because there was no need to.

Emilie smiled as tears filled her eyes and they shared another hug, each tightening her hold as they cried and laughed at the same time. Angeline imagined they could have held on to each other for hours if a small hand had not pulled on her skirt. "Who's the lady, Maman?"

Emilie reluctantly tore herself away from Angeline to see the boy standing by her, looking at Emilie with a worried wrinkle between thick, dark eyebrows. Emilie couldn't help but smile at the boy who looked almost exactly like her when she was six years old. She crouched down to speak to the child. "You must be Paul-Emile. I'm your aunt Emilie. And I'm so glad to finally meet you."

Paul-Emile skeptically studied the hand Emilie offered him and looked up to his mother, who confirmed, "That's right. Your aunt Emilie came to visit us all the way from Boston."

Joseph and Angeline had obviously talked to their children about her before because the boy's eyes suddenly lit up and he shook her hand enthusiastically. "Will you tell me all about Boston, Aunt Emilie?"

Emilie chuckled at his eagerness, remembering how much she'd craved hearing about other places when she was his age. "Of course, Paul-Emile. I'll tell you all about it."

"Paul."

"Pardon me?"

"Paul. Everyone calls me Paul."

"All right, then. I'll tell you anything you want to know, Paul."

"Everyone calls him Paul except me," Angeline said. Emilie looked up to meet her gaze as she added, "He'll always be Paul-Emile to me." Angeline smiled tenderly at Emilie, making her understand that the meaning of the second part of her son's name was too important for her to drop it. Emilie returned the smile.

"Aunt Milie," a small voice said by her side. Emilie looked to find a little girl she would have recognized anywhere walking toward her with open arms. She looked exactly like her mother.

Emilie hugged the child, who squeezed her neck without any restraint, as hard as her small arms would let her. "Hello, Marie-Ange. Such a beautiful little girl, you are." The compliment embarrassed the girl and she ran to her mother, where she buried her face in Angeline's skirt.

Emilie stood up and looked around for the blond boy she'd seen earlier. When she spotted him standing at the corner of the house, keeping his distance, she waved at him. "Hi, Victor." He looked at her defiantly but she couldn't help but smile at him anyway as she wiped a tear from her eye. Her father had written that Victor looked like Joseph, but seeing the boy now she realized she hadn't been prepared for such a height of resemblance. It was in his build and his features, of course, but in his expression as well. And obviously in his wariness of strangers.

"Victor, come here and say hi to your aunt," Angeline demanded, visibly upset with her son's behavior.

"No," Victor said before he hid by the side of the house.

"Victor," Angeline started before Emilie lightly shook her head at her, silently asking her to stop.

Emilie could still see the boy but she didn't think he was aware of that. She spoke to Angeline loud enough for him to hear. "It's all right. Victor and I will have time to talk later. He'll have to talk to me if he wants to see what I brought him from Boston."

Victor was intrigued enough to start walking toward them but he stopped a few feet behind Angeline and when Emilie smiled at him, the smile she received in return was brief, but gave her hope.

"Did you bring me something too?" Paul asked.

"Of course. I have something for all of you," Emilie answered, looking at Paul before she focused on Angeline.

As she and Emilie sat at the kitchen table after dinner, watching the children play with their toys, Angeline asked, "How long can you stay?"

Paul sat with them examining with care his small locomotive, made of metal, as if trying to understand how it was built, while Victor played with his own train on the staircase. He still needed to keep his distance, and Emilie understood. Marie-Ange sat in the rocking chair, singing a lullaby to her new doll.

Emilie knew the toys would please the children. She'd spent a great amount of her savings on them, wanting to give the children a part of the city, of her life. She also wanted Angeline to know she was doing well in Boston. She needed to portray the image of a happy, successful city woman. A portrait she had some difficulty believing herself as she sat quietly with Angeline and spent time with her family. She ran her hand through her short hair. A part of her wanted to tell Angeline she wanted to stay forever, but another part wanted to tell her she had to go back to Boston tomorrow, before she forgot who she was, or did something stupid.

She'd convinced herself she'd visit Angeline as a friend, but her body had awakened against her will in Angeline's presence. Angeline had gained a little weight, especially in the hips and buttocks, and her features betrayed fatigue and anxiety, but Emilie was as attracted to the mother of three, soon four, as she'd been to the young, fresh Angeline she'd known in Flint.

If she stayed, Emilie knew she'd have to keep that attraction to herself and fantasize in silence, as she'd done in the past, but she also knew it would be so much more difficult now. Now that she'd experienced sexual relations with another woman, now that she knew exactly what she'd do to Angeline if she had the chance, now that she knew the pleasure they could give each other. She wanted to answer that she'd stay until she went crazy, but instead she simply said, "I don't have a set date. As long as I'm not in your way."

"You're not in my way, Emilie. Stay as long as you want." Angeline didn't want Emilie to go, yet she wasn't entirely sure she wanted her to stay. Having her in the house she'd shared with Joseph seemed both natural and bizarre at the same time. Natural because Emilie was family. She was, or had been, her best friend and Angeline didn't doubt she'd be a moral support as well as a great help in daily chores with the house and children. Bizarre because the Emilie that was sitting in her kitchen now was not really the Emilie she'd known. Angeline didn't feel completely at ease with her. Emilie had changed, and the change was not only in the short hairstyle. She seemed so much more mature, like she'd experienced life in ways Angeline hadn't. Like she'd become the woman she'd promised Angeline she'd become all on her own. Emilie hadn't needed Angeline with her in Boston and Angeline couldn't help the way it made her chest tighten with bitter pain, even if it had been her own choice not to go with Emilie.

"There's one more present," Emilie announced as she rummaged through her suitcase until she found a small rectangular box wrapped in the same brown paper in which the children's toys had been wrapped. "For you," she said as she handed the present to Angeline.

"Me? Oh Emilie you shouldn't have," she said as she took the box and started to unwrap it carefully. Her heart was racing. She couldn't remember receiving a wrapped present before. The brown paper covered a simple wooden box in which she found a gold chain with a circular pendant. Angeline gasped her surprise and looked at Emilie, who was smiling proudly.

Angeline didn't own jewelry and her first thought was that Emilie had spent too much money on her. She didn't deserve the delicate gold chain she carefully took out of its box with trembling fingers. Then she took a closer look at the pendant and all her worries disappeared. "Oh, Emilie," she said again as she smiled at her, her eyes tearing up, before focusing on the pendant again. With her fingers, she traced the engraving within the golden circle.

To anyone else it would have been a simple tree, nothing worth crying over. But to Angeline it wasn't just any tree. It was a buttonwood tree, the tree that had witnessed their friendship grow, the tree that had sheltered their talks, their dreams and their confidences. Emilie hadn't forgotten.

"Thank you," Angeline said as she stood up to hug Emilie.

"I'm glad you like it. When I saw it I couldn't resist."

"I love it. It's perfect." She handed the necklace to Emilie and turned around, silently asking for help. She wanted to wear the necklace right away. She felt Emilie's touch on her neck and thought her friend was trembling. She didn't stop to wonder what made Emilie tremble. She was too perfectly happy in this instant and wanted to savor this moment of true bliss. They'd been too rare recently.

"It's beautiful, Maman," Paul-Emile said, approaching Angeline. She bent down so he could get a better look at her present. Marie-Ange also came to admire the jewelry, and soon even Victor couldn't help taking a peek.

"Well, now that we've all been properly spoiled by your aunt Emilie..." Angeline started, wiping the last of her tears with the back of her hand. With a quick look toward Emilie, who stood by her side with a satisfied grin on her face, she addressed the children gathered in front of them, "I'm afraid it's time to go to bed."

"Can we take our toys to bed?" Victor asked, holding on to his metal train.

"Yes," Angeline conceded.

Clutching his train, Victor ran upstairs before Angeline had a chance to change her mind, followed by his older brother and younger sister.

Angeline turned to Emilie and caught her yawning. "Poor Emilie. You must be so tired."

Emilie nodded and Angeline was taken with panic. She wouldn't have hesitated to ask Emilie to share her bed if they'd still been the girls who met under their buttonwood tree to gossip and discuss books. If everything hadn't changed the last time they'd met under that same tree, she thought as she absently caressed the pendant around her neck. But that last encounter had happened. They had shared a kiss, and now she was scared of simply sharing a bed with her best friend.

But Emilie simply picked up her suitcase and announced, "I can go sleep upstairs with the children, if you don't mind."

"No, of course, that's a good idea. I'm sure Marie-Ange will be happy to share her bed with her aunt Milie," she said with a timid smile.

Emilie returned her smile. "Good night, Angeline. Thank you for your kind hospitality."

"Good night, Emilie," Angeline replied, and she watched Emilie climb the stairs. She immediately felt lonely, a feeling that was only exacerbated when Yellow followed Emilie. The dog had always slept in Joseph and Angeline's bedroom, curled up on the wooden floor by Joseph's side of the bed. It looked like Angeline would be completely alone in her bedroom tonight, a fact that left her feeling abandoned.

CHAPTER TWENTY-NINE

September 1905

"Are you sure?" Angeline asked with an amused smirk as she studied Emilie's appearance.

"Yes, I'm sure. Harvesting potatoes is not a job meant to be done in a skirt."

"Women have done it for centuries," Angeline replied with a chuckle.

"That doesn't mean they were right," Emilie said stubbornly.

Emilie had started working in the garden the day before, wanting to make herself useful. While Angeline was busy with chores inside the house after they milked the cows and took care of the animals in the morning, Emilie wanted to stay outside, enjoying the country air she'd missed even more than she realized. She'd fought with her skirt all day long, cussing its length and complete lack of practicality. Of course, she lacked experience working with the shovel, spading fork and other tools she had to learn how to manipulate all over again, but her skirt definitely made things more difficult than they needed to be.

She'd come back to the house determined to ask Angeline if she could borrow Joseph's trousers to continue her work the next day. Angeline had hesitated but had finally accepted and Emilie was now standing in the kitchen with brown wool trousers and one of her own blouses tucked into the waist. She'd borrowed suspenders as well, or she would have lost the pants before making her way out of Angeline's bedroom.

"What's so funny?" Emilie demanded as Angeline kept laughing. Emilie wasn't quite as offended by the laughter as she made it sound. She took pride in making Angeline laugh. She'd only been in Rimouski for a week, but she could swear some of the distress in Angeline's face at her arrival had already disappeared.

The tension between them had also simmered down and they were more at ease with each other. Emilie still had to keep her attraction in check, but she'd managed well so far. She also enjoyed spending time with the children, even sharing a bed with her niece, despite the three-year-old's tendency to punch and kick in her sleep, a tendency Emilie could prove with several bruises on her body. She still preferred the bruises to sharing a bed with Angeline, which would have been a much worse kind of torture.

"Nothing's funny," Angeline said before she laughed even louder. "You just look like a circus clown."

Emilie looked down and joined in Angeline's laughter. Her brother's trousers were much too big for her and she floated in them, not to mention that the way they pooled on the floor, she'd be fighting with them as much as she'd been fighting with her own skirt the day before. She stopped laughing at the realization and sighed, discouraged.

"Don't worry, we'll make it work. Let me," Angeline said as she knelt in front of Emilie. She rolled up the bottom of the pants until they were no longer covering Emilie's leather boots. Then she stood up and adjusted the suspenders so they held the pants higher on her waist. The mere touch of Angeline's hands on her sides forced Emilie to hold her breath until Angeline backed up and examined her carefully. She smiled, satisfied. "There, much better."

Emilie looked down and studied the transformation. "Thank you," she said with a smile as she started walking around the kitchen table, testing her new working outfit. She crouched down, straightened back up, put one foot on a chair and stretched. The liberty of movement was as she'd expected and she couldn't help but grin at the newfound freedom. "So much better," she announced. "By nightfall, there will be nothing left in that garden but dirt. You'll see," she added for Angeline, who laughed at her antics.

"You're crazy, Emilie Levesque," Angeline said as she kept laughing.

"Not crazy, my dear friend. Forward thinking. If women knew how comfortable these are, we'd all wear trousers." She followed her declaration with a small dance that made Angeline laugh even harder, and then walked out of the house with exaggeratedly large steps. She kept walking with the same gait all the way to the garden, knowing Angeline was watching her out of the window. Knowing Angeline kept laughing. She took a deep breath, filling her lungs with the brisk September air and puffing her chest with pride.

"First short hair and now trousers. She's a little eccentric, isn't she?" her father said as he stood on Angeline's porch and they watched Emilie work in the garden. Angeline chuckled at her father's assessment. He'd come to see if Angeline needed anything from the General Store as he wasn't working at the mill that day and was about to get the horses and buggy ready for a trip to town.

"She sure is," Angeline admitted with a smile. "She says the pants make it easier."

"I have to admit she's fast. If those trousers don't fall to her ankles she might be done with the potatoes and beets before dinner," her father concluded with a low chuckle.

"I don't think she could have taken a step without suspenders," Angeline added, making her father laugh even more. She was glad and reassured that her father found Emilie's eccentric behavior amusing rather than threatening. Then again, as she watched Emilie work, she wondered how anyone could resist laughing at the situation. She'd found it funny at first too, but now she admired how quickly Emilie moved in the garden.

Most of all, she was touched and relieved that Emilie had managed to get Victor to help her. The four-year-old who'd been so angry since his father's death, often playing alone in a corner, was now helping his aunt harvest vegetables and seemed to genuinely enjoy her company. "I think she's good for Victor. She understands him better than I do," Angeline confided to her father.

"I think she's good for his mother too," her father said with a smile and a tender pat on Angeline's shoulder before he left her alone on the porch.

"Maybe," Angeline answered to herself, smiling as she watched Emilie pick up Victor and sit him on top of a pile of potatoes in the small wooden wagon she then pulled behind her with the help of two handles at her sides all the way to the *caveau*, the underground vault they used to store vegetables.

Emilie opened the trap to the *caveau* and she and Victor started taking the potatoes down to lay them on the ground. Paul was in school and Marie-Ange was never far from her mother, but Victor had been outside all day with Emilie. At first he'd lurked around the garden from a distance, curious about that crazy aunt wearing trousers, Emilie guessed. She'd waited patiently until he'd ventured closer and had finally asked him nonchalantly, "You want to help me put the potatoes in the wagon, Victor?"

The boy hadn't answered but started taking the potatoes she'd dug out of the ground and placed them carefully on the wagon. He wasn't a talker, but that didn't surprise her. Joseph had always been the quiet type. She didn't need Victor to talk to her. The fact that he was engaging in an activity with her was enough for now. He didn't protest the first time she picked him up to sit him on top of the potatoes in the wagon. He even smiled, and hurried to the side of the wagon every time Emilie got ready for the trips to or from the *caveau*.

Yellow stayed by their side at all times. At one point Emilie stopped digging potatoes out of the ground to catch her breath for a minute and watched as Victor petted the dog. "Why is his name Yellow?" she asked Victor.

The boy simply shrugged and Emilie went back to digging until she finally heard a hesitant voice. "Because his hair is yellow, I guess." The answer was followed by another shrug and Emilie stopped digging and grinned to herself.

"That's a stupid reason," she said, trying to get a reaction out of Victor.

"It's not stupid," he argued.

"Sure it is. If we gave people names based on the color of their hair, your name would be 'Yellow' too. And your brother and I would be named 'Black.'"

The boy giggled and Emilie couldn't help but smile. Even the way he laughed reminded her of Joseph. It was a sound worth waiting for. "And Maman and Marie-Ange would be 'Brown,'" he said before he laughed again, this time louder.

"Right, that's stupid, isn't it?"

"Yes," he agreed through his laughter.

"I think we need to find Yellow a new name, don't you think?" They spent the next hour proposing new names for the dog as they kept working together. Victor laughed at each of Emilie's suggestions like "Booger" or "Poopie." He even came up with a few ideas of his own, all in the same family of words any four-year-old would have found hilarious.

"No, I think your dog deserves a real name, something that will suit him well," Emilie finally suggested. She started examining the dog carefully, holding her chin between her thumb and index as if in deep reflection. She grinned when she saw from the corner of her eye that Victor was mimicking her. "I know!" she suddenly exclaimed, turning toward the boy who was staring at her with eyes open wide in excitement. "I think he looks like a lion with that thick fur around his neck, don't you?" The boy looked at the dog again and nodded in agreement. "So we should call him Lionel."

"Lionel," Victor repeated. "Lionel, come here!" he called to the dog, testing the new name. When the dog walked to him without hesitation, Victor jumped with enthusiasm. "It works! He likes it!"

"Of course he likes it. It's his name," Emilie said with confidence.

"I'll go tell Maman and Marie-Ange," Victor declared and he started running toward the house.

Emilie watched him leave and saw Pierre Fournier approach the garden, carrying a parcel wrapped in brown paper. She automatically looked at her trousers, self-conscious. She feared what Mr. Fournier might think of her forward-thinking ideas. She was only half-reassured when he got closer and she noticed he was smiling.

"What did you do to that boy, Emilie? I haven't seen a smile like that on his face since his father…" He interrupted his thought and looked at Emilie with a contrite expression. "I'm sorry. Victor hasn't been the same since we lost your brother. It seems like it's been worse for him than for Paul or Marie-Ange."

"It doesn't surprise me. Victor must have been very close to his papa. He looks and acts so much like him. I was close to Joseph when we were children. I think I have a pretty good idea how Victor thinks."

"I think you're right. And that's exactly what he needs."

Emilie felt the compliment heat up her cheeks and she smiled. Mr. Fournier looked past her to the garden and offered an appreciative nod. "You've accomplished a lot in just one day."

Emilie turned to the garden and realized that she'd not only harvested all of the beets but was also done with most of the potatoes. She'd be completely done by the end of the day and the carrots needed to stay in the ground a week or two before she could harvest them. "I enjoy doing this. And I had help," she said with a smile.

Mr. Fournier chuckled.

"Thank you all the same. My wife's arthritis makes it difficult for her to do this kind of work and your help makes it possible for Angeline to focus on other chores more suitable to her condition," he said with genuine appreciation.

"I'm here to help your daughter in any way I can, Mr. Fournier."

"Good. I think your presence is good for her and the children. That means your presence is good for us too, and I sincerely hope you're in no hurry to go back to Boston." Mr. Fournier cleared his throat, a little embarrassed by the sentimentality of his confessed gratitude.

"I'll stay as long as I can be useful," she promised.

"Good. I have something for you." He handed her the parcel he'd been holding and she took it carefully. Her expression must have betrayed her puzzlement because Mr. Fournier immediately offered an explanation. "It's just something I thought would make your life here easier."

"Thank you," Emilie said timidly as she tore the brown paper to reveal a pair of gray wool trousers. She looked up to Mr. Fournier and cocked her head in question.

"These are the smallest pants Theo had in the store. Theo's the owner of the General Store in town. I figured if you're going to wear trousers to work you might as well wear a pair that fits you. These might still be too big but Delphine can make adjustments if needed. Just let us know."

Emilie started caressing the wool of her very own, brand-new trousers as Mr. Fournier spoke. She couldn't believe how generous and understanding the man in front of her was. She imagined Angeline had explained why she was wearing trousers in the garden when he'd stopped by earlier. As much as Emilie had liked the freedom of wearing pants today, she didn't think she would ever have dared purchasing a pair for herself. Mr. Fournier's present meant more to her than he would ever know and she was tempted to jump to him and hug him to show exactly how grateful she was. Instead she simply looked into his eyes and said, "Thank you, these will be very helpful."

"Good. That's the point," he said and he cleared his throat again. He turned to start walking back to his house but hadn't made three steps before he stopped and turned back toward her. "Oh yes, there's something else I wanted to tell you about. You see, Theo's wife used to help him with the store but she's been sick for a few months now and the poor man can't keep handling the store on his own. I mentioned you and your experience working in a bookstore in Boston and he said he'd like to meet you. If you two get along he'd like you to work a few days a week. He'll pay you, of course."

Emilie felt compelled to throw herself at this man's neck again but managed to stay anchored to the ground, her heart racing at the possibility of working in a store and earning money to help Angeline.

Mr. Fournier said, "I hope you don't think I'm not minding my own business. I was trying to help and I figured if you had a job here you might be able to stay longer."

He took off his wool cap and started scratching his head nervously and Emilie smiled. Her respect and fondness for Angeline's father were growing stronger every second and she finally found the words to speak and take him out of his misery. "Thank you so much, Mr. Fournier. I'm very grateful you mentioned my name to Theo and I'll go meet him first thing in the morning."

"Good," he declared, relieved. "Do you need a ride?"

"Oh no, you've done enough already. I'll walk. I'm used to walking for miles in Boston and I walked here all the way from the train station so I'll be fine. Thank you for the offer, though."

"If you say so," he said.

"You're very kind, Mr. Fournier. Thank you again. For these," she said as she tapped the trousers still halfway wrapped in brown paper, "and for the potential job. I truly appreciate it."

"Don't mention it," he answered with a light blush on his face before he turned around once more and started walking all the way to his house this time.

Emilie held the gray trousers to her chest once more before she laid them on the ground so she could finish her job in the garden. When the dog went to sniff the parcel, she brandished her finger at him. "Don't touch, Lionel," she commanded firmly. The dog lay sheepishly down on the ground and instead guarded them for her.

CHAPTER THIRTY

September 1905

"Do you know how to work this kind of cash register, Miss Levesque?"

Theo Lepage stood tall despite a slightly rounded back. He wore a gray mustache that he rolled between his thumb and index finger as he observed Emilie with a raised eyebrow that failed to intimidate her. She'd witnessed him cuss out the cash register while serving a customer when she first entered the store. She knew he was desperate. The register had most likely been his wife's responsibility before she became sick, Emilie guessed.

While she waited her turn to step to the counter to introduce herself, Emilie had studied the store carefully. It was quite different from Mr. Flaherty's bookstore. There was a small round table at the entrance where two old men played checkers as well as a couple of chairs where customers could sit and chat while they waited their turn. Theo stood behind a large wooden counter that separated the store in two sections, and most of the merchandise was behind that same counter, well sorted onto floor-to-ceiling shelving. No books, Emilie had noted, except for a few Bibles. It was very different from the store where she'd worked for seven years, but the cash register was almost identical.

"Yes, of course. We used a very similar model at the bookstore where I worked in Boston."

"Hmm," Theo simply answered as he nodded and bent over the counter to take another look at Emilie, inspecting her appearance, starting with her shoes.

She'd cleaned her black boots and wore them with a brown skirt and a plaid double-breasted jacket. Although her short hair was pulled back behind her ears, Emilie couldn't hide the fact that it was, indeed, shorter than the hair of all other women in Rimouski. While Theo seemed satisfied with her overall appearance, he squinted at her in a mix of puzzlement and disapproval every time his gaze met Emilie's hair. At last he sighed and declared, "You're an odd girl, Miss Levesque, but I need help and Pierre thinks highly of you, so that's enough for me. When can you start?"

"I could start today, Mr. Lepage."

"Great. If you could handle customers and this darn register, I could focus on some bookkeeping." He slapped the top of the register with his large hand to illustrate his disdain. "If you start now we'll see how it goes and we can discuss your conditions at closing. Do we have a deal, Miss Levesque?"

"We do, Mr. Lepage."

Emilie got behind the counter and Mr. Lepage disappeared into the back office before the next customer entered the store. She used her experience at Flaherty Books and her common sense to make it through the day, limiting as much as possible the number of times she had to disturb grumpy Theo. Fortunately, pricing information was detailed in catalogs and what she couldn't find in catalogs she found in a handwritten book sitting by the cash register. Emilie imagined the book was the work of Theo's wife, who'd certainly wanted to help her husband and any future employee as much as she could before she finally had to stop working.

After they closed the store, she walked back to Angeline's house feeling exhausted but satisfied with her performance and her negotiations with Theo. He'd scoffed when she told him what she'd been paid in Boston and as she expected he could only pay her a small fraction of her former wages. That didn't bother her. She knew Theo couldn't pay her as much as Mr. Flaherty had and she also knew that as a woman in Rimouski she was fortunate enough to find any sort of remunerated employment that would allow her to help Angeline.

What gave her the most satisfaction, however, was that Theo had agreed to let her look into ordering catalogs from book suppliers and had even allowed her to purchase a few classics to see if any customer might be interested. He was skeptical, of course, but he admitted a few people, including the young Doctor Michaud, had inquired about secular literature recently.

Emilie promised herself she'd have a talk with Doctor Michaud next time he visited the store. They might have a passion for books in common, she hoped. The thought of possibly discussing books with a doctor again reminded her of Maurice and she swallowed the familiar lump of sadness that appeared in her throat every time she thought of her old friend, her kindred spirit. Then sadness was replaced with bitterness and Emilie swore that she'd keep her guard up with Doctor Michaud or any potential new friend. She couldn't trust anyone enough to let them find out who she truly was.

On Sunday, after they'd returned from church, Angeline was getting ready to get off the buggy, following her father, mother and the children, but instead of helping her down as he usually did, her father asked her to stay put. He stood by the buggy and held the reins with a smirk. Angeline was about to ask what was going on when she saw Emilie, who'd been the first to jump off the buggy, come back with her leather mailbag. She then climbed back onto the buggy to sit by Angeline and took the reins from her father. When Angeline saw her father wink at Emilie, she finally asked, "What's going on, you two?"

"Nothing, my girl. Your mother and I are about to have lunch with the children while you go on a short trip with Emilie."

Angeline turned to Emilie, who chuckled before she explained, "I need to celebrate my new job. And you just need to get out of the house." Before Angeline could protest, Emilie commanded the two horses into motion with a subtle movement of her wrist. Angeline couldn't help but smile at her friend, grateful for the attention, excited to spend a little time away from the house in good company.

Angeline's excitement only grew and her smile widened when she realized Emilie was guiding the horses and buggy toward the Saint-Laurent River. They stopped the buggy by the road before they got to the beach. Emilie helped Angeline down, set her mailbag across her own shoulder, and tied the horses to a tree.

They walked down to the beach where sand mixed with rocks of all sizes, and Angeline took in the views, sounds and smells of the sea. The sky was gray and the river so wide Angeline couldn't see the other side. The September wind was cold on her face and played with the rising tide, creating waves that crashed against rocks in a cacophony of splash Angeline found strangely soothing. Angeline filled her lungs with the marine air and reveled in its saltiness and its smell of kelp. She turned to where Emilie was standing.

"Thank you so much," she whispered. The cold wind and her emotions made it impossible for her to speak louder.

Emilie smiled and took her hand, leading her toward a large boulder that stood twice as tall as a grown man and was almost white in color. She got a wool blanket out of her bag and set it on the sand as she explained, "Your father told me how much you love the beach, and I wanted to do something special for you." She sat on the blanket and patted the spot next to her, inviting Angeline to sit by her. Angeline sat down on the blanket and Emilie handed her a piece of bread and an apple.

"Thank you. I do love this place." Angeline bit into the hearty bread. "We didn't come often because your brother worked so much, but I enjoyed every time we made it down to the beach. I haven't been here since he…" She didn't finish her thought, as usual, unable to speak the words.

Emilie offered an understanding smile. "That's a shame. We should start coming every Sunday after church. It will be a little like when we were children in Fall River, except this big rock will be our new buttonwood tree."

Emilie took a large bite of her own bread and Angeline started laughing at her contagious enthusiasm. She looked at the Saint-Laurent and declared, "This beats the Quequechan River, though, doesn't it?"

Emilie laughed and nearly choked on her bread. She followed Angeline's gaze and agreed, "There's no comparison."

They ate their lunch and talked about Emilie's new job at the store. Angeline laughed at Emilie's impersonation of old grumpy Theo and smiled at her elation over the books she might be able to order. Emilie's passion for knowledge would never die, Angeline mused. She found both reassurance and stimulation in that passion that made Emilie's black eyes sparkle, and she realized just how much she'd missed it. She'd missed hearing Emilie talk with such intensity.

They finished their apple, gathered their belongings into Emilie's mailbag, and started walking on the beach toward the Bic Islands. The wind made her shiver and she got closer to Emilie so they could keep warm, holding her arm as she'd done so many times on their walks to and from school or the cotton mill. The familiar touch reminded her that she'd missed their physical closeness too.

She couldn't let Emilie go back to Boston. That need to be in Emilie's presence ever since she'd met her, that need she'd thought she'd grown out of since she'd moved to Rimouski, it had only taken a little over a week for it to return stronger than ever. She couldn't lose Emilie again.

"How are we going to keep coming here every Sunday if you go back to Boston, Emilie?" The question surprised Angeline as much as it did Emilie, who stopped walking for a moment and looked at her with furrowed eyebrows.

"I'm not going back yet. At least not before you have that baby. I'll stay as long as you need me, Angeline." Emilie smiled and briefly placed her warm hand on Angeline's protruding stomach.

What if I need you forever, Angeline thought as they started walking again. Instead, she asked the question she'd wanted to ask ever since Emilie had arrived in Rimouski even though she couldn't admit it, not even to herself. "But isn't there someone waiting for you in Boston? A fiancé? Someone special?" Angeline ended her question before her voice broke, realizing she wasn't certain she wanted to hear Emilie's answer.

Emilie broke free of Angeline's grasp and walked a few steps ahead before she turned to Angeline. The crease between her eyebrows had grown deeper and she seemed upset. "Am I in your way? Do you want me to go back to Boston?"

"Oh no, of course not," Angeline answered quickly, closing the distance between them and taking Emilie's hands in hers. She should have known Emilie might interpret her question that way and she hoped that revealing her true desires would reassure her. "I want you to stay, Emilie. I love having you here. The children love having you here too. Even my parents love having you here. I was simply curious. I'm sorry."

Emilie's gaze was focused on their joined hands and Angeline waited nervously for her to speak again. "I love being here too, Angeline. But I guess if I'm going to stay a while longer you should know."

Angeline's heart raced as she waited for Emilie to continue. Her eyes were still fixed on their hands and she'd gone quiet for what seemed like hours. "What should I know? Look at me, Emilie. Please."

Emilie finally did look at Angeline but she let go of her hands and stepped away from her before she took a deep breath and finally spoke. "There was someone special in Boston but I ended it after Joseph died."

Angeline's heart tightened. "Oh. Henri never mentioned anything in his letters. You didn't mention anyone in your letter to Joseph either." She heard her own voice tremble and bit her lip in an attempt to regain her composure before she finally asked, "Who was he?"

Emilie took another deep breath and then looked at Angeline straight in the eye when she answered, "Her name was Kate."

"Kate? Wait, you had a relationship with a woman?"

Emilie was surprised at Angeline's expression, more intrigued and incredulous than shocked and repulsed. She'd imagined that Angeline might throw her out of her house, disgusted, if she learned that she'd been intimate with another woman. But she'd never thought it could be such a surprise. Not after the love she'd declared to Angeline and the kiss they'd shared years ago. Either way, she felt relief from telling the truth to Angeline. The only problem was that she couldn't run away from her friend's questions now.

"Yes, Angeline. We were together for five years." Emilie turned around and started walking toward the islands again. Angeline followed, but a few feet from Emilie, and wrapped her arms around her body to protect herself from the cold air rather than getting closer to Emilie. Angeline's choice to keep her distance didn't surprise Emilie. She was more astounded by the fact that she followed instead of running away.

"But, how is that possible? How can women be in love? That kind of relationship is meant to happen between men and women, Emilie. Men and women are supposed to get married, have children and raise a family together. How can you have that with another woman? It's impossible."

Angeline's tone was not accusatory. It was simply inquisitive, perhaps skeptical. Without looking at Angeline, Emilie answered, "Of course two women can't have children, Angeline. But they can still love each other. It's possible, and Kate and I were not alone. Every Saturday Kate's house was filled with other women like us, who loved other women. And there are plenty more all over the world. There are even words for women like me and Kate. Some call us Sapphists, but Kate and I preferred the word lesbian."

"Lesbian," Angeline repeated. "But the church?"

"The church doesn't dictate how I live my life anymore, Angeline. That said, I don't go telling everyone who I am. I'm discreet because I have to be. Especially here. But I couldn't stay under your roof any longer without you knowing. I want to stay at least until you have the baby, but it's up to you."

"How was she?"

Emilie was stunned by Angeline's question and she turned to look at her expression. All she saw was curiosity. "What?"

"Kate. How was she?"

"You want to know about Kate?"

"Yes."

"All right. Let's walk back to the buggy and I'll tell you anything you want to know."

Emilie couldn't help but smile at the turn of the conversation. She didn't know if Angeline's unexpected line of questioning meant that she could stay, but she took her eagerness to know more about Kate as a positive sign.

Emilie described at length Kate's physique and personality. She even told Angeline about Kate's marriage of convenience. When Angeline asked how their relationship ended, however, she simply said that Kate wanted to move to New York. She couldn't bring herself to admit how badly she'd hurt Kate, a woman who'd been so good to her and had helped her become the person she was in so many ways.

Angeline listened carefully and moved closer to Emilie as they walked back to the buggy. Emilie guessed the move was unconscious as Angeline wanted to hear Emilie's words through the noise of the waves and the wind. Yet she also allowed herself to interpret Angeline's closeness as a form of acceptance.

Emilie helped Angeline climb up to the buggy and sat by her, holding the reins. Angeline was quiet and Emilie figured she'd learned enough about Kate. She certainly didn't expect the next question.

"Did you kiss? You and Kate?"

Angeline's tone was hesitant but Emilie was shocked that she'd managed to ask that question at all. Her brain brought her back to the multiple kisses she'd shared with Kate and she had to swallow, her mouth suddenly dry. She was most uncomfortable thinking of Kate's lips on hers while sitting next to Angeline. But she couldn't be anything but honest with Angeline. "Yes, we kissed. Like couples do."

Angeline sat quiet for a few seconds. Emilie thought that Angeline knew more than enough already and hoped she wouldn't dare going further, but when she heard Angeline ask, "Did you make love?" her hopes crashed to the dirt road as a blush rose to her cheeks.

"Yes," she heard herself say in a hoarse, barely audible voice.

"But how?"

That was enough. Although she appreciated Angeline's interest and certainly preferred it to being called a pervert and put on a train to Boston, she didn't want to divulge details of her sexual life with Kate, details that only reminded her of the sexual life she could never have with Angeline. "That's personal, Angeline. I can tell you more about Kate if you want, but I can't share details of our intimacy with you. It wouldn't be right and it makes me uncomfortable."

"Of course. I'm so sorry, Emilie. It's none of my business." Angeline spoke sincerely and the pink that colored her cheeks confirmed that she was embarrassed by her intrusion. Emilie smiled at Angeline to put her at ease.

As they got closer to Angeline's house, Emilie dared asking what seemed most pertinent. "You haven't told me if you still want me to stay."

The question seemed to take Angeline off guard. She placed a hand on Emilie's arm to reassure her even before she spoke. "Of course I want you to stay. Thank you for telling me about you and Kate. And about being a...lesbian." The word was whispered even though no one could hear them. "I don't understand everything it means, Emilie, but I know it doesn't change who you are as my friend. I want you to stay. And your secret is safe with me."

Emilie was relieved that Angeline wanted her to stay but the shame she'd felt when she was forced to recall the way things had ended with Kate didn't sit well with her. She owed Kate an apology. She'd known from the moment she'd left the train station that day, and she couldn't wait any longer. She vowed to write a letter to Kate that night. Kate deserved an explanation and an apology. Emilie knew Kate would probably never answer, but she would write that letter nonetheless. She wouldn't feel comfortable under Angeline's roof until she did.

CHAPTER THIRTY-ONE

December 1905

Angeline sat in the rocking chair as she knit, regularly looking up at Emilie and admiring how absorbed she was by her book. Emilie had placed the rocking chair close enough to the kitchen table so they could share the light of the same oil lamp. She read and Angeline knitted while Lionel lay on the floor between them. Almost every night. It had become their routine in the past three months. They'd put the children to bed and spend an hour or two together like this, in peaceful silence, until Emilie shared a particularly interesting, touching, or funny passage in her book. Angeline cherished every minute of it. Sharing her life with Emilie had been her deepest desire since childhood and she felt like her dream had come true.

Angeline hadn't dared asking many more questions about Emilie's relationship with Kate since Emilie's confession shortly after her arrival. She'd limited herself to innocent inquiries about Kate's character and habits, purposefully avoiding the questions she still desperately wanted to ask. She wanted to know how Emilie and Kate could have been intimate with each other. She wanted to know if what they did resembled what happened in Angeline's recurring dream, the one in which she was in bed with Emilie, the one she couldn't get out of her mind, even awake, since Emilie's revelation.

Did Emilie touch Kate's breasts the same way she touched hers in that dream? Did she caress Kate's thighs in such a manner that Kate trembled as Angeline always did? What else did they do that she couldn't even dream of? She was dying to know and terrified at the same time. She couldn't deny that she felt jealous, envious of Kate and the relationship she'd had with Emilie. She knew her feelings for Emilie, her need of her, went beyond friendship and part of her wanted to live the kiss they'd shared again, to make her dream come true. Another part of her was still scared of what that meant. As much as Emilie said there were many other women like her and Kate, Angeline couldn't accept being one of them. Asking Emilie to leave, however, wasn't an option. She needed her too much.

"I think Renald will love this story," Emilie declared without looking up as she turned a page of her book. Angeline simply smiled at her. She still couldn't get used to Emilie calling young Doctor Michaud by his first name. Emilie had started ordering books for the General Store soon after she'd started working there and Doctor Michaud had been the first to take advantage of the new offering. He trusted Emilie's recommendations and whenever Emilie was late coming home from work, Angeline knew it was because she'd stayed to discuss a book with Doctor Michaud or to advise him on his next purchase.

Angeline winced and put one hand on her stomach when she felt a stronger contraction. She'd had small contractions throughout the day but this one was more serious. She recognized the pain and knew it was time. "Emilie?"

"Hmm?" Emilie asked without taking her focus out of her book.

"I think it's time for Renald to get out of his books and come here to deliver this baby," she announced calmly.

Emilie immediately jumped from her chair. "Really? All right. I'm going to tell your father and I'll be right back."

She kissed Angeline's forehead and rushed to put boots on and a heavy winter coat. They already had four feet of snow on the ground. Angeline knew it would be at least an hour before her father came back with Doctor Michaud. She got up from the rocking chair and walked slowly toward her bedroom, in pain. Soon Emilie would be back with Angeline's mother and they would put water to boil and stay with her until the doctor arrived and the baby was born. It would be a long night.

Emilie held the baby girl with pride and tenderness as she rocked the chair. She'd moved the rocking chair to Angeline's bedroom before the doctor, her father and mother had all left, leaving the baby in her arms. Angeline had fallen asleep right after giving birth, exhausted. Emilie had hated seeing Angeline suffer through endless contractions before she'd finally delivered the baby. Her mother and father and Renald had remained calm, obviously used to the natural phenomenon of giving birth. It was all very new to Emilie, however, and she'd felt powerless to help anyone in the situation. She hoped she'd be more useful helping Angeline take care of the baby. She definitely wanted to.

The sun would soon rise but Emilie hadn't shut an eye yet. Not even for one minute. She couldn't take her gaze away from the small pink creature wrapped in a blanket and sleeping peacefully in her arms. She realized that being here with Angeline and the children was the closest she'd ever be to having a family of her own, and holding this brand-new baby girl was the closest she'd ever be to giving birth to her own child. She'd never wanted children before. She'd never even dared wanting a family, but she was absolutely certain in this moment that she wanted to see this baby girl grow up. With Angeline. She'd never been so certain of what she wanted before. She couldn't go back to Boston. Her place was here.

"Hi there," Angeline said softly.

Emilie looked up to the bed where Angeline had been sleeping, surprised that she hadn't realized she'd awakened. She stood up, carefully holding the baby, and went to sit on the bed next to her. Lionel stood up from his post by the chair to follow Emilie, and lay on the floor by the bed. Angeline chuckled.

"What's funny?" Emilie asked.

"When I woke up after giving birth to Marie-Ange, Joseph was sitting in that chair in the exact same spot, holding the baby with such pride." Tears filled Angeline's eyes as she smiled.

Emilie fought her own tears, missing her brother. "I think he would have been very proud of this one as well," she said as she placed the baby girl in her mother's arms. "She's beautiful, isn't she?"

"Yes, she's a beauty, as her father would say," Angeline said with more tears falling to her cheeks as she appeared lost in her memories. She caressed the child's dark hair and added, "She looks like Paul-Emile. Like you."

Their eyes met and this time Emilie couldn't hold back her tears. She made herself more comfortable on the bed and placed an arm around Angeline's shoulders.

"Did you think of a name for this beautiful new niece of mine?"

"Since we're so close to Christmas, what would you think of Noelle? Noelle Josephine Levesque."

Emilie studied the baby in Angeline's arms. "Noelle Josephine Levesque," she said out loud to test the name. "That's perfect," she concluded.

CHAPTER THIRTY-TWO

Rimouski, January 1906

"How dare he?" Emilie said, her face reddened with anger and the wrinkle between her eyebrows deeper than Angeline had ever seen it.

Emilie was holding on to the back of a wooden kitchen chair so tightly her knuckles were turning white. She'd just come home from work and Angeline had told her about Father Roy's visit. A visit during which the priest had suggested it might be time to remarry and have more children.

"He's our priest, Emilie. He simply reminded me of my responsibility. I'm still fairly young and could carry and mother many more children. It's my Christian duty to do so."

"So are you saying you want to remarry, Angeline? Did good Father Roy already have a husband in mind for you?"

Angeline saw fire pass through Emilie's squinted eyes before she pushed the chair she'd been holding onto with a force that startled Angeline and reminded her of the rare occasions she'd seen Joseph angry. Fortunately, she thought, the Levesques didn't get angry too often, or they would certainly run out of kitchen chairs.

The sound of Emilie's enraged voice and of the chair hitting the side of the table alerted the children who were playing upstairs and all three rushed down the staircase. Noelle started crying from her crib in Angeline's bedroom.

"Dinnertime," Angeline announced before she shot her most serious, stern motherly look in Emilie's direction. The look always succeeded in effectively communicating "not now." Emilie took a deep breath and put the chair she'd pushed back in its place. Angeline went to get Noelle out of the bedroom, followed by Marie-Ange.

When she came back to the kitchen, Emilie was busy setting the table for dinner with Paul-Emile and Victor. Angeline smiled at the scene. Of course she didn't want to remarry. She wanted to keep living exactly the way they were living now. She wanted to raise her children with Emilie, share the house chores with her, as well as every moment of hardship and happiness. She wanted to go to the beach with her on Sundays, even in the bitter cold of January, when they just sat close together on the sleigh and gazed at the white sea in silence for a few minutes before turning the horses around to go back home.

Every moment with Emilie was precious and she didn't want to lose any of them to marry a man she didn't love. She didn't want to share her bed with a man, be forced to have sexual intercourse with him. Not when her most tender, intimate thoughts were filled with Emilie. Not when her attraction to Emilie kept growing every day to the point where she'd prefer not being touched again to being touched by anyone else. But she didn't know how she could avoid Father Roy's will, how she could avoid God's will.

Angeline went to the stove where Emilie had started to ladle soup into bowls and, holding Noelle in one arm, she caressed Emilie's back with her free hand. Emilie turned to her and Angeline brought her hand to Emilie's face, hoping Emilie could see in her eyes what she truly wanted more than anything. Emilie's smile told her she did.

Emilie lay in Angeline's bed wearing a simple white nightgown, her brain racing as she stared blankly at the ceiling. Since Noelle's birth, Emilie had started sleeping in Angeline's bed with her. It allowed her to help when Noelle needed something in the middle of the night. Angeline could feed her and then get some rest while Emilie rocked the baby back to sleep.

Emilie had hesitated when Angeline had first asked her to share her bed, but she'd figured she could smother her desires if it meant she was helping Angeline. Sleeping with Angeline was not always easy, especially when it was cold and Angeline snuggled against Emilie's body in the middle of the night, seeking warmth, but Emilie was getting used to keeping her needs and emotions under control. She'd even thought she was pretty good at it until she'd lost her temper earlier at the possibility of Angeline marrying a man.

She'd foolishly hoped they could keep living as they had for the past four months, but deep down she knew that even if Angeline didn't try to meet a man, the priest would eventually come around to remind her of her duty. It took her back to the day she'd heard her father defy Father Lavoie's will, telling his wife he wouldn't risk her life by having more children. She'd feared for her father that day, but now she wished she and Angeline were brave enough to stand up to Father Roy the same way her father had refused to listen to Father Lavoie.

Emilie turned to her side and propped herself up on her elbow, holding her head in her hand as she watched Angeline walk back and forth in front of the crib with Noelle in her arms, putting her to sleep. Like Emilie, she wore a white cotton nightgown, her curly brown hair falling to the middle of her back. Emilie never tired of looking at Angeline like this, in her most simple garments, made with such light fabric that Emilie could guess the curves of Angeline's body as she moved across the room in the faint light of the oil lamp burning on the nightstand. She was so beautiful.

Emilie kept watching and became nervous when she saw Angeline finally carefully lay the baby in her crib. Angeline would certainly want to address the reaction she'd had earlier, and she didn't quite know how to explain it without telling Angeline she wanted to be the only one sharing her bed for the rest of their lives.

Angeline climbed into bed but instead of killing the light as she usually did as soon as she got under the covers, she turned to face Emilie.

"I'm sorry about earlier," Emilie offered, hoping her quick apology would limit the conversation and especially Angeline's questions.

Emilie was taken by surprise when Angeline, instead of reprimanding or interrogating her as she'd expected, took Emilie's free hand and brought it to her lips to kiss it tenderly.

"Shh, I understand. I don't want to get married, Emilie. I really don't. You must believe me." Angeline's eyes welled up and Emilie let herself fall to her back so she could gather Angeline into her arms and let her cry against her shoulder. "I like our life the way it is," she added between sobs.

Emilie's heart swelled with joy. "So do I, Angeline. I don't even think of Boston anymore. My place is here with you and the children. I've never been so sure of anything in my life."

Angeline's sobs slowly subsided and she placed a hand on Emilie's stomach as she sighed. Emilie felt the heat of the contact through her nightgown and focused to keep her breathing regular. She was only briefly relieved when Angeline removed her hand from her stomach. She used it to raise her upper body and move her face over Emilie's, a smile on her lips. A smile on full lips that were just inches from hers. Emilie had to close her eyes to make sure her mouth wouldn't decide on its own to close the gap.

"But Father Roy won't let us keep living this way, Emilie. You know that."

Emilie opened her eyes to help convey the seriousness of her message. "If this life of ours is what you really want, Angeline, trust me. We'll find a way."

"I do trust you, Emilie. And this life of ours is what I want more than anything," Angeline whispered, her voice slightly breaking on the last words.

Emilie licked her dry lips and held her breath, wondering how long Angeline would hover over her mouth and how long she could keep herself from kissing her. She thought she imagined Angeline's lips getting closer to hers until she unmistakably felt the pressure of Angeline's mouth against hers. The kiss was brief and almost chaste but it was undeniably a kiss and Angeline had initiated it. Angeline pulled her mouth away but remained merely inches from Emilie's face. Emilie could see the flame of the oil lamp dancing in Angeline's eyes. She remained immobile, wondering what Angeline might do next.

"I want this too, Emilie," Angeline murmured, brushing her lips against Emilie's again.

"Are you sure?" Emilie asked, tempted to not wait for Angeline's answer to unleash her long repressed hunger.

"Yes, Emilie. I want you to show me. What you did with Kate. How you touched her. I want you to make love to me."

Emilie gasped. She didn't need more convincing.

She rolled Angeline over until she was the one on top, but not necessarily in control. She felt Angeline's hands roam through her short hair and enjoyed being pulled toward Angeline's lips. She knew she wouldn't be pushed away this time. Angeline wanted this. She'd asked for it, was demanding it with every move she made. There was nothing desperate in Emilie's kiss this time. When she took hold of Angeline's lips with her own, when she tasted her mouth with her tongue, every movement was purposeful, calm, assertive, and saying the same thing: this is what was meant to be, this is who we are.

Encouraged by Angeline's moans and the way she dug her fingers into the tender skin at the back of her neck, Emilie kept kissing her as she skillfully unbuttoned the four buttons of Angeline's nightgown. She tore her lips from Angeline's and before she moved her mouth to the newly exposed flesh, she made eye contact with Angeline. Reassured by eyelids heavy with desire, the undeniable yearning she read in Angeline's expression, she smiled her satisfaction and started kissing down Angeline's neck, pushing the cotton of the unbuttoned nightgown until she could access the soft flesh of one breast.

When she took an erect nipple into her mouth, she felt tears run down her cheeks to Angeline's breast. She'd wanted this for so long. She'd imagined the smell, the softness of Angeline's skin so many times, it was difficult to register that it was really happening. Angeline's nipple was really in her mouth, every flick of her tongue, brush of her lips and suction of her mouth making Angeline's body squirm with pleasure.

"Oh, Emilie, this is so much better," Angeline whispered through appreciative whimpers.

"Better than what?" Emilie asked before bringing her face back over Angeline's to hear the answer.

"Better than my dreams," Angeline confessed.

"You dreamed about this?" Emilie inquired with a playful smile, holding the nipple that had been in her mouth just a moment before between her thumb and index finger. Angeline simply nodded, bashful.

"And did you dream about this?" Emilie let go of Angeline's nipple and pushed the covers off their bodies to caress Angeline's nude thighs just under her nightgown. Angeline nodded again and closed her eyes tight, trembling under Emilie's touch.

"And what about this?" Emilie brought her hand higher under Angeline's nightgown and pressed it against the cotton of her underwear between her legs. She felt wetness through Angeline's drawers and Angeline cried out in surprise and elation. Emilie slid her hand into the waist of the drawers and went back to Angeline's sensitive mound of flesh. She sprinkled Angeline's neck and face with kisses as she maneuvered her fingers into Angeline's sex and familiarized herself with all of her folds, depths and the small bud she knew would bring her so much gratification.

Soon she knew what made Angeline sigh, moan, and writhe under the touch of her hand and she felt Angeline's pleasure build. She pressed her mouth hard against Angeline's just before she reached climax, feeling every vibration of her moans through her mouth and ever tremor of her ecstasy through her hand.

"Oh, Angeline, you're so lovely," Emilie whispered tenderly as Angeline slowly came back down from the heights of her orgasm. "I love you." She kissed Angeline again, this time more softly.

"I love you too," Angeline answered in a breath.

Emilie held Angeline throughout that night, feeling the weight of Angeline's head on her heart yet knowing that her heart had never been so light.

When Angeline woke up on her back with Emilie's hand on her stomach and her warm breath on her neck, she felt exposed. And panicked. She looked down at Emilie's hand and saw her own breast spilling out of her unbuttoned nightgown. She hurried to button up the garment and Emilie turned around in her sleep, freeing Angeline of any contact.

Angeline sighed with relief. She'd wanted Emilie's touch last night. She thought they could be together in every way. Been certain she wanted it. Convinced that it was meant to happen and that being intimate with Emilie would confirm the nature of their relationship and most of all would make her happy.

So why was she feeling so dirty this morning? Why were Father Roy's words swirling across her mind, reminding her of her purpose as a woman? Why did loving Emilie seem so selfish in the light of day? She needed time to think it through.

She sat up in bed but Emilie reached around her waist with her arms and she felt a soft kiss on her neck. The shivers that the kiss sent through her body, the same that had brought her nothing but pleasure the night before, made her entire body tense up.

Emilie must have felt it because she immediately let go of her and when Angeline got out of bed and turned around she saw Emilie sitting on her side of the bed, her chin on her bent knees and her arms tightly wrapped around her legs. Her position was defensive and her expression worried.

"Are you all right, Angeline? About what we did last night?" Her voice was small and hesitant. She seemed terrified. Angeline wanted to comfort her, but she needed to keep her distance even more.

"I don't know."

"Oh, I see," Emilie simply said, her eyes shimmering with tears.

"I think I just need to think about it, Emilie."

"It wasn't my idea, Angeline."

She was right. Angeline had been the one initiating the kiss. She'd been the one asking Emilie to make love to her. "I know. I thought…" Her voice trailed off and Emilie waited patiently. She didn't want to explain now. She couldn't explain now. She just needed time to think it through, she kept repeating herself. "I just need some space to think about it, Emilie. Please understand."

"Do you want me to go back to Boston?"

Emilie's question heightened the level of panic that had already paralyzed Angeline. Despite her doubts and questions about what had happened last night, Angeline was still absolutely certain she wanted Emilie to stay with her and the children. "No," she hurried to answer. "I don't want you to go, Emilie. Not ever."

At Emilie's tentative smile, showing a hint of hope, Angeline quickly added, "But I think it might be a good idea for you to sleep upstairs tonight." She turned around before she could see the effect her declaration had on Emilie's expression and went to the crib where Noelle had just awakened.

CHAPTER THIRTY-THREE

February 1906

Emilie stirred the pea soup. She rarely cooked in Angeline's kitchen. They agreed that Angeline was a better cook overall but Angeline had soon admitted that Joseph had been right. There was no pea soup as good as his mother's and Emilie had years of practice to replicate the recipe to perfection. Besides, Emilie was making the famous soup today because they were expecting her friend, Renald. They would discuss books over lunch.

Emilie glanced at Angeline, who was busy picking up things around the house, and she smiled. Renald might have been a good friend to Emilie, but to Angeline he was still the town's doctor and she was extremely nervous at the thought of welcoming him as a guest in her house. Angeline bent over to pick up the train Victor had left on the floor and Emilie turned back to her soup. If she stared at Angeline's buttocks too long she knew memories of the passionate night they'd shared a few weeks ago would come back to her mind and she couldn't let that happen.

Living under the same roof as Angeline without being able to touch her or kiss her had always been difficult, but since that night it had become pure torture. Now she knew what Angeline's body looked like, the way her skin felt, tasted and smelled. She knew how Angeline reacted to her touch and she knew her most intimate scent, the scent of her arousal. Emilie thought she'd missed what she'd never had before, but now that she'd had everything she missed it even more, with every fiber of her being. If Angeline said something or moved in any way that brought her back to that night, Emilie was left with an instant dry mouth and a lump the size of a wool ball in her throat. Torture, there was no other word for it.

She'd thought about going back to Boston, but she couldn't bring herself to do it. There was a lot more at stake than her relationship with Angeline and her frustration. There were four little creatures, five if she counted the dog sitting by her side, who'd grown used to her presence and needed her in their life. And she needed them just as much.

"The doctor's almost here, we saw his sleigh on the hill," Paul announced as he ran into the house.

"All right, you go and bring your brother and sister back inside," Angeline ordered and she busied herself straightening the Sunday dress she'd especially worn on a Saturday for Renald's visit.

"You look lovely," Emilie said in an attempt to reassure Angeline on her appearance. The dark blush that colored Angeline's face made her smile. "It's nothing more than lunch with a friend, you know. He's not here as a doctor today."

"I know," Angeline said as she smiled for the first time that day. "Thank you for reminding me again."

They stared at each other and Emilie noticed not for the first time how much the way they looked at each other had changed since that night she'd made love to Angeline. They'd always been able to understand what the other was saying through their eyes before. Now it seemed their eyes tried to communicate even more, but through a dense cloud of confusion that hadn't been there before. Paul came back inside, followed by Victor and Marie-Ange, just as Noelle was making herself heard from the bedroom, waking up from her nap. "I'll go check on her," Angeline said.

"Perfect, and I'll help the children become children again," she said mockingly as she approached Paul, Victor and Marie-Ange, who'd already started—albeit with great difficulty— peeling away the layers of snow-coated wool clothing they wore to play outside.

"All right, snowmen, tell me the truth. What have you done with my niece and nephews?" The children giggled and let Emilie help them remove the remaining layers of clothing. They were helping Emilie hang their wet clothes on hooks by the woodstove when Emilie heard a knock on the door.

Angeline, who had had time to come back from the bedroom with Noelle in her arms, got to the door before Emilie. "Father Roy?" she heard Angeline ask.

What in the hell was he doing here?

"What a surprise," Angeline continued.

"What a surprise indeed," Emilie added as she hurried to the door and stood ready to take the priest's heavy overcoat.

"I thought we could continue the conversation we started last month, Angeline," the priest announced. "I thought you'd be at the store," he added to Emilie as he handed her his coat.

No such luck, Emilie thought before she answered the priest. "Theo didn't need me today."

"Will you stay for lunch, Father Roy?" Angeline asked politely.

"Of course, please join us. We'll be ready to eat as soon as Doctor Michaud arrives," Emilie added as she went to hang the priest's coat on the hook that was the farthest from the stove. She didn't want to keep the children's clothes from drying and she honestly didn't care whether Father Roy was forced to wear a cold coat to get back on his sleigh.

"Doctor Michaud?" the priest asked incredulously, as if a doctor didn't belong in Angeline's humble home.

"Yes, he's a good friend of mine." Emilie enjoyed the expression of shock in Father Roy's pale, wrinkled face.

"In that case I'll stay, thank you. It smells delicious in here."

"Emilie made her mother's famous pea soup. You will love it, Father."

The priest squinted at Emilie as if he couldn't believe she could cook. Fortunately Emilie heard another knock at the door before she could tell him that women who work and wear short hair can still, by some miracle unknown to men, manage to make a perfectly good pea soup.

"Renald, hi. Welcome."

"Thank you, Emilie. Hello, Mrs. Levesque," the doctor greeted Angeline. "Father Roy," he said with a nod, obviously surprised by the priest's presence.

"Doctor Michaud," the priest replied with a similar nod.

Emilie was relieved to see the priest and doctor didn't seem overly friendly toward each other. Their greetings had been polite, but cold. Renald's reaction led her to believe they both could probably add a certain aversion to men of cloth in general and to Father Roy in particular to the already long list of things they had in common.

They all sat at the table and Emilie served soup with bread and butter. During lunch Father Roy and Doctor Michaud took turns to make pleasant and amiable conversation with both women and the children, who were as well behaved as children were expected to be in such situations. Emilie glanced a few times at Angeline, who seemed uncomfortable in the presence of the two men who represented the highest forms of authority in their town, but still smiled with pride at the way her children acted.

After lunch Angeline made tea and the children went upstairs to play. Emilie was holding Noelle as they shared tea and the priest came dangerously closer to the topic of conversation he was most interested in. Emilie had hoped he wouldn't dare talk about such a personal matter as marriage in front of the doctor, but she should have known better. Father Roy was not here for pleasantries.

"I was hoping, Angeline, that you had considered what we discussed last time."

"I have," Angeline started anxiously before a knock on the door surprised them.

Emilie went to answer and was relieved to see Pierre Fournier. "Father Roy, Doctor Michaud, I thought I recognized your horses. I'm sorry to interrupt but I couldn't pass up the chance to say hello. It's not every day a priest and a doctor are both under my daughter's roof, you know," Pierre said with a chuckle as he removed his boots and coat and made himself comfortable sitting across from both men at the table.

Emilie saw Pierre place a large hand on his daughter's and noticed the grateful smile she gave him in return. The three men started talking about town matters and bought Angeline and Emilie precious time until the name of Stanislas Pelletier was brought up. Mr. Pelletier's wife had died recently after giving birth to their second child and all three men around the kitchen table agreed about the great tragedy the situation represented.

"Such a good man, that Stan," Pierre said as he shook his head. "And all alone to take care of two children and his farm. It's not fair."

"I hear his sisters have been of great support," Renald said, trying to shed a positive light on the widower's circumstances and making Emilie proud to call him a friend.

"Sisters who have families of their own to take care of," argued the priest. "What Stanislas needs is a new wife."

Here we go, Emilie thought. Now was her chance to act. An idea had been taking shape in her mind as she'd listened to the men talk, an idea that only the doctor's presence made possible and that she found more and more ingenious. His participation was crucial to its realization, of course. So was Pierre's, but for some reason she trusted Pierre would do the right thing. She just needed to talk to Angeline alone before she put her brilliant plan into motion. She took advantage of Noelle's quiet whimpers to excuse herself and went to the bedroom.

"Angeline, could you please come here for a second? I need help with Noelle," Angeline heard Emilie call out from the bedroom. Relieved that she'd been temporarily saved, once again, from the priest's questions, she quickly excused herself and joined Emilie.

"What is it?" she asked as she saw that Noelle was already in her crib and seemed content. Emilie put her hands on Angeline's shoulders and held her at arm's length, staring into her eyes as if she were trying to read through her. "What is it, Emilie? We have guests."

"I know we have guests, Angeline. But I need you to answer me one question before we go back out there. One very important question that you have to answer with the absolute truth, you hear me?"

Angeline nervously locked her gaze on Emilie's. She feared the question, but it seemed important to Emilie so she agreed. "All right, what is it?"

"Promise me you'll answer truthfully," Emilie repeated, slightly tightening her grip on Angeline's shoulders.

"I promise."

"Do you want to get married again and have more children? Yes or no?"

"No," Angeline answered without hesitation, relieved that the question was one she could answer so easily. She didn't want to get married to Stan or any other man. She wanted to sort through her feelings for Emilie and find a way to live happily with her. She didn't know what level of intimacy she felt comfortable having with Emilie yet, but she knew she loved Emilie, and no one else.

"No, I don't want to get married, Emilie. I still want our life. I love you." She hadn't meant to say it in this moment, and judging by the dark red color on Emilie's cheeks, she hadn't expected to hear it either, but it was said, and it was true.

"All right. That's all I needed to hear. Now let me do the talking, will you?"

Angeline nodded. Emilie had a plan, and Angeline trusted it would get her what they wanted, so she nodded. She watched Emilie close her eyes and take a deep breath to ready herself, then followed her back to the kitchen.

"Stan is a good man, Father Roy. I was the first to say so earlier, but Angeline doesn't know him," Pierre was explaining to the priest when the women sat down again at the table.

"She'll get to know him, Pierre. Surely she'll learn to appreciate his qualities," the priest insisted.

"I don't doubt that if Stanislas Pelletier is as good a man as you all say he is, Angeline would be very happy with him," Emilie started.

Shocked, Angeline threw a furious glare in her direction, but Emilie wasn't looking at her. She was staring at the priest.

Then Emilie lowered her gaze and smiled sadly before she continued, "Unfortunately I'm not sure Stanislas would be quite as happy with her, considering the circumstances."

"Why wouldn't Stan be happy with my daughter?" Pierre asked defensively.

Angeline squinted at Emilie, wondering where she was going, but Emilie continued to ignore her. Emilie covered Pierre's hand with hers to calm him.

"Pierre, I know we didn't want people to know, but don't you think we should say something now before some poor man marries Angeline? It wouldn't be fair to him." At Pierre's puzzled look, Emilie continued before he had a chance to say anything, turning to Doctor Michaud next. "Renald, I know we asked you to be discreet but I think Father Roy deserves to know the truth now."

Doctor Michaud seemed as puzzled as her father but straightened up in his seat, on alert.

Emilie turned back to the priest.

"Father Roy, the truth is that Noelle's birth was a very difficult one. Doctor Michaud managed to save both child and mother, but I'm afraid Angeline can't have any more children." Emilie spoke solemnly and wiped fake tears with the back of her hand.

All three men turned to Angeline and she lowered her head. She hoped they would see her stance as one of pain and sorrow, but the truth was that Angeline was scared she might laugh if she met any of their gazes, especially Emilie's.

She didn't condone lying, especially to a priest, but it was for a good cause. Besides, the numerous miscarriages she'd gone through during her marriage with Joseph led her to believe giving Stanislas Pelletier more children might not have been as easy as Father Roy had hoped. Her reasoning helped her accept the lie.

"Is that true?" Angeline heard the priest ask. When she looked up, she saw his stare go from her father to Doctor Michaud.

Both men cleared their throat nervously but Doctor Michaud was the first to speak. "Yes, it is," he affirmed with an understanding side glance at Emilie. He grew more confident in his own deceit as he continued, "Angeline lost a lot of blood and the placenta wouldn't dislodge so I was forced to perform an emergency hysterectomy."

The priest wrinkled his nose in disgust and waved his hand in the doctor's face. He'd obviously heard enough of the medical details. He turned to Pierre next.

Angeline watched as her father studied her first, then Emilie. In that very moment, in the tender smile that followed his scrutiny, Angeline could swear her father understood the nature of her relationship with Emilie. He might never imagine they could be or had been intimate with each other, but he knew they wanted to keep living together as they had. He knew they wanted to share their lives. She smiled back at him and when he nodded she knew he would support them.

"Yes, Father, it's all true. We didn't want to talk about it because Angeline was embarrassed. She felt like she was less of a woman, as you probably understand." He never took his eyes off Angeline as he spoke, and she offered him a grateful smile.

The priest nodded with forced compassion, then he sighed. "You gave God's family four beautiful children, my child. That's something." He then looked at Emilie and hesitated before he dared asking. "I don't imagine you're interested in marriage, young lady? You might find a husband if you grew your hair as nature intended."

"Me?" Emilie scoffed incredulously. "Oh no. I'll be back in Boston eventually. If I marry it will be there," she lied.

Angeline found it difficult not to chuckle.

"Well, I guess I'll go back to town without a wife for that poor widower," Father Roy declared as he stood up. "Thank you for the soup, Miss Levesque. It was delicious."

"You're welcome," Emilie said as she went to get his coat, still as cold as it had been when he'd arrived.

"Stan will find a wife, Father. I'm certain of it," Pierre assured the priest as they all stood at the door to bid their good-byes.

"I hope you're right, Pierre."

Once the priest left, Emilie and Angeline thanked the doctor and Angeline's father for going along with Emilie's story. Doctor Michaud seemed amused by Emilie's cleverness.

Pierre was more shaken by the turn of events but nonetheless declared, "I do think there is such a thing as a white lie, and I trust God will look kindly on this one. I don't want you to marry anyone you don't love, my girl, and I know you're happy living here quietly with your friend. You and Emilie are good for each other, and I'll support the two of you in any way I can."

Angeline hugged her father tightly, grateful for his kind nature and his blessing. The words he murmured to her ear, however, surprised her. "Love is love, my girl."

Long after he and the doctor were gone, she wondered what her father had meant. Did he understand even more than Angeline had thought? Did he know she loved Emilie with all of her heart, the way she'd been expected to love a man? The way she hadn't been able to love anyone else, not even Joseph? Or did he simply mean that friendship was another form of love, one that was also worth defending? She would never know what her father really meant and would never ask, but one thing was certain: no one would ever come to threaten her life with Emilie again. She would never be forced to marry another man, and Emilie would never be forced to leave her. The thought left her heart light with hope.

They went through the rest of their day and Angeline noticed that Emilie seemed as lighthearted as she was, laughing freely at anything Angeline or the children said. Angeline loved hearing her laugh. That night, when they got ready for bed and Emilie started to climb the stairs to join the children, who were already asleep, Angeline stopped her by grabbing her hand.

Emilie turned to her. "Did I forget anything?"

"No. I was hoping," Angeline started nervously, fearing Emilie's response.

"What were you hoping, Angeline?"

"I was hoping you'd sleep in the bedroom with me." Angeline caressed Emilie's hand with her thumb and squeezed it lightly as she licked her lips, dry from apprehension.

"Tonight?" Emilie asked, incredulous.

"Every night," Angeline answered in a whisper.

Emilie took a step toward Angeline and joined their free hands. "Are you sure? I don't think I could go through you changing your mind again."

Angeline freed one hand to place a finger on Emilie's lips. "Shh, I won't change my mind, my love." Emilie's lips formed a smile under her finger. "I never really changed my mind, Emilie, but I couldn't see how we could keep living the way we were. I was afraid it would all be taken away from us, so I kept it from happening myself before anyone else could. It was wrong of me."

"It's understandable," Emilie started despite Angeline's finger still pressing on her lips.

Angeline replaced her finger with her lips to stop Emilie from talking. She noted her kiss was less hesitant than the first one she'd initiated. She knew the amount of pressure Emilie liked, and she knew how to use her tongue to tease a whimper of pleasure out of her.

When she heard the sound she'd wanted to provoke, she interrupted the kiss to continue her statement. "It was wrong of me, Emilie," she whispered. "I should have trusted you."

"That's right," Emilie agreed as she tried to resume the kiss that had apparently left her hungry.

Angeline dodged Emilie's lips and brought her mouth to Emilie's ear instead. "I should have trusted that you'd find a way. What you did today secured our lives, Emilie. It made me see once and for all that I can let myself love you. That I can let you love me. And that you'll always find a way to protect our love."

Angeline looked at her then and was surprised to see tears in her eyes. Emilie closed her eyes as if to hide her emotion. Angeline kissed each of her eyelids before bringing her lips to the wrinkle between her eyebrows, the wrinkle she'd grown so fond of.

When Emilie opened her eyes again, her lips quivered as she spoke, "I'm so happy you can finally see it. I'll do whatever it takes to keep our love safe. Always."

"I know now. Please, come to bed with me."

They shared another kiss. It was soft, unhurried and sensual. Each movement of their tongues, each brush of their lips was filled with love. It was the kiss that marked the beginning of their own kind of marriage, one Angeline had no doubt would grow and make them blissfully happy. Still holding Emilie's hand, she pulled her toward the bedroom and Emilie followed willingly. They would never sleep apart again. Angeline knew.

EPILOGUE

Rimouski, July 1906

"It's my birthday today, Joseph," Emilie said to her brother as she placed a bouquet of wild daisies in front of his humble tombstone. She knelt on the ground that covered her brother's body and took a deep breath.

"We're happy, Joseph. I know you see it from wherever you are. I hope you're happy for us. Sometimes I'm scared you hate me but then I remember that of all of us, you always had the best heart. You *are* happy for us, aren't you?"

Emilie sighed. When Angeline had asked her what she'd like to do on her twenty-seventh birthday, Emilie had surprised both of them by saying she wanted to visit her brother's grave. She'd been to his grave when she'd first arrived in Rimouski but the visit had been brief. Her pain over his death had been too recent and she'd found staring at a cold tombstone unbearable. Today she felt the need to speak to her brother, to explain herself, and to ask for his forgiveness.

"You see, you're not the only one who fell in love with Angeline the day she saved you from those Irish bastards," she said with a chuckle thinking of the day Joseph had confessed his love for Angeline as he walked her to the Banvilles.

"I dreamed of being with her, just like you. And I was so jealous when your dream came true, when you took Angeline from me and brought her here. That day, Joseph, my own dream was shattered. That's why I called you a coward. I was blinded by my own jealousy. You'd won. And I hated you for it. I will always regret the way I reacted and the way I treated you. I'm so sorry, Joseph." She started crying. She cried for a long time, releasing all of the guilt she'd felt through the years over the last time she'd spoken to her brother.

"The funny thing is, I think your dream needed to come true first before mine could come true. I didn't know it then, but my dream was flawed. It turns out your dream was better, brother. I'm starting to love this place as much as you've always loved it. And if your dream hadn't come true, I would never have known Paul, Victor, Marie-Ange and Noelle. You have four beautiful, smart, wonderful children, Joseph. You'd be so proud of them." Emilie smiled tenderly as thoughts of the children rushed through her mind.

"Don't go thinking I'm glad you died so I could have it all, though. Not a day goes by that I don't wish you were alive, my dear brother. I wish you could see your children grow up. I wish you could meet Noelle. Most of all I wish I could ask for your forgiveness in person. I would fight you for Angeline's love, Joseph, don't you doubt it. I would fight with all I have. But I would do it honestly, and openly."

She paused and took one daisy out of the bouquet, caressing it as she gathered her thoughts. "I hope you can see I love her the way she deserves to be loved, the way I'm sure you loved her too. I'll protect her, and cherish her, for as long as I live. I hope that you can find comfort in knowing that, even if you can't forgive me."

"He forgives you," Emilie heard Angeline say behind her as she felt a hand on her shoulder. "More than anything, your brother wanted me to be happy. He sees how happy you make me, Emilie. He forgives you."

Emilie looked up to Angeline and smiled. Angeline smiled back and then she asked, "Are you ready?"

"Yes." Emilie put the lone daisy back on top of the bouquet and stood up. "I love you, brother." She kissed her hand and bent forward to place her palm on the tombstone.

Then she turned around and offered her arm to Angeline, who held it tightly as they started walking side by side away from Joseph's grave.

A lone daisy followed the women for several footsteps, blown by the wind.

Bella Books, Inc.

Women. Books. Even Better Together.

P.O. Box 10543
Tallahassee, FL 32302

Phone: 800-729-4992
www.bellabooks.com